THE RUSSIAN CLASS

THE RUSSIAN CLASS

JOHN HOOKHAM

The Book Guild Ltd

First published in Great Britain in 2018 by
The Book Guild Ltd
9 Priory Business Park
Wistow Road, Kibworth
Leicestershire, LE8 0RX
Freephone: 0800 999 2982
www.bookguild.co.uk
Email: info@bookguild.co.uk
Twitter: @bookguild

Typeset in Garamond

Printed and bound in Great Britain by 4edge Limited

ISBN 978 1912575 886

British Library Cataloguing in Publication Data.
A catalogue record for this book is available from the British Library.

Printed on FSC accredited paper

This book would not have been possible without the love and support of the three most important women in my life – my fabulous wife Marian and my beautiful and talented daughters Bohemia and Claire.

DISCLAIMER

The Russian Class is set in a particular historical period and consequently references some actual events and real people. It is, however, a work of fiction. All names, characters, businesses, places, events, locales, and incidents are either the products of the author's imagination or used in a **fictitious** manner. Any resemblance to actual persons, living or dead, or actual events is purely coincidental.

PROLOGUE

JAMES

Although I am not without imagination, I don't believe I could have imagined this. Certainly at my age you don't expect surprises, especially not this kind. I thought all my adventures were behind me and all my battles fought. So when Sarah's email arrived, I was simply blown away. This could not be happening to me, I thought. Not now, not after all this time.

What distressed me most about getting the email was that I knew it would plunge me back into the past, into the darkest time of my life. A time of despair when the only way I could deal with my pain was through drunkenness and debauchery.

For years I had lived a life of self-destruction and self-hatred. I had tried to find refuge from my personal loathing by seducing other men's wives and girlfriends, cavorting in brothels, binging on mindless sexual gratification. And drinking. Drinking and drinking. Anything to get my mind off my inability to change what had happened and what I was powerless to prevent.

And now this email drawing me back, making me face the past again while forcing me to remember what I had so hoped to forget. But which I was unable to forget. Just when I thought I could find some peace. Just when I thought I had some stability in my life. Reminding me of what I had tried to escape from.

With the memories came everything else including the fear and the horror of knowing that I had been in the presence of real evil, that I had seen its face and knew it intimately.

Naturally, I've encountered similar brutality before. My work as a documentary film-maker has taken me all over the world and I've seen a great deal of human cruelty. Once, some years ago, on a shoot in Cambodia, I visited the Tuol Sleng Genocide Museum in Phnom Penh. It is a ghastly place and most harrowing to witness. The building used to be a high school until the Khmer Rouge took possession of it and turned it into the notorious Security Prison 21.

Outside the former classrooms and on the verandas, there is chicken wire to prevent the prisoners who were kept there from committing suicide by leaping to their deaths. More than 17,000 people were interrogated, tortured and killed at Tuol Sleng. Many of the torturers were children who used techniques like waterboarding, beating, suffocation and hanging to grill the prisoners. All over the museum the gruesome tools of their trade can be seen – pliers to pull out human nails, shackles on the prison floor and even a modified children's swing used to plunge victims into a drowning pool.

In some of the rooms, posted all around are photographs of the dead victims. They are truly appalling to behold. I found the experience deeply depressing. And haunting. Overall the building gave off a profound sense of human suffering that emanated from the walls, from the stones. Not only that, but I could feel an overwhelming barbarous presentiment, an aura that could not be ignored.

All these crimes against humanity were carried out at the behest of Pol Pot or Brother Number One as he was known. For me there is no doubt that the man was an abomination, contaminated by ideology, impossible to comprehend.

But despite Tuol Sleng's horrors, despite the terrible savagery I had seen there, it was still possible for me to distance myself and remain somewhat detached. After all, these crimes had been inflicted upon strangers, people I did not know.

But now it was personal. Now I was intimately involved. There was nothing remote about it. The arrival of Sarah's email was forcing me to recall and reconsider the acts of another depraved individual, a man whose heinous deeds changed, irrevocably, the course of my life and the destinies of those closest to me. The people hurt had been my loved ones, the harmed victims, kith and kin. The iron cage mine.

But this is too simple, too one-sided. It's not an accurate representation of what I really felt at the time because Sarah's correspondence also carried with it something else, something entirely different. Hope. Reconciliation. The chance to live a richer, more complete life and the promise of so much more.

Nevertheless, the email's arrival was totally unexpected and I was unprepared for it in almost every way. I was caught off guard both emotionally and intellectually. It felt like the universe was tossing me another curve ball, bushwhacking me as it had done so many times in the past.

And yet, perhaps I should have anticipated it. After all, there were hints, intimations of what was to come.

Only the day before, I was given a most prophetic foreshadowing. As is my wont, I had checked my astrological prediction on Jonathan Cainer's website. In some circles, Jonathan had a reputation for being "spookily accurate" and I had been reading his column for a number of years. I had never personally experienced his much reputed precognitive gift and occasionally his horoscopes could be way off the mark and downright obscure but the day before Sarah contacted me, he wrote:

Sagittarius, Thursday 6 February 1997

'Wednesday morning at five o'clock the day begins…' So begins one of the Beatles' most famous songs. It's a melancholy piece all about a sad situation. "She's Leaving Home" can still bring a tear to the

eye of the listener. But, not if, just for a change, life has stopped presenting them with reasons to be nervous and has begun instead to offer much-needed signs of support and reassurance. The question now is not, who or what is leaving? It is who or what is arriving? You are going to like this next visit.

Anyone who is familiar with the song knows it is about a daughter leaving home. But what Jonathan seemed to be suggesting was someone (perhaps a daughter?) arriving home. On reading the horoscope at that time, I did not really take much notice of it. It seemed cryptic and abstruse. I could not imagine it having any direct relevance to my life.

The next morning, however, I drove in to work to attend a staff meeting at the Melbourne Film School where I teach cinematography. The semester was only due to start the following week so there were no students and I was able to easily find parking. In the meeting we discussed preparations for teaching and our technical support needs. My colleagues are fairly easy-going and the session was amicable and courteous.

After the meeting I went to my office, booted up my computer and began checking my emails. Nothing seemed different, nothing out of the ordinary. But then things changed. After reading about half a dozen boring and banal administrivia emails, I encountered one by someone I did not know. It read:

I'm sorry to bother you but I'm trying to contact the James Morrison who studied at Wits University and the London Film School in the seventies. Is that, by any chance, you?

Regards,
Sarah Basinger

I wrote back acknowledging that it was, indeed, me and asked how I could be of assistance. She replied that she wanted to contact me about a personal matter and that it would probably be better if I gave her my private email address.

At this point I started to become quite anxious. The writer was unfamiliar to me and I was wary of Internet scams. I was once the victim of identity theft so I thought I should be careful. But something about this felt different. It seemed too personal, too intimate. Whoever she was, she seemed to know something about my history. I began to worry that it might be an enemy from the distant past. Very reluctantly, I sent her my private email address.

I logged out of the university system and logged into my private email account. Then I waited. After what seemed like a very long time but was probably only a few minutes, I received the following email:

Hi James,

I'm sorry for contacting you suddenly. There is no other way to say this other than I understand you dated my mother Carol and I believe there is a strong possibility you are my father.

Sarah

Well, it's almost impossible to describe my reaction to this bombshell. Talk about a curve ball! I think something of the disquiet I was feeling can be inferred from my reply. I wrote:

Hi Sarah,

You are really freaking me out here!!!!! Please can you give me some more information? Could you perhaps tell me who your mother was, how I met her, how I knew her? Why am I only hearing about this now??? Please!!!!

James

I felt short of breath and my right arm was aching. It was impossible to concentrate on anything and I knew I would not be able to do any work. I thought of contacting my wife, Karen, and telling her about the email but I wasn't sure how she would react. So I shut down the computer and went outside for a walk.

Although it was still early, the sun was beating down and it was brutally hot in the Melbourne summer. My breathing became more laboured as I stumbled into our local coffee shop and ordered a cappuccino. When my order came, I stared distractedly into the chocolate-sprinkled froth. Nothing seemed real.

Across the street I could see graffiti painted on an old warehouse. The building was empty and abandoned and recently homeless people had broken into it and started sleeping there. But now they were nowhere to be seen and the site looked deserted and neglected.

My thoughts were racing, jumping all over the place. For some bizarre reason, it occurred to me that it was the 7th of February and that this was Charles Dickens's birthday. I remembered that as a young boy the writer had felt abandoned by his father, "cast away" and forced to work in a boot-blacking factory.

But what had any of this to do with me? Unlike Dickens's father, I had not ditched or forsaken a child. Of course I had a daughter but she lived with me and had been with me from birth. I had always loved her and looked after her. I didn't have any other children and if I did, I would certainly know about them.

So clearly there was something wrong here. This must be some kind of error or misunderstanding. It had to be either a simple case of mistaken identity or a sophisticated scam. There was no real threat to me and nothing to be afraid of. I should talk it over with Karen. See what she had to say.

Back in the office, I booted up the computer and called my wife. I read the email to her.

'Do you think it's genuine?' she asked.

'I don't know. Seems like a pretty elaborate hoax if it's not.

I don't recognize the name at all. Sarah Basinger. I don't know anyone by that name.'

'It might be a married name. Do you know how old she is? Or where she lives?'

'It's a UK email address. That's all I know,' I replied.

'Not South Africa? Not from home?'

'No, she's definitely writing from somewhere in England,' I said.

'She seems to know a lot about you. Where you studied, that kind of thing.'

'Well my academic history is on the school's website. She could easily have read up on that. There's also quite a lot of information available about me on the Internet.'

'You know,' Karen casually remarked, 'I've always thought this was a possibility. It's always been in the back of my mind that this could happen. You screwed so many other women before we met.'

'None after,' I quickly added.

'Hmph! So what are you going to do now?'

'I'm not sure. Never been in this situation before. Maybe I'll ask her for more information.'

So I wrote back to Sarah asking her for more information. Within minutes there was a new email which read:

Hi James,

Sorry to drop this on you so suddenly. My mother's name is Carol Basinger. I believe you knew each other in the 70s. I am 20 years old. I still live with my mother. We live in Elephant & Castle in London. I only found out about you (who you were that is) two weeks ago. Only recently has my mother wanted me to contact you. My mum and I are very close. I don't know what else I can tell you.

Sarah

I wrote back:

Sarah,

I don't know anyone called Carol Basinger. I know no one by that name. Are you sure you have the right James Morrison?

James

There was no reply for several hours and I was prepared to dismiss the whole episode as a simple case of mistaken identity. Then she wrote again and everything changed.

Hi James,

Sorry I took so long getting back to you. I had to get hold of my mum. She was in a meeting at her work. She said to tell you two things. She said you would understand. She said to tell you:

Cookie. The Russian class.

Fear burst through my body in a shuddering wave. It felt like a hand was reaching up through the past and squeezing my heart.

***

It's been two weeks now since Sarah first contacted me. There has been a flurry of emails between us. In the beginning I tried to ascertain if this was all true, whether it was possible and if indeed she was my daughter.

She began by telling me about her interests – the fact that she liked literature and films, the theatre and history. She told me she was very outspoken, direct to the point of sometimes being tactless. I guess she figured some of these personality traits were inheritable and maybe we were similar in many ways. And, of course we were but all kinds of people can have these qualities. There was nothing definitive about any of this.

Then I asked her to send me a photograph. When I saw it there was no longer any doubt. She could not be anything other than my daughter. She had my smile, my plump cheeks, my colouring, my eyes, my hair, my nose, my lips, my face. It was uncanny.

Sarah also very closely resembled my own sister at that age. They had the same platinum blonde hair, the same demeanour and countenance. We discussed having a DNA test and I even made enquiries about how to go about that when one party was in Australia and the other in the UK. And then I seemed to lose her. She became reticent and withdrawn, a little wary and a touch hostile and combative. I wondered if she was hiding something. Why should she resist such a simple and definitive test?

And then it occurred to me. She wanted me to care about her because of who she was and because she believed I was her father. She wanted my acknowledgement without some scientific evidence. So I wrote to her and told her the test was unimportant, I did not need it. If we lived in the fifteenth century, I said, no such corroboration would have been available to us. We would have had to go on trust and gut instinct and that every fibre of my being already told me that she was my daughter. I felt that immediately and unquestionably. I told her I wanted her in my life and that, if I had known about her, I would have wanted her in my life before. She was a part of me.

We made a time to speak on the phone. When I heard her voice, despite the London accent, it sounded so familiar, so intimate. At first we were a little shy with each other and the conversation was strained, but soon we opened up.

'I managed to track you down because I was watching an Australian movie and I saw your name on the credits. "Director of Photography: James Morrison".'

'What was the movie called?' I asked.

'*Four Horsemen,*' she replied.

'Oh yes. Did you like it?'

'I thought it was fabulous! Very inventive and beautifully photographed.'

'Thanks. It was fun to work on.'

'I was a little confused though,' Sarah said. 'I thought you lived in South Africa. What are you doing in Australia?'

'I immigrated a few years ago. It's a long story which I'll tell you one day.'

'I know so little about you. I wish I had known you when I was younger.'

'We'll get to know each other. You must come to Australia to visit. I really want you to come here and meet us. We are all dying to see you in person. You are part of my family. You are my daughter and I love you.'

After that things between us improved. Sarah was much less guarded, much more open and forthcoming, much more inclined to tell me things. But there was one thing she could not tell me and that was why I was only finding out about her now. Why had I not even known of her existence until very recently? Sarah's only answer to this question was that her mother had wanted to protect her. But she did not know exactly from what or from whom. She only knew that, for some reason, her mother had been compelled to live a secret life. To hide her true identity and to keep the truth from her daughter. Sarah suspected it had something to do with what was going on in South Africa at the time. Something political.

This was, I told her, only partly true. There was much more to it than just that. The whole story was much more complex, much darker. Despite the fact that I knew it was going to be painful, I knew that I would have to go there. I knew that I would have to travel back in time and unravel the truth, visit some of those places that haunted me. Enter once again the Russian class.

THE 1970'S

1

JAMES

The first classmate I really got to know was Marty Lehman. This was in the late summer of 1971 soon after I had completed my compulsory military service in the South African army. I had no idea what I wanted to do with my life, other than take photographs, watch movies and read books so I decided to enrol in an arts degree at the University of the Witwatersrand (affectionately called "Wits" by the locals, the "W" pronounced the Dutch way as "V", so "Vits") in Johannesburg.

It was deep into the *apartheid* era so all universities were segregated and Wits only admitted white students. During Orientation Week, just before the semester started, you were expected to sign on, in person, for the subjects you had selected. This took place in a large, open-plan room called the Exam Hall on the fourth floor of the Central Block just above the Great Hall. Tables were stacked around the perimeter of the room and each subject was allocated a particular table. Coloured posters identified the subject and a lecturer responsible for coordination sat at each table. Students would line up in front of the tables and wait to sign on and arrange tutorial times.

Nowadays, with computerization and on-line enrolments, the

whole process has been simplified but then everything had to be done manually and laboriously. It might have been cumbersome but there were some distinct advantages to the old method in that it gave you face to face contact with your lecturer who could answer any of your enquiries and personally assist you.

I had made a very eclectic choice of subjects – Law, English, Drama & Film and Russian. To graduate, I was obliged to pass at least two language courses and I was really hoping to enrol in Spanish but it clashed with my Law course so, on a whim, I decided to join the Russian class. It sounded offbeat, glamorous and the queue was very short. There was only one person ahead of me. Strange how one's whole future life can be set in stone by such an arbitrary and capricious decision.

There was a rather lively discussion going on between the student ahead of me and the lecturer so I let my mind drift off. In my youth I was a notorious daydreamer, often escaping into my own private thoughts, so I was caught unawares when the student suddenly turned around. Very abruptly, I broke out of my reverie and noticed that he was wearing a bright pink tee shirt with a copy of the poster for Eisenstein's film *Battleship Potemkin* blazoned across the front. Even though the print was in Cyrillic script which I could not yet read, I nevertheless, immediately recognized it.

Confused and surprised, I blurted out: '*Battleship Potemkin*. It's a famous film.'

The young man looked at me quizzically and seemed about to say something. Then he simply shrugged his shoulders and smiled in a sort of lazy, knowing way. Very casually he slipped past me and was gone. I could feel myself blushing self-consciously. Fumbling with my papers, I signed on to join the Russian class.

About twenty minutes later, after I had enrolled in my other subjects, I was standing in the line for Drama & Film when I felt a gentle tap on my shoulder. I turned around and there was Potemkin tee shirt again.

'We must be the only students in the entire university who have enrolled in both Russian and Drama & Film' he said grinning. 'I hear the intake for Russian is very small and there are fewer than a dozen people doing the subject.'

'*Ja*, apparently it's the first year that they've offered it. People are still not sure about it. I doubt if it will ever be very popular though.'

'So what do you know about *Potemkin*?' he asked, smiling.

And that's how I met Marty. He had a scraggly, half-grown beard, curly brown hair and the most disarming smile. He seemed very laid-back, loose-limbed and nonchalant. He was not tall but he had a relaxed confidence in his angular, thin-framed body. Marty was very talkative; on first meeting him he would look you straight in the eyes and bombard you with twenty unrelated questions in no particular order.

'Do you like Eisenstein? Personally, I've always thought some of his montage ideas are crap. What about Welles? Have you seen *Citizen Kane*? Just saw it in London over the holidays. Have you been to England? The weather was dreadful. Nearly froze my arse off. Saw some good stuff though. Movies and shows. Are you into the theatre? I thought I'd explore that. Do some acting? That's why I'm enrolling in this course. Drama & Film. Should be fun. Are you a performer? I see you have a camera. Is that an SLR? Are you any good? Have you heard the new Stones album? The guitar riffs are brilliant…' etc.

After this initial onslaught, this barrage of questions, he would ease off and listen to your responses in an amiable and empathic way. Normally I am quite reticent about telling people, especially strangers, anything about me. But Marty was so sympathetic or should I say, so unthreatening, that I began to tell him about my interest in the cinema. He showed a genuine understanding and we chatted together as we worked our way to the front of the queue and then signed on for the course.

Outside, while we continued talking, Marty suggested we

get something to drink. Although he was a freshman like me, he seemed to already know his way around the campus and he led us, with an easy familiarity, to the student cafeteria.

Over coffee he told me about the Wits Film Society. This was great news as I was a committed *cinephile* fascinated by the whole cinematic storytelling process. I loved all kinds of movies and devoured whatever I could see (which was not much in South Africa at that time).

'They have screenings every fortnight. The first one is this Sunday. You must come. Apparently they will be showing some really good stuff this year – Truffaut, Godard, Mizoguchi, maybe even some Eisenstein.'

'Fantastic,' I replied. 'Perhaps now I'll get to see *Potemkin.*'

Marty spoke with some authority about all these film-makers. Travelling abroad with his parents he'd seen many seminal films. I found myself both delighted and intimidated by his erudition. I had read about many of the directors he mentioned but had never seen their work and I dared not mention this. So I simply nodded sagely as he continued to drop names.

The conversation shifted to other things. He told me that most of his ancestors were from Lithuania and had fled the Russian Empire pogroms. This was one of the reasons he had decided to enrol in the Russian class. He wanted to get in touch with his origins.

Despite all the hardships we both experienced later, our friendship endured. I still miss him terribly. But then I was captivated by his easy, self-assured manner as he talked of his love for drawing and how he used charcoal in a sparse, expressionist way. His goal, he told me, was to broaden out his talents as an artist and apply them to a wide range of creative media – theatre, animated film, architectural design, installation and gallery exhibition.

Marty seemed, in so many ways, to be the very antithesis of me. He was poised, urbane and sophisticated whereas I was clumsy, naïve and provincial. He knew exactly what he wanted and how he planned to get it. I, on the other hand, had no expectations, no clear trajectory for my life. I had some vague notions about making films but that was all. I hoped that I would be happy and successful but I had no real goals, no vision.

The following Sunday evening at the film society screening Marty introduced me to his girlfriend, Ruth Jacobson. She really blew me away. She had mousy-brown, curly hair, intense grey eyes and an aquiline nose. If you took each of her features individually, they might seem mundane, quite ordinary but the way in which they were all put together just seemed, to my mind, magical. I found her enchanting.

She was quiet but self-assured. A good listener, by which I mean she could entice you into talking about yourself. Unlike Marty who had a privileged childhood and came from a wealthy family, Ruth's background was very different. Her parents were immigrants and Holocaust survivors. Her mother had been liberated from the horrors of Bergen Belsen and her father had been a *häftling* in Dachau. They were the only living members of their immediate families to have made it through the *Shoah*.

After the war her parents met in a Displaced Persons' Camp where they married. They originally intended going to Israel but the British were restricting immigration. Ruth's father, Benjamin Jakubowics, had a cousin in Johannesburg who offered to help him if he came to South Africa. Destitute and desperate to make a home for themselves anywhere outside Europe, the site of such pain and suffering to them, Ruth's parents boarded the first available ship for Cape Town.

From the outset, life in their new country was extremely difficult. They spoke only Yiddish and German so they struggled to communicate with people. Eventually they acquired jobs and learned English but never lost their heavy foreign accents. They anglicized their name to Jacobson and, in time, made a life for themselves. Benjamin gave private piano lessons to schoolchildren and his wife, Sadie, became a bookkeeper.

These experiences were etched into Ruth's very being. They defined her, shaped and branded her just as the numbered tattoos on her parents' arms forever marked them. Throughout her childhood she was always conscious of her father and mother's struggles to make ends meet. She knew that, in relation with the vast majority of black people in the country, they were well off but compared to her white peers, her family lived in genteel poverty.

They had a small yellow-brick bungalow in the predominantly Jewish suburb of Orange Grove. During her high school years, Ruth seldom invited friends home as she felt ashamed by her modest home and the foreign manners of her parents. At the same time, she experienced guilt about these feelings and grew irascible and angry with herself for what she considered to be self-centred.

Given what they had lived through, Benjamin and Sadie doted on their only child and were extremely overprotective. Ruth responded with a quiet rebellion and a firm commitment to finding her own way in the world. She was determined to make something spectacular and meaningful of her life. In time, she would fulfil even her own great expectations.

I can no longer recall what movie we watched that night at film society. I have a feeling it was something Nordic, very pretentious and forgettable. I do, however, remember that after the show we met up with some of Marty's friends and ended up at a flat in Hillbrow. There must have been about a dozen of us sitting on cushions on the floor in the living room. We were all drinking cheap *Lieberstein* wine, smoking and talking.

That was the first time I had ever smoked *dagga* which was bountifully passed around in big, fat joints. I can't say that I really took to it. I vaguely remember feeling high and getting into a giggling fit but after that I felt a little paranoid and edgy.

Later on, a guitar suddenly appeared and people began belting out Beatles numbers. I usually hate sing-alongs but something unique and entrancing seemed to happen when Ruth picked up the guitar and started playing. She opened slowly building up to a complex hybrid picking style that allowed her to run a couple of musical lines at once. I remembered that her father taught music and it was in her blood, her genes. The first song she sang was Dylan's haunting *Farewell Angelina* which Joan Baez had made legendary. Ruth's interpretation was heart-rending, her voice pure, ragged and fragile with no trace of vibrato.

Nobody sang along. We all listened quietly. Then she played a couple of Ewan MacColl ballads starting with *Black and White,* a savage, political number about the Sharpeville Uprising that I had never heard before. Ruth seemed to strip the song down to its basics, respecting its rustic folk origins but somehow managing to emphasize the primal human emotions at the song's core. She followed this with a sublime and idiosyncratic rendition of *The First Time Ever I Saw Your Face,* the gentle guitar arpeggios and sobbing strings perfectly complementing her brittle, soulful voice. Exquisite and tender.

It was probably as a consequence of smoking that dope but, by the time Ruth finished singing, I was weeping and tears were running down my face. I felt completely overwhelmed by a complex mishmash of emotions. One part of me was rejoicing, grateful for meeting my new-found friends and the dawning of my life at university. At last I could be liberated from the shackles that had confined me for so long – boarding school, the army, my parents. Finally, I could release myself from the restrictive conventional values that had held me captive all my life. Once and for all I could be what I wanted to be. Do what I wanted to do. I could live a bohemian lifestyle without guilt or fear. I was free.

But at the same time, I felt crushed by feelings of inadequacy. I was deeply aware of my own limitations. Marty and Ruth seemed so bright, so talented, so self-assured, so centred and when I compared myself to them, I felt incompetent, useless. Hopeless. I had no skills, no special abilities and no aptitude for anything. Of course I had my photography but what I was doing with it seemed inauthentic, derivative. Narrow and circumscribed. Somehow pointless.

If only I had been able to see what lay ahead. To look into the future and predict all the hardships, all the crises and adversities that were waiting for us. If I had known then, what I know now, I could have changed it all and done something to make it different. But prescience is a gift we are never given. We can never look forward, we can only look back.

2

JAMES

One thing Marty was wrong about was that he and I would be the only students enrolled in both Russian and Drama & Film. There were three others; one of them was Ruth but also Marty's good friend David Kastner and an Afrikaans girl, Marie le Roux who everyone called Cookie.

David and Marty went to the same high school and had known each other for ages. Together with Ruth, the three of them were united in their commitment to local theatre. They were inseparable, always together, tight.

David was the natural leader of the group. Charismatic and self-confident, very assured of his opinions and secure in the knowledge of the place he would make for himself in the world. He was tall and carried himself with an aristocratic bearing that was almost patrician. His hair was cut in a severe, pageboy style in the manner of the Hal Foster comic book character, Prince Valiant. Open, convivial and affable he never distanced himself from others but he seemed to come from another planet, a more refined one.

Marie (or Cookie) had long, dark, almost black hair, down to her shoulders. In class, I watched it shining in the sunlight pouring through the window. I wanted to touch her hair, stroke it. Her eyes were hazel, her nose straight, pronounced cheekbones. She had fine features which I considered very beautiful. Right from the start I had a serious crush on her but was too shy to do anything other than exchange pleasantries. So I secretly hid my adulation, my ardent yearnings.

Cookie had some impressive skills. She was excellent at languages. She had an ear for them and was majoring in both English and Afrikaans. She would have liked to also enrol in French but it clashed with her timetable so she ended up, by complete chance, in the Russian class. Despite it not being her first choice of subject, she liked the course and enjoyed the sound of the language on her tongue. *Paroosskie. Ya panee mayu paroosskie.* It sounded good, exotic and sophisticated.

Cookie was also an accomplished actress with an exquisite phonetic ear and a phenomenal gift for mimicry that enabled her to reproduce a range of different accents both local and foreign. She spoke priceless cockney, with appropriate rhyming slang, imitating to perfection both Michael Caine and Barbara Windsor which we all found hilarious.

Through her I met the only other Afrikaans student in the class, Antoine Pienaar. He was camp and flamboyant, and called everyone darling. Big and well-built, his huge muscles bulged through his half-unbuttoned chambray shirt. He pretended to be mellow, carefree and extroverted but I soon found out this was all an act. In truth, he was really very private and introspective. He liked to kid me, call me a "gadget queen" because I was always fooling around with my camera and taking photographs.

The Russian class was very small and we soon got to know each other. There were only three other students all seemingly committed to left-wing politics.

Rory Callaghan usually sat in the front of the class. He was a little older than the rest of us and was earnest, single-minded and self-disciplined. With his bright ginger hair and sparkling green eyes, he was unmistakably Irish. Rory was keen to learn and always came across as restless and impatient, waiting for the class to start.

Then there was "Fat Bill" Saunders who seemed to always be fooling around with his pens and pencils. Unlike my handwriting which was spidery and untidy, Bill wrote in this very precise, ornate, florid manner. He spent a great deal of time refining his letters, thin going up and thick coming down. Someone once told me this kind of opulent handwriting signalled a narcissistic personality. But at the time, Bill seemed jovial and sociable, a hail-fellow-well-met type, the party animal.

Finally, there was Diane Wilkins who almost always arrived late. She dressed impeccably in exclusive designer clothes, never jeans like the rest of us. Pearls around her neck, a cashmere sweater loosely draped on her shoulders, a somewhat outdated look, her mother's style. Diane was charming and sophisticated. To me she seemed an exotic anomaly with eyes that gave nothing away. I found her difficult to ignore but impossible to comprehend.

That was it – just nine students and our lecturer, Dr Vladislav Ivanovich Kozar, a genuine Russian émigré, born way out east in Vladivostok but educated in the capital, Moscow. He was an urbane, erudite man, balding with a pronounced and ugly comb-over that occasionally impeded the vision in his left eye. He was passionate about nineteenth-century Russian literature but unfortunately, he also had an injurious dependence upon alcohol in particular 80-proof Polish vodka.

I remember that he always used to say: 'In French you can only make love. In German you can only make war. And in English you can only make money. But in Russian you can do all three!' He was a first-rate teacher, articulate and patient. Dr Kozar would spend lots of time explaining grammatical intricacies and he had a prodigious knowledge of Russian literature having written an excellent book on Pushkin.

He had this ritualistic way of starting the class. He would walk forward (in my mind's eye this always happened in slow motion) up to the lectern and then bow formally to us and say: '*Zdrastvoitya.*' Then the Russian class would begin. A class made up of a small circle of friends. Well, maybe not friends – acquaintances or fellow students. Classmates. Yes, that's it, classmates. Nothing more really, nothing else to tie us together. When I think about it now, after all these years, that's the only thing that connected us. Such an arbitrary, random relationship. And yet so much sprang from it.

3

FAT BILL

The first time William ("Fat Bill") Saunders spoke to his future wife, he thought he was on his way to prison.

On the day in question, Fat Bill and about fifty other students had been involved in a demonstration on the steps of Wits University's Central Block. They were protesting against the country's oppressive security legislation and the recent detention without trial of an academic professor in the anthropology department.

Wits was known as a liberal institution and the mainstream press often portrayed students as "long-haired dissolute lefties". But in truth, most of the students were pretty conservative, content to leave politics to others and enjoy the fruits of the status quo. This was, after all, a segregated institution.

There was, however, a small radical group made up of secretive and tightly-knit left-leaning intellectuals who kept to themselves and only selectively admitted outsiders to their ranks.

Of course, Fat Bill knew that Diane Wilkins was part of that crowd. She was in his Russian class and he had seen who she hung out with. For some time, he'd wanted to find an excuse to talk to her but no opportunity had really arisen. But now she was the one taking the initiative and conversing with him.

It was cramped in the back of the police van and Diane had to reach over someone else to touch him. She gently pressed his hand, a light almost imperceptible brushing across his fingers.

'Are you alright?' she asked. 'The cops whacked you pretty hard. That was very brave of you. You just stood your ground. The moment they charged us, I shat myself and ran.'

Despite the slight chill in the air, Fat Bill was sweating profusely. He wondered if she noticed. He was acutely aware of a pungent odour but he expected they were all sweating in the confined spaces of the overcrowded van.

Everyone was talking rather excitedly. For many of the students it was the first time they had experienced being baton-charged by police and dogs. It was like the aftermath of a battle and they were just coming down from the adrenaline rush. Some of them were still shaking, their nerves jingle-jangling all over the place. In the far corner a young woman was quietly weeping. Fat Bill could hear someone else whispering '*Jesus, jong!*' over and over.

He felt slightly elated. He touched the welts on his back where one of the cops had *sjambokked* him. Some of the wounds were raw, bleeding through his shirt. None of this worried him and Diane's observation about his lack of fear was pretty accurate. Certainly he had felt no anxiety when the baton charge began, rather he had watched in awe as all around him his fellow students panicked and scattered in different directions.

But then none of this was entirely new to him. He'd participated in baton charges before but from the other side. Then he had been one of the ones charging, not being charged; one of the hunters, not the hunted. Because for the last two years, Fat Bill had been a policeman.

At that time in South Africa, all young white men were conscripted into the armed forces. Unless you had some serious illness, you were required to serve in some branch of the military

16

for at least a year. For the average Joe, with no political connections, there was no choice about where you found yourself. If you were lucky, you were assigned to either the air force (the glamorous option) or the navy (the safest option). The unlucky ones were drafted into the army where they could end up fighting on the border against insurgents. Not only was it the most dangerous option but it was also the most psychologically debilitating and many veterans of the border war returned home haggard and *bosbefokked* with emotional problems brought on by combat stress.

The only way to avoid this was to volunteer for the police force. The advantage was that you were stationed in your home town and you evaded fighting in a guerrilla war. The disadvantage was that you served for a longer period – two years rather than one.

Ever the pragmatist, Fat Bill opted for this choice.

As a policeman, it was his job to enforce the law and in *apartheid* South Africa that meant not only preventing criminal activity but also implementing racial segregation. So Fat Bill found himself arresting black men and women for Pass Law violations, for living in "whites only" designated areas and for other petty offenses that restricted their mobility and freedom of movement. He witnessed lovers being imprisoned for sexual liaisons across the colour bar. He observed the detention and torture of political activists and dissidents. And he saw the callous and reckless exercise of power.

All of this, Fat Bill would later tell people, profoundly changed his views about the country. He realized that a vicious and perverted ideology could only be enforced by brutal means. He was able to see, first hand, what kind of cruel means had to be used to put down political foment, to silence dissent. The scales, he said, had fallen from his eyes and he experienced a kind of epiphany.

And now here he was, in the back of this paddy wagon giving Diane Wilkins, *the* Diane Wilkins, his most disarming smile.

'I'm fine,' he said, beaming at her. 'Just a little shook up. Any idea where they're taking us? John Vorster Square?'

'No. I believe Hillbrow Police Station. It's closer. Apparently they are not taking this very seriously. They'll book us and let us go.'

She sounded very English. No trace of the lazy South African inflections there. Quite snooty and almost condescending. A private school accent. *An accent not unlike my own,* Fat Bill thought. *God, we're all still so defined and confined by class, victims of privilege.*

Diane was right. Within a few hours they had all been fingerprinted and released. They were required to appear before a magistrate the next week.

Fat Bill was one of the last to be processed and when he left the police station he found most of the others hanging around outside, smoking and chatting loudly. Diane was in a small group and she smiled warmly as he joined them. He offered her a Texan which she declined. As he was lighting up his own, the guy next to Diane, a scrawny kid with long blonde hair, began to tell a story about when he was in the army and how the corporal they had always arrived on parade demanding: '*Ek soek* Lucky Strike, Texan or Gunston. *Wie het dit?*' ('I'm looking for Lucky Strike, Texan or Gunston. Who's got it?')

Everybody laughed. It was a story they all understood. The bully who thought he could take whatever he felt like. Whatever he thought was owed to him. A story about *baasskap.* The white man must always be boss.

Then someone suggested the Devonshire Hotel (the Dev), a student pub in Braamfontein. There was a general murmur of assent, approving nods and smiles as they all began drifting off in that direction.

'Coming?' Diane asked.

'Absolutely!' replied Fat Bill beaming once more.

There were booths in the pub and Fat Bill found himself sitting opposite Diane squeezed in with four other young men he only vaguely knew. People seemed to be flickering and flittering around her, the queen bee. It was now late afternoon and the pub was crowded and smoke-filled. Everybody seemed in good spirits, flushed with victory. The enemy drubbed. Several people came over and toasted Fat Bill. Clearly he was the hero of the moment. The fearless defender who had not submitted. They patted him on the shoulder and expressed concern over his injuries.

Diane was telling him about *Bonnie and Clyde*, a film she had recently seen and liked. Fat Bill listened attentively, watching her carefully. He knew he would remember this day forever and he wanted to savour every detail. He found the cadence of her voice, its slight breathless quality, captivating. Leaning in closer, he smiled, holding her gaze with his own. Her eyes large, the colour of iron ore speckled with copper.

'Like it's really violent but it's got this kind of gentle, very fairy tale kind of quality as well. Nostalgic but with a cool overlay. These criminal outsiders taking on the system. It's weird. Almost epic but also banal at the same time. Very eerie.'

Fat Bill had seen the movie so he understood what she was on about. He knew Diane was identifying with the Faye Dunaway character in some way. Seeing herself as living that kind of role. The last romantic couple on the run. At once free but at the same time trapped by destiny and fate. Believing she could choose in a world where everything was pre-determined.

Fat Bill wished he could tell her that both of them were the victims of powerful historical forces that were dragging them along. Shaping the events that would unfold. Binding them together irrevocably. But he knew he should keep silent. *Do with me what you will*, he thought. *Just let it happen. And don't show your hand too soon.*

He felt reconciled to what he believed would be inevitable. And so, when a short while later, Diane got up to leave, he did not try to persuade her to stay. He just smiled and gently kissed her cheek. She had to get home – her mother was expecting her she said.

'See you on Friday,' he said. 'In Russian.'

'Yes,' she said. 'In the Russian class. With all the other irregular verbs.'

Then she was gone.

Fat Bill kept drinking. He began working his way around the pub, on the lookout for some "stray", some piece of "*los*". Someone asked him where he got his nickname from. He felt like punching the guy's lights out. Instead he merely lifted his shirt and stuck out his gut. This got a few laughs. In truth, he liked being called Fat Bill. It marked him, set him apart from others, gave him status and authority. Like some Western gunman – Wild Bill Hickok. A man doing what a man must do.

He found a small group that looked promising. He started talking to a brunette called Nicole who was studying sociology. She had the kind of slovenly looks he liked. He flattered her and told her she was beautiful. Told her all kinds of little white lies.

They were both a little unsteady on their feet when they finally left the pub at closing time. It was cold and Fat Bill was freezing. Someone lent him a sweater. Nicole had a small one-bedroom flat a few streets away and they made their way to it.

In her bedroom, just before he kissed her, Fat Bill told her he loved her in Russian. '*Ya loobloo tebya,*' he whispered. That seemed to please her.

He was thirsty when he woke up. He had a slight hangover but overall he felt happy with the way things had gone. In the kitchen he poured himself a glass of water and drank it over the sink. The sociology student was still sleeping when he went back into the bedroom. She looked vulnerable in a corrupt/innocent way. Fat Bill wished he could remember her name. Nicolette. Nicki. Something like that.

He kissed her lightly on the forehead and she stirred slightly in her sleep. Then he pulled on the borrowed sweater and walked out the door without looking back.

In the street he smiled. 'Progress, Billy Boy!' he told himself. 'You're making progress.'

4

COOKIE

In South Africa, they have this biscuit called a Marie. It's pronounced in the Afrikaans way, sort of like Mars without the s and then a long ee sound. Nothing like how Americans say it – you know the Elvis song *"Marie's the name of his latest flame"*. Not like that at all.

Anyway, when she was a kid, Cookie's brother used to tease her and call her "Marie biscuit" which she hated. It really upset her and she would burst into tears every time he did it, which only spurred him on to doing it again and again. So her father, who Cookie adored, came to her rescue. He said: 'Marie's much too nice to be a biscuit. She's really a cookie.' And that's how she got the name – Cookie. It was her father's special term of endearment for her. He always called her that when he hugged and cuddled her.

And then, when she began attending school, on the first day, the teacher asked her what her name was. She said 'Marie'. The teacher said: 'But what's your other name?' She replied: 'Cookie.' The teacher smiled and from that day on that's what she called her. And the name stuck, right through junior and high school and university. That's how everyone knew her. That became her name. Cookie. Cookie le Roux.

Cookie was both highly sociable and outspoken. She never hesitated to let people know what she thought on any subject and was, at all times, forthright and direct. Because she was gregarious and loved meeting new people, she decided to make the most of her time at university and joined a number of sporting clubs, playing amongst other things, bridge and badminton.

She also signed on to the theatre group that David Kastner set up with Marty, Ruth and James. The group would meet at least twice a week for workshops and rehearsals at a scout hall in the western suburb of Melville. These extramural activities resulted in a number of complications and difficulties for Cookie. Her family lived in Brakpan and she was obliged to catch trains to and from Johannesburg every day to get into university. With these other activities, she was often forced to travel late at night and the constant to-ing and fro-ing was becoming onerous and burdensome. She decided to try and find a place to stay near the university.

The opportunity came through a student whom she had met in the Wits badminton club. Bob Elliot captained the men's team and had occasionally partnered with Cookie in a mixed doubles match. After one particularly high-powered game, he told her that he shared a communal house in Melville and that recently someone had moved out and the commune was looking for another young woman to lend a hand with the rent.

This was an ideal location and Bob assured Cookie that, if she was interested, she would be able to get a large sunny bedroom. Everyone in the commune, he told her, was friendly and they shared the chores, like cooking, in an equitable and responsible manner. Together they all contributed to the wages of the domestic servant, Rosie, who cleaned the house and tended the garden.

They agreed to meet on Stiemans Street the following Wednesday afternoon. The sky was darkening and a thunderstorm was brewing when Bob drove up in his battered Ford Cortina. He reached over and opened the passenger door for Cookie to get in.

'Hi,' he said. 'I wasn't sure if I should call you to remind you in case you forgot.'

'Not necessary,' Cookie replied as he drove off, turning the car into Jan Smuts Avenue. 'I never forget anything.'

'How's that?' Bob asked.

'I've got this weird memory. I guess you could call it photographic.'

'Really! You mean you remember absolutely everything?'

'Not exactly. But if I read something just once, like a poem, I'll remember it all. I'm not sure how to explain it…'

Cookie wondered how she could describe her prodigious memory. She had once read a short story by Borges called *Funes the Memorious*. It's about a man who has an accident falling from his horse and as a consequence, is paralysed but acquires a miraculous memory that allows him to relive and recall every moment of his life. But to remember a day, takes him a whole day. It is a gift but also a curse. Cookie's memory did not work like that but she could conjure up images and incidents from the past in ways that often surprised people. She would read something just once and then repeat it verbatim.

'There's no trick involved. In fact, I don't even know how I do it. I suppose it involves mnemonics of some kind but I'm unconscious of it,' she said.

'You mean you make some kind of associations with what you're trying to remember?' Bob asked.

'Well that's the theory. Most experts think it works that way because they argue that true eidetic or photographic memory doesn't exist,' Cookie said.

'And what do you think?' Bob asked.

'I'm not sure. In my Russian class, our lecturer told us about Solomon Shereshevsky who apparently could memorize complex mathematical formulae or read a book and repeat it word for word. It seemed he had some kind of synesthesia whereby the stimulation of one of his senses caused a reaction in another one. So if he heard a musical note, he would see a color or if he touched something he might then notice an odor with it. This helped him to remember things through association. It probably works like that for me but like I said I'm not consciously aware of it.'

'Did this suddenly happen?' Bob asked. 'Or did you fall off a horse or something?'

'No,' Cookie laughed. 'I've always been cursed like this.'

'You're right,' Bob joked. 'That is weird.' And they both laughed.

By now it was raining quite hard, a typical brief Highveld thunderstorm. She had only met him recently but driving along Empire Road in his battered Ford Cortina, Cookie found Bob to be both likable and charming. He had long, wavy, shoulder-length blonde hair and a droopy moustache in the style of David Crosby. Bob favoured a relaxed hippy lifestyle and dressed accordingly – cheesecloth shirts, cord bellbottoms, sandals. Cookie found herself responding positively towards his self-assured and affable manner which put her totally at ease so she was more communicative and forthcoming in his company.

By the time they reached Melville, the storm had passed and the sun was breaking through the clouds. Cookie noticed that the house was built in a Victorian style with traditional white walls, a green corrugated-iron roof and large, expansive verandas facing north and east. It was pleasant and appealing and she immediately felt comfortable and secure. The house seemed familiar, as if she was returning home after a long journey. She knew at once that she would be happy there.

She calculated that, with her bursary and the money she made from her part-time waitressing job, she could easily afford the rent. By cutting out her daily train trips, she would also save money and have more time to herself.

So it was decided and they began to discuss the details of Cookie's house move. They sat in the deep shade of the veranda while the sun slowly descended in the violet sky. The house stood on a slight incline and below them was a large rugby field which stretched all the way to the Melville *koppies*. A group of men, in shorts and rugby jerseys, were coming on to the field.

While they watched the men warming up, stretching and jogging around, Bob casually began to roll a joint. He lit up, inhaled deeply and then offered Cookie a hit. She declined with a nod of her head. Although she had no objections to others partaking, Cookie never touched drugs.

Now, the swell of rainwater was gently streaming down the *koppie*, the bright sunlight reflecting off it so that the rocks sparkled and glinted. Cookie was reminded that this was how these rocky ridges got to be named the Witwatersrand or white waters reef. She loved this sight, felt the landscape was every bit of her, that it defined her and was part of her essence. That she could never leave it.

And so it was with much anticipation that she looked forward to her move to Melville and getting to discover more about her new friend. It was impossible for her to know then how significant and beneficial this friendship would later be for her.

5

'Call me George Kaplan,' he said, grinning madly.

He was a big man, a very big man. Chunky. A slight pot belly, balding with grizzled, mousy brown hair. He wore a powder blue safari suit with short pants, the ubiquitous black comb poking out of one of his matching long socks. He wasn't what you'd expect of a spy – nothing at all glamorous about him, certainly no James Bond.

It was the first time Rory Callaghan had met his "control", the man who was to be his only contact with the communist underground. They were sitting on the veranda of a suburban hotel just off Corlett Drive, watching the traffic and drinking ice-cold Castle beers. Kaplan had picked the location, someplace where neither of them were known.

'I'm sure you know the drill,' he said, still grinning. 'We only meet when absolutely necessary or in emergencies.'

Kaplan had a broad diastema like the Wife of Bath who was similarly "gat-toothed". Rory recalled reading somewhere that it was thought to be a genetic marker for sensuality and that Chaucer had used the description to alert the reader to her licentiousness. He wondered if Kaplan was equally lascivious.

'I've acquired a postbox for you at Parkview Post Office. It's in the name of Bruno Anthony.' He reached into his side pocket. 'Here's the key.'

Rory noticed some light chalk marks on Kaplan's safari suit and deduced that he was probably a schoolteacher.

'From time to time, I'll be sending you literature to this postbox. Here's the number – 79165.' Rory took the key and a slip of paper from Kaplan. 'Be careful. It's all banned stuff, mostly from the ANC or the SACP. You need to make copies and then send them out to the people in your cell. People you have recruited. No more than six or seven comrades. And screen them carefully. Make sure they are absolutely trustworthy. You are going to have to copy each document by hand. Retype them and make carbon copies. It's a hassle, laborious I know, but it's the only safe way to do it.'

'*Samizdat*,' said Rory.

'What?'

'*Samizdat*,' Rory repeated. 'It's Russian. It's what they called underground publishing. Typing carbon copies and passing them on to your friends. It's how they distributed banned books under Stalin. And recently it's how people in the Soviet Union got to read Solzhenitsyn.'

Kaplan smiled, 'Very good, *tovarich*!'

It was no accident that Rory found himself meeting Kaplan in secret like this. Long before he became a student in the Russian class he knew where he stood politically. Rory's dreams were not for himself but for the emancipation of his country and the enlightenment of his fellow citizens. He was an idealist who believed revolutionary change was both imperative and inevitable. As a committed Marxist, he saw the material conditions in South Africa as a larger manifestation of capitalist imperialism rather than simply racist colonialism. In his view, the working class, were, by some historical accident, black Africans and the bourgeoisie, who exploited the workers, by the same accident of history, happened to be white.

Naturally, Rory identified with the working class and considered himself to be one of them. His father was a gold miner and his mother had a junior clerical position at Barclays Bank. They lived in Rosettenville, an old working-class residential area in the southern suburbs. The Deep South. Where one lived if one wished to commit social suicide. A place of no importance. A place from which to escape.

Throughout his childhood, Rory dreamed of travelling to other, more exotic locales, far away from the narrow provincialism that he felt surrounded him. Every Saturday morning, he and his cantankerous Irish grandfather would walk down Mabel Street to the public library where they would trade their weekly supply of books for a new stockpile.

From his grandfather, he heard about the dignity of labour and the "manifest destiny of the working class". Rory became captivated by his grandfather's chivalrous stories of the heroic Bolsheviks overcoming their oppressors and fighting to establish the glorious October Revolution. In his mind's eye, he developed a highly romanticized and idealized portrait of the Soviet Union. In later years he re-assessed the naïvety of this vision and voiced criticism of "the excesses of the Stalinist era", but he never entirely lost his boyish enthusiasm for the country he most associated with the socialist dream.

After finishing high school, Rory was drafted into the army. He considered conscientious objection but his grandfather persuaded him that there were "bigger fish to fry". That year seemed to fly past him incredibly quickly and he discovered, much to his surprise, that there were aspects of military life that he enjoyed. All the physical exercise was energizing and he lost his chubbiness and grew lean and strong. He liked the army's hierarchical structure, its orderliness appealing to his fastidious makeup. He found himself volunteering for advanced training in guerrilla warfare which alerted his superiors to his leadership qualities and he was selected for an officer's course which he passed with flying colours.

Command came naturally to Rory and by the time his national service ended, he had grown in stature, confidence and authority.

After the army, he planned to go to university but his parents could not afford the fees, so he worked on the West Rand gold mines for five years, saving as much money as he could. He applied for a scholarship which he was awarded and, with a small donation from his grandfather, enrolled at Wits University. While there, Rory became an outspoken opponent of *apartheid* and what he regarded as the hostile and repressive regime that spawned and sustained it. He joined the Student Radical Group, which is where he first met Diane Wilkins. She introduced him to a number of people in her circle.

And then, suddenly, everything changed. In a private, clandestine meeting Rory was recruited into the South African Communist Party underground. It would prove to be the most challenging and momentous decision of his life. He knew from that moment on, he would have to be incredibly careful about how he conducted himself. Now would begin a secret and conspiratorial life of stealth and espionage. A life that Kaplan was now laying out for him.

'Stay away from the black townships and don't associate with anyone of colour,' he warned Rory. 'You'll stand out like a sore thumb,' he said. 'Leave that to our black operatives. We've got plenty of them in the field. You stick to the whiteys. And be careful who you associate with. Hang out with conservatives. Pretend to be one of them. Learn to think, talk and act like them. And keep your mouth shut. Don't let anybody, and I mean anybody, not even the chick you're *schtupping*, know what you really think and who you're working for. Be wary of everyone. You think we're the only ones with an underground network. They've got their spies too – stacks of them!'

They discussed how they would communicate and put in place emergency procedures. Rory had a locker on campus in the gymnasium. He gave Kaplan a spare key so that they could leave messages for each other there in the event of the postbox being compromised. They agreed that if something disastrous happened, if security was ever totally breached and there was a meltdown, whoever first got wind of it would leave a warning signal in the locker. A small red handkerchief would signify danger. If this was accompanied by the lines:

"The broken wall, the burning roof and tower
And Agamemnon dead."

It would mean total catastrophe. Flee. Don't look back.

Rory was impressed. This last fanciful, romantic flourish had been Kaplan's idea. Of course, he knew that the phrase came from *Leda and the Swan*. Yeats. His grandfather's favourite poet. It would seem that he had underestimated Kaplan. The slob had some class.

And so it began.

After the meeting with Kaplan, Rory went about the process of enlisting people into his distribution network, his cell. From the Russian class he only recruited Diane and Fat Bill, dismissing the rest as "aesthetes, dilettantes and questionables". The other five cell members he found in his law and anthropology classes.

Kaplan would regularly send Rory material which he would dutifully copy and then distribute, by hand, to his group whom he jokingly referred to as his "cabal". Most of this material was pretty tedious and usually consisted of prosaic propaganda pieces by the South African Communist Party and the African National Congress. Occasionally there were spirited, militant calls to arms from *Umkhonto we Sizwe* and sometimes there were even intellectual tracts from the writing of Althusser and Gramsci. Rory found the whole exercise quite tiresome and dreary. He craved action and soon he would get it.

But in order for that to happen there would have to be a seismic shift in the balance of power in the world. A rift that would allow a kind of leaking out of energy that would give license to the possibility of destined intervention.

It happened in the only place it could happen – across the Atlantic in Portugal. Military rule in the country was brought to an end by a popular uprising that peacefully defeated *Estada Nova*, the longest running authoritarian regime in Western Europe. Rebel soldiers and ordinary citizens ran through the streets of Lisbon bearing red carnations and calling for the cessation of martial law. In the aftermath of what became known as the Carnation Revolution, a new constitution was drafted, freedom of speech implemented, political prisoners released and, more importantly from the South African point of view, the Portuguese colonial wars in Africa ceased and Angola and Mozambique were given their independence. Although most South Africans hardly noticed these events, their significance was not lost on Rory.

Some months later he opened the Parkview postbox and found a note from Kaplan requesting a meeting. This time he was invited to lunch at the Spurs Steakhouse on Louis Botha Avenue.

Kaplan was already seated, scanning the menu when Rory arrived. They both ordered rump steaks and then exchanged pleasantries while waiting for their meals. Nothing personal was said as neither man knew much about the other.

When their order came, Kaplan sliced off a large chunk of meat which he promptly wolfed down. He took a deep swig from his beer.

'Do you have a valid passport?'

'No. Why?' asked Rory.

'We're going on a little trip. To Mozambique. Lourenço Marques. LM. Maputo. Better get one.'

'Sounds like fun. And what, may I ask, is the purpose of this trip?'

Kaplan grinned, 'As you know, the *Porros* have been pulling out of Mozambique. Thousands of them are heading back to Portugal. Some are moving here as immigrants. Frelimo are going to be taking over the country. Samora Machel will be in charge. He's sympathetic to our situation. He's just won an anti-colonial war and

31

he wants to help us win ours. So he's going to give us some toys to do just that.'

'Toys?'

'Guns and explosives. Dynamite. AK47s. I was told you knew something about them. From your time in the army.'

'*Ja*, I can deal with that. Count me in. When do we go?'

'As soon as you've organized that passport.'

6

JAMES

I have some home movies from that period. Originally they were on super 8mm but recently I've had them dubbed to DVD and I've taken to watching them on the computer. Most of them were shot by me so I'm usually behind the camera and not visible. It's mainly of all the members of the Melville Theatre Group. Naturally David, Ruth and Marty feature prominently but there is also a lot of footage of Cookie and others in the Russian class.

It's pathetic I know but sometimes when I view the films I can't help crying. Not because of what's there on the screen, the content, but because I remember so vividly what we were like. Our tremendous idealism. Our deep moral fervour. We had such high mountains to climb and we lived up there where the air was thin. Where we breathed nothing but the expectancy of dreams fulfilled.

David was the most driven. He was the one who knew exactly what he wanted and he directed all his fierce energies towards realizing his goals. He dragged us all with him just by his charisma and the force of his will.

I remember that first time he came back from overseas. In London he'd seen some productions that opened up a whole new world to him. Beckett and Pinter. But also iconoclastic approaches to staging and directing. Peter Brook's stuff. And innovative ways of mounting Shakespeare. In particular, he was interested in what people like Jonathan Miller and Peter Hall were doing. He was fascinated by their flouting of theatrical conventions and their imaginative use of *mise-en-scène*.

New York had an even more profound effect on him. Productions on and off Broadway. He was taken by Richard Schechner's experimental theatre group. It was where his mind was heading – into the establishment of a local drama company, with the emphasis on local.

David wanted to create theatre that reflected the social tensions, the inner turmoil of our own experience. You must remember that, at that time, theatre in South Africa was totally unsophisticated. It consisted mostly of re-staging popular West End plays. Drawing room comedies. What the butler saw. All done with posh, hoity-toity pseudo English accents. Very superficial. There was also a kind of cultural cringe driving the agenda. You know, anything home-grown was no good. Only stories from abroad would do.

And naturally, David challenged all that. He wasn't the only one. Probably not even the first. There were others but what he was able to do was make it his own. Make the personal political and the political personal. And also universalize it. He did that in a way that made the parochial comprehensible. At once complex as well as popular.

We started off by adapting existing material. Stuff we knew. What we were familiar with. In our Russian class we had been reading Gogol's *The Government Inspector*. In translation, of course, as our command of the language was not quite up to the original yet. That was still to come. Our professor, Dr Vladislav Ivanovich Kozar had, in his lectures, discussed in quite some detail Meyerhold's famous staging of the play. The text is a pretty savage satire on Russian provincial bureaucracy, but in Meyerhold's hands it becomes something more, an absurd comedy that reveals a world of self-deception and lies, hopelessly corrupt.

David thought it would be perfect for us. We could set it somewhere in the parochial heartland of the country. Somewhere in the Transvaal Bushveld. Herman Charles Bosman territory. So we went about "localizing" Gogol, transforming his play. Ruth was responsible for the adaptation and she wrote this extremely dark piece that satirized everything that we hated about the government of the day. The main characters became Afrikaner bureaucrats, intent upon implementing the administrative trivia of *apartheid*. The villagers were ignorant, prejudiced and insular. It was brilliant and devastating!

My role was to record the rehearsals and stage productions on film. Marty did the art direction and designed the sets using his charcoal drawings as stylized backdrops. In later years this became a feature of our productions but at that time, it was a purely pragmatic decision as we had inadequate resources and our knowledge of naturalistic stage craft techniques was somewhat limited. Nevertheless, it seemed to work as it was in keeping with David's anti-illusionist direction of the play.

The only real problem was the venue. We wanted to stage the play "in the round" but, unfortunately this was impossible in the Great Hall which had a traditional proscenium arch. In any event, we managed but thankfully, soon after that the Market Theatre was opened. This was a much more sophisticated and versatile theatrical space which allowed us far greater freedom to successfully explore our aesthetic vision.

That's where we performed our first original production. Looking back now it seems to me that *Sunday's Journey* marked a real turning point for all of us. After that, nothing would be the same again.

But before that was possible, an event occurred which spurred our efforts on. It took place on 16 June 1976. The Soweto Uprising. On that day, a large number of black Soweto students staged a series of protests against the introduction of Afrikaans as the medium of instruction in schools. Many of these students felt that the *apartheid* government was forcing them to submit to the "language of the oppressor" and they were determined to resist. The South African Police responded with force and at least 176 high school students were shot and killed.

This act of aggression left us shocked and outraged. Ashamed. Ashamed of our country and of our people and most of all, ourselves. We could no longer sit idly on the sidelines while atrocities like this were committed on our doorsteps. We had to take a stand. We had to become engaged, immersed in the struggle.

But the first thing we had to change was ourselves. At that time the Melville Theatre Group was made up exclusively of young white liberals. We had no black actors or writers in our circle. How could we address the majority of the people in the country, our intended audience, if we were only an elitist clique, preaching from a place of privilege? If we wanted a non-racial society, a non-racial country, then we had to make our theatre company non-racial. We were adamant about that.

That's when David first started bringing Churchill Khumalo to our theatre meetings and rehearsals. Once he had joined the group, more would follow including Dorothy Makhene, Bongane Gumede, Zakes Nyeki, Jimmy Congwane and others. But Churchill was the first and he stayed with us through the good and bad times. Even in those early dark days when the Black Consciousness Movement was urging all black people to have nothing to do with whites and not to be "co-opted into the system", he remained firmly dedicated to the ideals of non-racialism and fought constantly for a truly representative theatre group. He was true blue and I miss him dearly.

Right from the start, his presence had a profound effect on our output and our methods. Trained as we were in literature and the written word we were bound by the text. We always started with writing. But Churchill had no such deference to what was on the page. For him, the theatre was a much more living thing and performance was a more organic process that came out of experience. He worked in a looser, freer way than we were accustomed to. He would disdainfully toss out the script (sometimes driving Ruth mad!) and begin to improvise at the drop of a hat.

His was also a more athletic, muscular kind of theatre. Not only would he use free association to open up new dimensions to the characters he was playing but he would leap and bound all over the stage. In some ways, it was like a *commedia dell'arte* type of approach but without the reliance on stock types. In contrast, we had become, due to our Russian influences, much too slavishly mechanistic. Churchill liberated us from that. We were still able to bring complex ideas and staging techniques to our productions but, with his input, our work became less derivative. More vital and elemental.

Without Churchill's contribution, *Sunday's Journey* would have been impossible. The inspiration for the play was a real event that had come to Ruth's attention. Sunday Mazibuko worked as a cleaner in the accounting firm where Ruth's mother was employed as a bookkeeper. For many years, Sunday had been regarded as an exemplary worker by the company's management. But suddenly, out of the blue, his routine changed. He stayed away from work for days at a time never offering explanations for his absence. He would return looking bleary-eyed and distracted. Some staff members complained about the standard of his work dropping. They thought he was goofing off and probably drinking heavily. But Sadie Jacobson noticed that Sunday was inattentive, preoccupied and seemed lethargic and depressed. It was not good. She had seen people like this in the camps.

Eventually she approached him and persuaded him to tell her what was wrong. The story that Sunday told was horrific and harrowing even to Sadie who had witnessed the depths of human cruelty and depravity.

The events are as follows. Sunday's teenage son, Jabulani,

attended school in Soweto. He had been an active campaigner in the uprising and had been a leader in some of the riots that followed the police massacre. Then suddenly he disappeared. No one knew where he had gone. Sunday searched for him everywhere and reported his disappearance to the police but they seemed indifferent to his concerns. He even went to the notorious John Vorster Square and tried to ascertain if the police had Jabulani in custody. They denied it. Then after some weeks, he received a call from a police constable who informed him, in the most callous and insensitive manner, that he could come and collect the corpse of his son.

When Sunday finally got to see his beloved son's body, he was appalled. Jabulani had clearly been tortured and beaten before his death. His left arm was broken, his torso covered in bruises and abrasions and the flesh on his scalp soft and spongy, his back scarred with deep *sjambok* lacerations. Sunday wept knowing that his son's last moments must have been wretched and fearful.

Sadie tried to assist Sunday by hiring a lawyer and paying for his legal counsel but there was nothing that could be done. As in so many of these cases, the perpetrators got off scot-free.

Ruth was so unsettled and disturbed by these events that she immediately drafted an outline for a possible play which she brought to our next rehearsals. We had been looking for material without success for some time and this story seemed to most of us to be profoundly moving and deeply significant. We embraced the idea wholeheartedly.

There was one problem though and that was our own insecurity. Many of us whites felt inadequate dealing with this subject. It was too big, too overwhelming. We felt we did not have the right life experiences to cope with it. We felt unworthy and incompetent. How could we possibly give truth to this story? We were in awe of it.

That's where Churchill was so helpful. He had no such qualms. This was his world and he knew it intimately. There was nothing to be afraid of. For him we could not turn our backs on this story. He had little patience with our sensibilities which he thought were hindering rather than helping matters. So he took the play and ran with it.

By that time, Dorothy Makhene and Zakes Nyeki had already joined the group and together with Churchill, they became the main cast members, central to the core of the piece. Cookie also had a major role in the production playing a much older Jewish woman loosely based on Sadie Jacobson. With a flawless Yiddish accent, she was fabulous.

While the play was taking shape we rehearsed three times a week in the evenings. Often these would begin with some kind of background research which we would use as a catalyst for improvisational story construction. Through his contacts in the black townships, Churchill brought in a range of people to come and tell us tales of their own experiences at the hands of the South African Police. Then we would improvise around these accounts and Ruth would record it all in longhand and then go away and rework it, rewrite it. This more "organic" process formed the basis of all our future collaborations. From that moment on, "workshopping" became our preferred modus operandi.

Once the play had taken shape we invited Abe Cohen, the artistic director of the Market Theatre, to one of our rehearsals. He was over the moon about it and immediately booked *Sunday's Journey*. So now we had a venue and date for our opening night.

Everything was going along swimmingly, it was all copacetic and then suddenly there was a hitch. An obstacle we had not thought of, something that threatened to ruin all our plans. Abe had heard through the grapevine that we might have censorship problems. It appeared that there was some kind of leak or a spy in our midst who was feeding information to the security police about what we were doing. *Sunday's Journey* was clearly very critical of the police and could be seen as inflammatory and provocative. All that had to happen was for a member of the public to submit a complaint to the Publications Control Board and the play could be shut down. Banned. Abe Cohen told us he could not afford to take that kind of financial risk. He would have to pull the plug. Cancel our scheduled six-week run at the Market Theatre.

As you can imagine, we were devastated. All our hard work for nothing. Not to mention the fact that we all thought this story needed to be told. We had no idea what we were going to do. David, Ruth, Marty and I decided to drown our sorrows. We went drinking at some hotel bar in Hillbrow and were so depressed that we all got completely "motherless".

I don't remember how or why but for some reason, we ended up in Melville sleeping at the communal house that Cookie lived in with Bob and some other people. There was a spare bedroom which Ruth and Marty shared while David and I crashed on the floor in the lounge. In the morning I had a dreadful hangover. David was still asleep so I went into the kitchen to make some coffee. It was a stunning day, the sun low in the sky, the *koppie* purple in the early morning glow, a turtle dove's vibratory purring song coming through the window.

Cookie, Ruth and Marty were sitting at the table sipping from hot mugs of coffee. Although my memory is hazy about so many things, I remember this conversation vividly. Marty was telling Cookie about a film he and Ruth had seen the previous week at the Wits Film Society.

'Extraordinary, you really must see it!' he told her. 'Black and white with subtitles, some of them are a bit burned out so it's hard to read but the dialogue is not that important. It's what Jancso does with camera that's so amazing. The film is about imprisonment, so you never see the sky or the horizon. The camera always tracks or cranes so that we only see land, never sky. The camera's moving anyway, he uses all these long takes, some almost ten minutes long so there's very little cutting, it's all in the *mise-en-scène*.'

'What's the movie called?' I asked.

40

'*The Round-Up*. It's Hungarian. Really amazing. Made after the Soviets invaded the country. Remember the tanks in 1956?'

I just nodded my assent.

'Anyway,' he continued, 'the film is set in 1848 and it's about these guys who rebelled against the Hapsburgs. They are imprisoned and then these interrogators start subjecting them to mental and physical torture. I'm not sure about the historical facts… It's not really important to understanding the film. In any event, the film's not about the past. It's really about the present and the Soviets torturing people in the recent past.'

'How do you mean?' Cookie asked.

'Well, it's kind of an allegory,' Marty said. 'Jancso was worried about the Soviet censor. He had to hide what the film was really about so he set it in the past. It alludes to what is happening in the present but it's not so obvious. At least not to the censors.'

I remember it was like a gear sliding into position. I could almost hear the soft click as it snapped into place.

'That's it,' I said, getting very excited. 'That's what we'll do. We'll turn this on its head and beat them. We'll beat the censor! By George,' I said mimicking Henry Higgins, 'I think I've got it.'

And I had. I had a plan. So, what we did was exactly the opposite of what we had done with *The Government Inspector*. There we had taken a Russian play and adapted it to South Africa. With *Sunday's Journey* I proposed we take a South African situation and set it in Russia under Stalin. Make an allegory. And that is just what we did.

Naturally, no one was really fooled. Especially as we had African actors playing Russian peasants. But then we weren't trying to kid anyone. We wanted it to be absolutely clear that the play was alluding to the situation in our own country at that moment. But, at the same time, we wanted to ensure that the censors could not stop us. They could not claim that we were being incendiary. But, of course, we were.

As you know, *Sunday's Journey* was a huge success both locally and abroad. It really put us on the map theatrically. The opening night at the Market was truly momentous. Remarkable. We were given a standing ovation and the applause for Churchill and Cookie was literally deafening. I only had a small part in the play but as I stood on the stage bowing to the audience, the thunderous clapping and cheering roaring in my ears, I thought: *What a moment! What a moment! I will never forget this.*

It seemed to me then that the future lay mapped out in front of me, the path straight and unencumbered. There was now a clear trajectory to my life. 'Do with me what you will,' I told the gods. Soon I was to learn that the legal equivalent of this was *nolo contendere* or "no contest". It is a plea someone enters when they do not admit guilt but will accept punishment.

But back then I knew nothing of guilt or innocence. I had little concern for justice or retribution. I had not, as yet, fed on the "bitter bread of banishment". Instead I was just enjoying the moment. All I could see were bright, happy faces applauding. I could not see what was being prepared for me. The crimson rupture, the scorched earth.

No, I could see nothing then. I could not see that there was a bigger stage out there, bigger than the one I was standing on. Nor was I aware that even then, that other larger stage was being prepared, the props carefully moved into place. I was blind to the actors dressing and applying their make-up. Putting on their masks. No, I could not see the orchestra warming up or the audience shifting restlessly in their seats waiting for the performance to begin.

And certainly I was totally oblivious to the villain waiting patiently in the wings.

7

RORY

Three weeks later they hit the road heading east in Kaplan's inconspicuous looking grey Volkswagen Kombi. At midday there was still smog clinging to the earth though the sun was bright and sharp. Rory and Kaplan sped through the dreary coal-mining town of Witbank where the landscape was bleak and deep red fissures scarred the drought-ravaged earth, the wide plains blackened, scorched by veld fires.

Kaplan drove fast but competently. He and Rory sat in the front. In the back was a double mattress on top of a steel frame. Kaplan explained that there was a storage area under the bed but directly below that he had installed a false floor with a secret compartment and that is where they would hide the guns and explosives.

'It's all been fitted out by experts,' he bragged. 'Soviet trained. None of these fascist monkeys will ever be able to find anything. It's safe as houses, safer than the uranium in the wine bottles in *Notorious*. But that's just a MacGuffin anyway.'

'A what?' asked Rory.

'A MacGuffin. It's what Hitchcock uses as a plot device in all his films. It's the thing the spies are after but the audience doesn't care about at all. The audience is interested in the love story. They don't give a shit about the uranium in the bottles. It's irrelevant.'

It turned out that Kaplan was a *cinephile* and a Hitchcock aficionado. He'd seen almost all the master of suspense's films and could talk about them at length. Knew them backwards. Only many years later did Rory discover that the pseudonym, "George Kaplan" had been purloined, adopted from *North by Northwest*. In the film, James Mason plays the heavy, VanDamn, who mistakes Thornhill (Cary Grant) for a non-existent CIA agent called George Kaplan. But Kaplan is a fiction. The CIA created a non-person to mislead the villains. George Kaplan is a suit with no body.

The "real" George Kaplan was now on a roll. He'd shifted slightly and was rambling on about *Torn Curtain*.

'Politically the film's up to pawpaw. It's got this real corny Cold War backdrop. Paul Newman pretends he's a defector to East Germany. But then this bodyguard, I think his name's Gromek, discovers the secret mission and Newman has to kill him. It's in this farmhouse kitchen. The farmer's wife is there. And they both have to kill Gromek. She has to help Newman. There's a taxi waiting outside so they have to do it quietly. No guns. They have to use the weapons they can find. Newman is wrestling with Gromek. The farmer's wife picks up her kettle and smashes it against Gromek's head. *Bupkes*. Nothing. She gets one of her carving knives and stabs him. There's blood pouring out of him but the knife breaks. She is desperate as Gromek is getting the better of Newman. She makes some kind of exasperated sighing noise and then finds a spade for shovelling coal into the stove. She smashes it against his shins. Bang! Bang again! He falls down but still with a hold on Newman. They struggle on the floor and then slowly, ever so slowly, Newman and the farmer's wife drag Gromek over to the stove. They shove his head in the oven and turn on the gas. After a long time, the German finally dies. Gassed. The allusion to the ovens of Auschwitz is obvious. But what's so extraordinary about the scene is that it's so brutal. Hitchcock makes sure that the audience knows it's difficult to kill a man. It's not some elegant, balletic sequence like those crappy karate movies. Chop! Chop! No, it's clumsy and bumbling. It's hard. Arduous. It's not an easy thing to kill a man... Have you ever killed someone?'

Rory thought a while before answering.

'Probably. But from a distance. Firing on the enemy. I'm sure it's nothing like close-up. Nothing like looking in someone's face as you drag him into the gas oven.'

The landscape outside the car was changing. Gradually the bleak grasslands of the Highveld were giving way to lush subtropical forest as they got closer to Mozambique. They drove south of the Kruger National Park and made the border crossing at Lebombo. The disinterested passport control officers paid little attention to them. Just another two white *jollers* looking for a good time.

Rory's thoughts returned to Kaplan's question and the ethical dilemma of killing. He saw himself as a soldier, albeit on the side of the irregulars, fighting a just and righteous war. Rory knew, with certainty, that the battle against *apartheid* was morally incontrovertible but he, nevertheless, had grave doubts about the taking of human life.

The guns and explosives they were planning to bring back to South Africa would definitely be used to destabilize the government. There were already plans in place to blow up power stations and disrupt communication networks. But Rory realized that very little real damage could be done given their limited resources. Rather the benefits would be more symbolic, a gesture to tell the people that resistance was possible, that freedom lived.

Still there would be casualties, probably on both sides. He was certainly not naïve and he knew that violence begets violence. There would, he felt sure, ultimately be a price that he personally would have to pay. But he decided that he had no choice. He could not simply walk away from this. It would be a denial of his humanity to not take up arms against the evil he believed was devouring his country. The die was cast. There was no turning back. And yet, and yet...

8

RORY

Maputo wasn't quite what Rory had expected. That is not to suggest he was disappointed by the place. Quite the contrary. He actually found the city intriguing and appealing. But it was just not what he originally had in mind. Not what he had anticipated.

The city's name had only recently been changed from Lourenço Marques to Maputo and Rory had romantic notions and nostalgic associations with the capital of the former Portuguese colony. During the sixties and the early seventies, Lourenço Marques or LM as it was commonly known, had come to symbolise freedom and openness. A place where anything was possible. In contrast to the conservative values and rigid repressive constraints at home, the city was seen as a beacon of spontaneity and abandon. LM had pizzazz. Superb beaches, great hotels, bars, casinos, nightclubs and brothels. LM was impregnated with a breathtaking and boundless aura of *laissez-faire*. It was where you escaped to and where you found yourself.

The mystique surrounding the city had, no doubt, partly originated around the radio station that broadcast pop and rock songs to South Africa on short wave. Unlike the local radio stations which were operated by the South African Broadcasting Corporation and were rigidly controlled, LM Radio had a very liberal program and was free to play music that was often banned in the Republic. While LM was celebrating the urban ballads of Bob Dylan and Rodriquez, the SABC was busy gouging deep scratches in their records. LM was hip and pounded the airwaves with a vibrant beat that culminated on Sunday nights in the LM Hit Parade.

The station had the coolest disc jockeys who fuelled their repartee with the latest lowdown on all the with-it bands and performers. David Davies, John Berks, Evelyn Martin and Darryl Jooste (DJ the DJ) were household names to South African teenagers in the sixties and early seventies. Rory spoke no Portuguese but he could recite LM's station blurb off pat – '*Lourenço Marques transmitindo em ondas curtas e medias. Check your time by the BP chime…*'

But now the radio station was no more. Late in 1974 there was a bloody battle on the streets of Lourenço Marques. Frelimo troops routed the colonial forces and occupied the broadcast facilities. The following year the communist government decided to nationalize all the country's major assets and shut down LM Radio for good.

When they arrived in Maputo, Rory noticed that Kaplan seemed to be quite familiar with the city and drove through the streets confidently and purposefully. The boulevards were wide and spacious, lined with the town's distinctive acacia trees. In many ways, it still looked like a typical colonial outpost with evidence of European rule in many of the administration and commercial buildings, the main municipal complex still proudly boasting "This is Portugal" on its esplanade.

Rory thought the architecture was charming and idiosyncratic and especially liked the marvellous modernist structures that he recognised as being designed by Pancho Guedes. Passing the famed Polana Hotel, Kaplan remarked: 'We won't be staying there unfortunately. Our hotel is much more modest.'

'Pity,' said Rory, 'I hear the food is excellent.'

'You can find good *chow* all over the city, if you know where to go,' Kaplan replied. 'We will just have to be quite circumspect. Try not to draw any attention to ourselves. The *Boere* have got spies all over the place. They could be watching our *ouks* and we need to ensure the coast is clear before we make contact. But don't worry, it's all been thought out in advance.'

'I'm not worried,' Rory said.

The streets were getting narrower, the traffic more congested. Most people were, however, either pedestrians or cyclists. Garbage littered the sidewalks and the neighbourhood they were entering seemed overcrowded and seedy. It had a down-at-heel Third World feeling with hawkers selling live chickens, goats and fruit on the pavement.

There was a large military presence, a number of armed soldiers patrolling the area. Rory noticed some of them harassing the vendors, quite openly demanding bribes. The city seemed much more regimented than he expected and there was a tension in the air, an anxiety and edginess that he found disquieting. People seemed wary and fearful and when he looked at them, their eyes would slide away, avoiding direct contact.

They checked into a run-down but quite charming little hotel and agreed to meet later for dinner. It was hot and humid so Rory tried to cool down by having a cold shower. He lay on the bed in his khaki shorts and resumed reading Dostoevksy's *Crime and Punishment* but he was distracted by the dripping sound coming from the leaky shower rose. The plumbing left much to be desired.

He tried to sleep but it was far too warm. Watching the sweat run down his chest he whispered to himself: 'Well, you've done it now, *boykie*. No turning back! *A luta continua* as they say here in Mozambique!'

By the time Rory met with Kaplan it had cooled down somewhat and they enjoyed the balmy night strolling along the verdant avenues. They found a little restaurant where they sat outdoors under a string of coloured lights and drank crisp green *Gatao* wine which perfectly complimented the grilled prawns served with a fiery *peri-peri* sauce.

After the meal, pretending to be tourists, they drifted around until they (seemingly by chance) ended up in a pool hall. Kaplan challenged two local black men to a game which he and Rory managed to win. Then the bets were doubled. Everything was going along swimmingly when, all of a sudden, one of the men appeared to be upset by the break Kaplan had just made. The man seemed to be complaining that Kaplan had played out of turn. He started shouting in some strange language which Rory thought sounded like a mixture of Portuguese and Shangaan.

All at once, a dozen or so black men surrounded Rory and Kaplan. There was a great deal of shouting and a kind of melee or skirmish broke out. People were pushing each other around and a punch was thrown. Rory felt both his arms being held very tightly, a man on each side of him. Another man was in front of him and a fourth man at his back. They boxed him in completely and led him towards the back of the pool hall. The crowd parted, letting this compact phalanx through and closing the ranks behind them. Just ahead of him, Rory could see Kaplan being manipulated by a similar team.

Then they were outside in a small dark alley being led away from the pool hall. The men released Rory's arms and smiled at him. The man in front turned around and said: 'Let's *vai!* We need to keep moving.'

If anyone had been watching or if Rory and Kaplan had been under surveillance, it would have been almost impossible to ascertain that the entire venture had been carefully stage-managed. Their exeunt had been carried out seamlessly and any attempt at pursuit had been effectively sealed off. A very professional operation. Rory was impressed.

The men led them down a number of alleyways, past corrugated-iron shacks, bomb-damaged flats and ruined dwellings. Finally, they entered a *shebeen* smelling strongly of spilled beer. Sitting at a large circular table were the people they had come to meet. Kaplan seemed to know almost everyone and began the introductions. There were too many for Rory to remember all their names but he knew a few of them by reputation. Duma Mokoena, Bambata wa Luruli, Precious Selinda, "Spanner" van der Merwe, Jack Mohlala, Brigit Britten and, of course, the infamous leader "*Oom*" Isaac Spiegel.

Rory was very warmly welcomed into the group. A space was made for him to the left of Spiegel and he was served an ice-cold beer. At first Rory felt a little bashful and uncomfortable but Spiegel soon put him at ease.

Rory had seen photographs of the great man but being with Spiegel in the flesh was quite different. He was larger than expected, fleshy with meaty jowls, big crooked teeth and a broad smile. A web of veins on his cheeks and a bulbous nose that reminded Rory of the actor Karl Malden. Spiegel would look at you intensely and seemed interested in whatever you might be telling him. He made you feel as if you were the most important person in the room. It was a great asset in a leader.

Spiegel talked to Rory about all manner of things – Marxism, the struggle against *apartheid*, the unfortunate need for an armed struggle, the difficulties of exile, his love for his family, the importance of friendship, freedom and most of all, hope for the future.

Rory spoke about his fleeting impressions of Mozambique – the poverty, the fear in people's eyes, the militarization of the society, the corruption.

'*Ja*, there are lots of problems,' Spiegel acknowledged. 'Frelimo made some bad mistakes. When they took over the country about quarter of a million Portuguese living here left almost overnight. Some went to South Africa but most returned to Portugal. These were all the people who had been running the country, people who managed the infrastructure. Gone. Just like that.' He clicked his fingers for emphasis.

'They took all their assets with them. All the wealth of the country and there was this tremendous brain drain. There was nobody left who could manage things. It was a big *gemors*, a fuck-up.' Spiegel leaned forward and looked straight in Rory's eyes.

'That's one thing we need to ensure doesn't happen when we take over in South Africa,' he said. 'We need the whites. We don't want them all splitting and running off to Australia and Canada and God knows where else. We need to let them know we are not going to impoverish them, nationalise the mines and the banks and stuff. Try not to freak them out!'

'But what about what they stole from the people under *apartheid*?' Rory asked. 'Surely we need to redistribute the wealth? Put all the assets in the hands of the proletariat?'

Spiegel smiled. 'Sure, we'll do all those things. Our aim is to transform the country, create a more just society. End racism. But we can't do this overnight. It's going to take time.' He winked at Rory and said: 'Remember one thing – softly, softly catchy monkey.'

Later, when he was back at the hotel, Rory thought about some of what Spiegel had to say. He had to admit that he found it a little disturbing. He understood the need for pragmatism, but Spiegel seemed too keen to sacrifice principles to achieve results. It was very much a case of the end justifying the means. Rory was at heart an idealist but he was enough of a realist to appreciate that sometimes flexibility was called for. Sometimes one had to make compromises in order to achieve the greater good. But something about Spiegel's easy and flippant manner, his careless cynicism worried Rory. It felt like throwing out the baby with the bathwater. It felt wrong.

He brooded on this for some time. The heat was still making it difficult to sleep. It was a little cooler outside on the veranda and he stood there for a while listening to the sounds of the city. Far off in the distance he could see a house on fire, the flames licking the night sky. There was very little traffic noise but he could hear voices, the occasional shouts of anger or joy. Finally, the mosquitoes drove him back indoors.

Rory lay on the bed, anxious and distressed. He read more

Dostoevsky. It made him more anxious. Sleep was a long time coming.

Two days later Rory and Kaplan left Maputo. Twenty miles outside the city they turned off the main highway and drove along a gravel road for about ten minutes. Then Kaplan stopped and parked the Kombi on an isolated section. This was the spot chosen for them to meet Spiegel and his guerrillas.

Rory and Kaplan did not have long to wait and at the appointed time, they could see a truck racing along the road towards them. The landscape here was flat without any hills. The odd acacia tree and grassland, the endless savannah. A perfect place for a secret rendezvous. Any approaching vehicle could be seen from miles away. It would be impossible to have them under surveillance without being aware of it.

Once the truck reached them, the switchover was very swift. The guns and explosives were quickly loaded into the truck, the men working efficiently and with great haste. Rory and Kaplan were treated to a quick handshake, hug and a warm farewell from Oom Spiegel and then he and his men were gone. It almost seemed as if it had never happened. For Rory they appeared to disappear as fast as the dreams he often tried to hold onto in his waking moments. You thought they were so real but once you tried to recall them, they were gone.

One evening three weeks later Rory was coming home from university. He was on the top floor of a double-decker bus. Down below on the street corner there was a black vendor selling newspapers. Rory could see *The Star* headlines on a poster: **"Bomb Explodes in Bryanston Shopping Centre."** He felt sick, nauseous and jittery. He jumped off the bus and bought the paper. Anxiously reading it, he discovered that there were some minor injuries but no one had been killed. It did not make him feel much better.

For weeks after that he felt disorientated and shook up. His sleeping patterns were disturbed, his concentration limited. He was filled with deep uncertainty. He was not sure if he could continue running guns.

9

FAT BILL

Fat Bill loved nothing better than to see a plan coming together. From one perspective, his entire course of action seemed to be falling into place. Mostly he had been able to predict likely outcomes but when unexpected events had occurred, he had usually been able to adjust his strategies accordingly. Consequently, there had not really been any serious crises to take him off track.

Of course none of this would really have been possible without Diane's input. She had all the important social and political contacts he needed and she was able to pave the way for him. Make all of this attainable.

Take the elections for example. In order to establish the right cover, Bill was convinced he needed to be elected to the Students' Representative Council (SRC). This was a highly politicized body that was fiercely anti-*apartheid* and noted for having a liberal agenda. Elected members of the council gained automatic affiliation and access to the inner sanctum of the National Union of South African Students (NUSAS).

Although NUSAS was predominantly for white students, it had become, since the Soweto Uprising, radicalized and had moved sharply towards the political Left. Bill's goal was to infiltrate it but to do that he had to get himself elected to the SRC.

To become eligible for election, it was necessary to obtain personal endorsements from at least twenty students. With Diane's backing, this became a formality and Fat Bill was able to secure the necessary signatures within two hours of declaring his intention to run for office.

How was this possible? Simple. Diane had impeccable political credentials by virtue of the fact that her father was a famous human rights lawyer who had defended numerous anti-*apartheid* activists. Her mother too had all the right connections having been a member of the Black Sash for many years.

Like other members of the organisation, Myra Wilkins could often be seen standing on street corners in silent and passive protest against the barrage of unjust legislation in the country. Donning opaque dark glasses and a black sash of mourning, she affected a presence that was both hieratic and striking. Very dramatic.

From her mother, Diane had inherited this confidence and poise. So, given her support and open campaigning for him, Fat Bill was easily elected to high office in the SRC. This was exactly where he wanted to be as it accorded him the appropriate cover for espionage.

On the romantic front, things also seemed to be going to plan. Bill and Diane had been dating for a few years now and everyone accepted them as an ideal couple. They did all the conventional activities of young lovers – partying with friends, drive-in movies on Saturday nights, making out in the back seat of cars, drinking too much, planning for the future. They had even discussed marriage but agreed that they should probably wait a year or two.

Bill made sure that his future in-laws approved of him and he presented himself as the perfect potential spouse for their beloved daughter. Courteous, caring, selfless, concerned. A match made in heaven.

Not that Mr and Mrs Wilkins did not have some concerns. For, even though they fully supported the stand he was taking against *apartheid*, they were worried that perhaps he was *too* actively involved in the struggle. Was it necessary to be at the forefront of every student protest march? How many times had he been arrested already this year? Three? Four? Maybe he was drawing too much attention to himself and putting himself in harm's way. The police had him in their sights. They were watching his every move. Perhaps he should tone it down a bit, back off for a while?

But, like Diane and almost everybody else, Bill's future in-laws did not, in their wildest dreams, imagine that maybe he was not exactly what he seemed to be. They never suspected that he might be leading a double life. No one considered the possibility that he could be a police spy. It never entered their heads.

Bill himself believed that he had established the right cover and that his real motives remained hidden. It was as if he had donned some magical cloak of obscurity, as if he had become, as Winston Churchill once described Russia "a riddle wrapped inside a mystery inside an enigma."

Yes, most of the time, Bill was happy with the progress he was making. But occasionally, like now, he would begin to feel restless. Dissatisfied. Troubled and edgy. He would get an urge that Diane certainly could not fix.

He would get this craving and this itch that gnawed at him. He wanted to scratch at it but it ate away at his insides. It was a yearning that he knew only too well. A hunkering that he could not resist.

It only happened to him every two months or so but when it occurred it felt like he was going to be devoured. It was like a deluge that assaulted all his senses. Overwhelming him. He was incapable of curbing his desires. Capitulation was impossible, he had to surrender.

And so tonight he found himself at the Adelphi on the ground floor of the Klein Hotel in Hillbrow. It was a gay bar that he had discovered while participating in a raid on the establishment when he was a policeman. Since then he had been back quite often.

On his first visit, he had felt like he was running the gauntlet as he walked across the pub. He could sense the men sizing him up, rating him, their lust so palpable it leached through their clothes. But now he was used to it, the mood of longing and appetite that pervaded the saloon. He liked it. It made him feel comfortable, relaxed. He was in charge. He was in control. He was *die Baas*.

He ordered a Scotch and soda and patiently sipped on it, the ice cold on his tongue, the heat of the alcohol filling him with expectation. He knew that there were numerous codes operating here, a signifying process at work. Blue shirts if you were a "top", a red bandana protruding from your back pocket if you were a "bottom" but he was indifferent to the complexities of any stylized argot. Bill just knew what he wanted and he knew he would recognise it as soon as he saw it. So he waited, enjoying the moment, the anticipation.

Three twinks arrived together and gave Bill the once-over but he just ignored them. He kept to himself, aloof and self-contained. Then he saw what he was after. A dark-haired, short but muscular young man. A bit lacy. A hint of mascara. *That's it*, he thought. *Just my cup of meat.*

Bill didn't hesitate. He went straight over.

'Hi,' he said. 'Can I buy you a drink?'

'Sure. Bacardi and Coke. Haven't seen you around much. Get much action?'

'Some. What's your name?' Bill asked casually, not giving too much away.

'You can call me Josie.' A demure smile.

They drank and chatted for a while. Nothing substantial. Small talk. Feeling each other out. But it was not long before they left. No point in sticking around when you both saw where this was heading.

Bill had a small flat in Banket Street, near Joubert Park which he kept for special adventures. Not too many people knew about it. An intimate little place on the second floor. Soft lighting in the living room.

He poured them both a drink and then excused himself to go to the toilet. When he came back, Josie had already undressed and was sitting on the couch naked, gently stroking his small, erect penis.

'You're way ahead of me,' Bill slurred. He could hardly speak, his lips and tongue swollen and thick. There seemed to be something happening to the time; like his pulse it was racing. He thought he needed to slow everything down, so he had a sip from his drink. A big sip.

Josie came over and stood in front of him. He undid a few buttons on Bill's shirt, gently tugged a couple of chest hairs.

'Kiss me, Mr Bear,' he whispered.

Bill obliged, plunging his tongue deep into Josie's hot little mouth. Josie undid Bill's fly and slipped his hand in. He gently touched Bill's phallus which, surprisingly, was still somewhat flaccid. But soon, as he stroked, it began to harden and grow exponentially.

'Wow, a regular accordion,' he said approvingly.

'Shut up and suck it!' Bill murmured.

Josie knelt down and slipped Bill's now erect penis in his mouth. He slowly ran his tongue up and down and around the shaft. Bill sighed and let out a slight grunting noise. Josie eased off for a while and, barely audible said: 'I want you to fuck me in the bootyhole.'

That's the moment when everything changed...

Bill's countenance altered dramatically. The lustful, confident lothario suddenly mutated into a panicky, lily-livered screaming thing. His voice high-pitched and childlike.

'Why, you horrid little queer!' he screamed and punched Josie in the face. 'Fucking *moffie!*'

Josie cried out and fell to the floor. Bill sprang on top of him and pinned Josie's arms with his knees. Grabbed his throat and squeezed hard. When this happened to Fat Bill he was always transported to a very dark place. Way back in the past. He was a little boy again. In the shed at the bottom of the garden. Bent forwards, his short pants at his knees while his stepfather beat him with a cane. Beat him so hard he would almost pass out.

And then after the beating there was always more. His stepfather having his ugly way with him. Even now, Bill could feel the wet tongue in his ear, smell the sour breath on his neck. The spittle drooling on his back. The pain in his anus. The hatred in his heart. And all the while this thrusting and panting. Until the last groan of delight. His stepfather's final moment of triumph.

But Bill made sure he got his revenge. Settled the score. One day, after school when he was sixteen he stole a car. A Chevrolet Impala, big and heavy. He parked it on a side road, waiting. He knew that at 6pm, regular as clockwork his stepfather would leave home and go for a jog.

When he heard the outside gate clicking shut, he gunned the engine, turned the corner. He had timed it perfectly so that as his stepfather left the pavement, Bill ploughed through him. The beefy car slammed into his body, the momentum so great he was flung high in the air. In the rear-view mirror Bill could see his stepfather smacking into a street pole. No one could survive that he thought.

There were no eye-witnesses to the accident. The police called it a hit-and-run. They had no suspects. Some days later a wrecked Chevy Impala was found on Rifle Range Road, a short distance from Uncle Charlie's Roadhouse. The car had been set alight and was burned out. Impossible to get fingerprints.

Back in the flat, Fat Bill's vision was now blurred. He saw through a red haze. There was a throbbing sensation behind his left eye. He felt a terrible fear and a flaming anger. With his right hand he squeezed harder on Josie's throat. He held his cock tightly in his left hand, milking it up and down furiously. Josie struggled but Bill's knees pushed down hard on him. The pressure on his throat increased. As Josie started to lose consciousness, Fat Bill ejaculated, hot sperm squirting all over the young man's face.

10

I don't know how the rumour began or who started it but it spread like wildfire. Everybody was talking about it. And they all had an opinion about who it might be.

Fat Bill was the first person to tell me. I was sitting on the library lawn reading a book when he sauntered over. He came straight to the point. Bill never beat around the bush, never equivocated.

'Have you heard the news?' he asked his voice earnest and concerned. 'Apparently there's a spy in the Russian class. Someone is working for the security police and giving information to them about us.'

'What?' I said shocked. 'How do you know?'

'It's all over the campus. They even discussed it at the SRC executive meeting. People are pissed off! Fucking hell! Fascist pigs!'

Of course it made sense when you thought about it. The Cold War was still on. The Soviet Union was the enemy of the West. Russians were to be feared. The pro-*apartheid* Nationalist government had been exploiting these anxieties for ages. They were paranoid about "reds under the beds" and the "communist menace". In fact, they were able to persuade other countries like the

USA and the UK that they were allies of the West and an effective bulwark against the threat of socialism.

So they would have assumed that anyone who was studying Russian at Wits must be a communist sympathiser. From their eyes, the entire Russian class probably consisted of left-wing zealots and radicals. They obviously saw us as representing a potential danger to the state. We needed to be watched, to be placed under surveillance. A spy should be ensconced in our midst. A mole to report back to the security police.

'So who is it?' I asked.

'Fucked if I know,' Bill said and shrugged. 'Has to be someone we're unlikely to suspect. A person we trust.'

'You think the security police are that good? How do you even know that it's true?'

'I don't know,' Bill conceded. 'Maybe it's bullshit. It could be just a rumour. But I had to tell you about it.'

Thereby ensuring he would be the last person I would suspect. A kind of double bluff. Very smart. This rumour was not entirely new though. It had partly come up when we were about to stage *Sunday's Journey*. Then there was the suggestion that a spy or informer had raised the spectre of censorship. Fortunately, on that occasion, we managed to sidestep the problem but the supposition that there could be a permanent and deeply camouflaged plant in our midst was much more disturbing. Especially if that person was reporting back to the security police. As far as I knew, there was no one in the Russian class who was involved in any clandestine or illegal activities but the mere fact that our conversations could be relayed to a secret intelligence agency made my skin crawl. It was creepy and sinister. No wonder everyone was talking about it.

The rumour was certainly on most people's minds when we held a party to celebrate the end of the highly successful second run of *Sunday's Journey*. The entire cast, crew and all our friends came over for a *braaivleis* and drinks at Bob and Cookie's communal house in Melville.

When I arrived the sun was just beginning to set and the surrounding *koppies* were bathed in a crimson glow. The jacarandas were in bloom and a purple canopy covered the street. Blossoms were scattered on the pavement and the air was fresh and lilac-smelling after the usual afternoon electric storm. I could still hear the occasional rumble of thunder in the background. A crackle of lightening.

Churchill and Dorothy turned up at almost the same time and I warmly greeted them outside the house. Across the street I could see one of the neighbours sitting on his *stoep*, smoking a pipe and giving us the hairy eyeball. Although the recent influx of alternative types into the area was changing the suburb, Melville was still a conservative place with mostly Afrikaans residents. It would still have been highly unusual for non-racial social events to take place there and Cookie and Bob could have been prosecuted for serving alcohol to people of colour. All that was necessary was for someone to make a complaint. But fortunately no one did.

In the yard, on the lawn there were two big charcoal-filled *braais*. Most of the guys were standing around them sipping Castle lagers and chatting. There was a slight tangy odour of charred *boerewors*. A cordial, sociable atmosphere. A sense of community, male bonding over the fireplace, an ancient ritual. I felt comfortable, relaxed. There was music in the background, coming from inside the house. I remember the record playing was Sam Cooke's magnificent *A Change is Gonna Come*. To this day, I still associate the song with that night. A night on which so much changed.

I wandered around vaguely, chatting to friends, dancing, sipping wine. Later in the evening David arrived with his date, Celeste. She was tall, statuesque with long, flowing auburn hair to her shoulders. Very striking, very self-assured. Celeste was a couple of years older than us, had just completed a medical degree and was planning to do an internship at Baragwanath Hospital in Soweto.

'I'm really looking forward to it,' she said, running her long fingers through those chestnut locks. 'The hospital is one of the largest in the world and has excellent teaching staff. You can't get that kind of experience anywhere else. Especially in an emergency ward.'

David had only recently met her but he was bowled over. Madly in love with her. Sometime later in the evening he, Marty and I were standing on the veranda, getting some fresh air away from the crowd when he told us that he was planning on marrying her.

'But you've only been dating for two months,' I said.

'I know but this is the real thing. She's the one for me. She's my *beshert*. We just hit it off perfectly.'

'Are you sure?'

'Absolutely,' he assured me.

'But she's a *shiksa*. What will your parents say?' asked Marty.

'Well that's tough. They'll come around to the idea. Maybe she'll convert. Anyway it's not a problem for me, so my folks will just have to get used to it. Which reminds me, there's something else I wanted to talk to you about. It's partly related to this. Well, it's kind of come about because of all this. Because of Celeste.'

'*Ja*, so what gives?' Marty asked.

'Well, you know how we've been talking about finding somewhere to live? You and Ruth have been looking at flats?'

Marty nodded.

'I think I've found it. The perfect solution… There's this house for sale. It's huge. A double-storey place. The ground floor has a big lounge that you could use as a studio. And a good quiet space with a view of the garden for Ruth to write in. Outside there are the servants' quarters. They're a bit run-down now but we could fix the rooms up. Break down the connecting wall and turn it into a rehearsal space. It would be perfect. We could live there and run our theatre workshops from there.'

'It sounds great,' Marty said, 'but it must be expensive. We would never be able to afford it.'

'No,' David said. 'That's the best part. It's going cheap. The catch is it's not in a great area. It's in Belgravia. The houses around there are all run-down. It's kind of a slum district but this house is different. It's got a whole acre of land with a lovely oak tree in the middle. It's really an old Randlord's house and it's insulated from the rest of the suburb by this high brick wall. It's ideal for us. You and Ruth could live downstairs and Celeste and I upstairs. Only thing is we'd have to share the kitchen.'

As usual, David's enthusiasm swept Marty along. He was already sold on the idea but pretended he would have to think about it.

'Sounds good,' Marty said, 'but I will have to talk to Ruth.'

'Great,' he said, 'and while you're about it, the two of you should also think about getting married.'

Well, what could we say to that? Marty just laughed good-naturedly and I found myself blushing. I knew it had been on Marty's mind but, as in all matters relating to love, it was the woman's call. It would only happen if that was Ruth's wish.

Later in the evening I drifted off to get a beer from the fridge. Often at those kinds of parties you would always be guaranteed to find a small group casually leaning against the cupboards, drinking and chatting together in the kitchen. Not surprisingly on this occasion, the subject of their conversation was the spy rumour. It seemed that there was a general consensus that the informer was most likely one of the two Afrikaans students in the class – either Cookie or Antoine, and the kitchen group (which included Antoine) were debating this assumption.

'That's crap!' I angrily interjected, coming to the defence of Cookie. 'It would be too obvious to use an Afrikaner. The security police are not complete idiots. They wouldn't put an agent in place who could so easily be identified. You're thinking group politics now. You're thinking that if there's an enemy in our ranks, then it must be someone from the other group. The outsider. The Afrikaner. The rock spider. What bullshit! I think the spy is much more likely to be an insider. It's got to be someone we are unlikely to suspect.'

'You mean someone like you, darling?' Antoine purred.

'Yes,' I said. 'Someone like me. But you know it's not me so fuck off!'

The kitchen had two doors, one on each side of the room. From where I was standing the opposite door that led into the garden was half open. There was a sudden blur of movement there that caught my eye. I thought maybe someone was standing behind the door. I couldn't be sure. Whoever it was decided not to come in. Was he or she listening? Or just getting some fresh air? Impossible to tell.

Antoine smiled then added quietly, 'You know the only person no one has really mentioned as a potential suspect is Fat Bill. What about him?'

Jack, a long-haired folk-singing hippy type laughed. 'Oh that's a good one. That's why the cops are always *sjambokking* him and sticking him in jail.'

Again I was vaguely conscious of a presence outside the door. At the time it meant nothing but in retrospect...

'Think about it,' Antoine said, not smiling now. 'He used to be a cop. He was in the police at one stage. They could have recruited him then.'

'Bill's never tried to hide the fact that he was in the police,' I said. 'He's always said that his time in the police politicised him. Made him see what this country was really like. It enabled him to see the fascist policies at the coalface.'

'*Ja*, it just couldn't be Bill,' said Jack. 'Not the way he is.'

'What do you know about the way Bill is?' Antoine asked. 'What do any of us *really* know about him? I've heard some things about our friend Fat Bill. I've seen him hanging out at some of the gay bars in town. People have told me he's into some very weird stuff. Apparently he goes for B&D and very rough trade. Some of the fairies are really scared of him.'

'No way!' said Jack.

'But that's horse shit, Antoine. Are you saying that because he goes both ways, we can't trust him? You of all people should know that just because you have "different" sexual tastes,' I protested, using my fingers to illustrate the inverted commas, 'it doesn't mean that you're unreliable or deceitful.'

'I'm not saying that we should treat him with suspicion because he goes flip flop or because he's a flamer,' Antoine explained. 'But what I am saying is that he is not what he appears to be. He has gone about creating this image for himself. The straight guy who's going to marry Diane. That's the way he presents himself. That's the way he wants us to see him. But that's not what he is. He's really living a double life. We should bear that in mind. We should be wary and careful around him. If there is a spy in the Russian class, then we need to be cautious. That's all I'm saying.'

Was Antoine saying too much? Was he ignoring his own advice? Was he being indiscreet? Was someone listening at the door? Could it have been Fat Bill? With hindsight it seems possible that Antoine's careless and imprudent remarks might well have sealed his fate. But, after all these years, there's no way of knowing for sure.

All I can tell you is that two weeks after this, two weeks after the party, Antoine's once beautiful body was found naked, mutilated and abandoned on a dirt road a few kilometres outside Roodepoort. He had been badly beaten about the face and his features were hardly recognisable. Identification was only possible through dental records. His wrists were bruised and bore the marks of bondage, probably the result of being bound by steel handcuffs.

The cause of death was not the beating but something much more gruesome. A small plastic pipe, about six inches long, had been inserted into his anus. Then expanding Polyfilla foam had been pumped into his rectum. On entry, the foam had swollen and expanded. As it coagulated, his stomach would have distended and all his organs would have been put under extreme pressure until they burst and tore apart. It would have been a most painful death.

An autopsy was carried out by a police pathologist. The official cause of death was determined to be "sexual misadventure". Unofficially some of Antoine's friends (gay and straight) questioned this hypothesis. For us, it just did not seem likely given his known sexual proclivities.

But, for most people the official verdict prevailed. Antoine was assumed to be the victim of an accident involving some kind of weird, kinky and dangerous sexual gig that had gone tragically wrong. No one even considered the possibility of assassination.

Recently, while watching some movie, I came across the acronym TWEP which, I learned, stands for "Terminate With Extreme Prejudice". Was this what happened to Antoine? Was he simply "terminated"? Did his indiscretion cost him his life? Was he killed to shut him up? To silence him?

It should be noted that the security police had put a great deal of resources and effort into establishing a "cover", an armour-plated identity for Fat Bill. He was seen as their best asset, their mole in the liberation movement. They simply could not have all of this sabotaged by the brash speculations of some *moffie*. Antoine would have to be silenced. It was unfortunate, they would have argued. Unavoidable. But when you were fighting a war there were always bound to be some civilian casualties, some collateral damage. The poor faggot just couldn't keep his mouth shut. That's the way they would have rationalised it.

But that night I wasn't thinking about politics or espionage or violence. There was nothing dark or sinister on my mind. All my energies were directed towards imagining a new future. A future where I could escape from the turmoil and destruction that seemed inevitable in our land. A future where I could be liberated from everyday constraints and hardships. I envied the plans that David and Marty had to move into the house in Park Road, Belgravia and establish a true community of artists. I was jealous of their friendship and their vision. I too wished to create work that was visionary, thought-provoking, ambitious and above all, human. Work that celebrated the integrity of our lives. I wanted to find a way through the madness that surrounded us and to, like them, find a haven and a sanctuary where genuine love and caring was possible. But most of all I wanted to be liberated and for my life to change. And that night it did in ways that I could never have imagined.

Sometime after nearly all the revellers had left, I was on the veranda sitting on the swinging couch when Cookie came over and sat down next to me.

'I believe I should thank you for coming to my defence,' she said smiling.

'I hardly did that,' I said. 'I just didn't believe you could possibly be a spy.'

'Well I assure you I'm not. Not even close.'

We both laughed and began talking of other things. And then all of a sudden she was in my arms. It was the first time we had kissed. I know many of my friends put a great deal of store in the first kiss a woman gives you. If that is good, everything else will be fine. That's what they say. Well, that kiss, Cookie's first kiss, was perfect. A Goldilocks kiss. Not too hot or too cold. Just right.

I slept over that night. In the morning I woke early and pulling on my jeans, went outside onto the veranda. It was early summer and quite warm. A cerulean sky slowly lightening and gently shifting to a soft orange glow. In the distance I could hear the sound of a train whistle, a melancholic, wistful note, full of promise. I sat and watched the shadows slide down the *koppie*. My emotions were all jumbled up. One part of me felt serene and at peace, at one with the world. After all, I was young and in love and hopefully about to take control of my life, set a path for it. Another side of me was unsettled and disturbed by the enormity of what had transpired. It seemed so big, so heart-stoppingly awesome.

Then Cookie stepped outside. She was wearing my blue long-sleeved shirt, half unbuttoned. I could see the gentle curve of her breasts, the merest hint of a brown nipple, her dark hair all messed up, a radiant ring of light encircling her, an aureole. She looked magnificent, smiling at me.

'What's up, my man? Why so contemplative? You look lost in thought.'

I smiled back. 'I was just thinking about how gorgeous you are. How right this feels. And how overwhelmed I feel.'

She came and sat next to me. 'Poor boy,' she said, taking my hand in hers.

We sat there silently watching the sun now streaming across the rugby field, the dew glittering off the grass. Cookie never looked at me; her gaze was directed outwards towards the distant hills.

'So how do you feel now?' she said.

'I feel fine. Just fine,' I said. 'At one with this bloody great universe!'

11

Later in the day, after we had cleaned up the booze bottles and beer cans, Cookie and I took a walk on the Melville *koppies*. We were at ease with each other and talked of random subjects. She started telling me about her friendship with Antoine Pienaar.

'You know,' she said, 'he's not really an exhibitionist. I know he comes across that way but he's really very private. I think he's scared of showing people his true nature so he hides behind this outrageous exterior. This camp persona he puts on is really a disguise, a subterfuge that masks his true character.'

'I think you're right. I've noticed that he's actually very sensitive,' I said.

I knew that because they were Afrikaans both Cookie and Antoine probably felt like outsiders and that's partly why they found themselves drawn to each other. But at the same time I knew that it was very easy to share confidences with Cookie because she was so empathic, so caring.

We were getting near the top of the *koppie*, the climb a little more challenging so we were quiet for a while until we reached the summit. At the top, there was a large yellow rock that we rested on, looking north towards the expansive vista unfolding before us.

There was something about being so high, looking down on the city that gave that moment a uniquely charged quality. I could feel the electricity between us and somehow I knew that Cookie was going to share something of inestimable importance with me. Something precious. What she told me helped me to realise why she was so compassionate and responsive to the pain of others. It was because her own wounds were so deep and abiding.

According to Cookie, until she was eleven years old, she had a relatively happy, ordinary, if somewhat restrained, childhood. Then her world collapsed. Her father, Johan, was under a great deal of stress at work. His job was excessively demanding with near to impossible deadlines and he was trying to please a despotic and bullying boss. Suddenly something snapped, fractured.

'My father,' Cookie said, 'started to behave in rather strange and bizarre ways. He became withdrawn and did not seem to care about anybody or anything. His feelings seemed blunted, dulled. He claimed that everyone was "out to get him" and that work colleagues were trying to castrate him. He said my mother was poisoning him. There were voices in his head, shouting at him. He was constantly depressed and once when I came home from school I found him in the shower trying to hang himself.'

At this point she became emotional and was struggling to talk. I put my arm round her shoulder and drew her to me. 'It's okay,' I said. 'Just breathe in slowly. Don't worry, I'm here for you.'

It took her a while to get control but she clearly wanted to continue with her story.

'I'll never forget that,' she continued. 'Seeing him in the shower with his dressing-gown belt wrapped around his scrawny neck. It scared the hell out of me. I phoned my gran in a panic and she got hold of the hospital. A little while later an ambulance came by and took him away in a straitjacket.'

Apparently her father, Johan, was hospitalized and diagnosed with "late onset schizophrenia". Cookie went with her mother, younger brother and sister to visit him in the Johannesburg General

Hospital. She found her darling father unrecognizable. He was heavily sedated, unshaven and unkempt. He slurred his words and spoke of random, unconnected things. It was as if a stranger had taken over his body.

'Then my father was transferred to Tara, the psychiatric hospital where he received treatment in the form of multiple electric shock therapy,' Cookie went on. 'Finally, after about a year he was allowed to come home. He remained a shadow of his former self and was now drug dependent and unable to work. And from that time on, my mother became the family's principal breadwinner.'

'Whew!' I said. 'That is one of the saddest stories I've ever heard.' I hugged her and gently stroked her hair. She was weeping quietly, the tears running down her cheeks.

Naturally, these events had a profound effect on Cookie. She became less gregarious, more reserved and introverted. Books offered her an escape route, an imaginative deliverance from the baggage and hardship of everyday life. She became a voracious reader, and combined with her eidetic memory she was able to almost magically recreate images and pages in her mind. This mimetic gift frightened her as it was so graphic, so hallucinogenic. She was concerned that it was a manifestation of the illness that had afflicted her father and she feared, knowing its genetic predisposition, that she too might be schizophrenic.

'That's the main reason I don't touch drugs at all,' she said. 'I want to be in control of my thoughts. I don't like the idea that I might have to become dependent upon chemicals to silence the voices in my head, if I ever had any.'

I guess her telling me this story became a turning point in our relationship. It meant that she trusted me as she seldom told anyone about her past. I was very moved by her account. It explained so much about her and it bound me to her in irrevocable ways.

12

JAMES

Antoine's funeral was a sad affair. It was held at the Dutch Reformed Church in Linden. Cookie and I decided to attend the service together. I wore my best navy suit with a white shirt and dark tie. She looked very elegant in a sleeveless black dress set off by a simple gold crucifix around her neck. Cookie told me that she had a sentimental attachment to the crucifix as her father had given it to her as a child.

When I turned my old Volvo down D F Malan Drive (which has now been renamed Beyers Naude to honour the Afrikaans church activist) I started to tell her about what I had overheard at the party and Antoine's misgivings and disquiet regarding Fat Bill. She listened attentively not making too many comments since she had been very close to Antoine. We both expressed a certain uneasiness about Fat Bill but at the same time we thought it was just too far-fetched to conceive he could have had anything to do with Antoine's death.

'We'll see if he comes to the funeral,' Cookie said. 'If he stays away, then he's more than likely guilty. Even so I would still find it hard to believe.'

But, of course, Bill was at the church, friendly and relaxed as always so we had no definitive validation one way or the other. Nevertheless, from that time on, I remained cautious and suspicious of him.

The funeral service was sober and relatively unemotional. Antoine's family all seemed to accept his sexuality and were prepared to discuss it openly. Even the *predikant* was sympathetic and open-minded. Antoine's father delivered the main eulogy in a dignified and precise manner but clearly the old man was broken inside. He was tall and patrician-looking, his face drawn and lined as he struggled to keep his emotions in check.

The family had asked Cookie to speak on behalf of all of us, Antoine's university friends. Everyone knew they were close but she was also the logical choice as she was comfortable speaking in Afrikaans. I don't remember everything she said but she emphasised that his life had been cruelly cut short by tragic circumstances. She talked articulately of lost opportunity and unfulfilled promise emphasising Antoine's warmth and kindness to her. Cookie spoke sincerely from the heart and I could tell that everyone in the church was deeply moved.

After the service we drove to West Park Cemetery where the previous familial restraint was replaced by deep turmoil and turbulence. Antoine's mother was overcome by emotion and tried to throw herself into the grave after her son's coffin. She had to be forcibly held in check by her elder sons who like her were weeping and wailing uncontrollably. It was all very distressing and Cookie's and my nerves were jangled and jumpy. We decided to leave early and not attend the tea that was scheduled to be held at the church hall.

Cookie was still pretty tightly wired when we got back to the house in Melville. I poured us each a stiff glass of Scotch and we sat at the kitchen table gingerly sipping our drinks.

'I've been thinking over what you said in your speech,' I said after a short while. I took our drinks over to the sideboard and topped them up with a little more Scotch before coming back to the table. 'About unfulfilled promise and opportunity. And I've been thinking about myself. I feel I've been underachieving. Everyone else I know, all my friends – you, Marty, Ruth and especially David are doing so well. Getting somewhere. But I feel like I'm just drifting. Aimlessly going with the tide. I'm fed up with it.'

'So what are you going to do?' Cookie asked.

'I'm thinking of going to film school. Doing a postgraduate course. I've been reading *Sight & Sound* magazine a lot. It's a British publication. All about movies. And there are always advertisements in there for the London Film School. It's got a good reputation. It's not theoretical. All hands-on stuff. You learn about cinematography, editing, sound recording, directing. And you get to make your own short films. I thought I would apply. But I wanted to talk to you about it first. See what you thought.'

'I think it's a marvellous idea,' Cookie said. 'It's exactly what you've been dying to do ever since I've known you. You must do it. And living in London would be fantastic for you. Go for it!'

So I wrote to the school requesting information about their enrolment process. It took about six weeks for them to get back to me (in those days it was all snail mail) with an application form and details about what they required. There was not a straightforward acceptance based on academic merit, instead the school selected their students via a creative portfolio consisting of amongst other things, a short screenplay and a shooting script illustrated by still photographs. Rather than being intimidated by what was required, I was stimulated and enthused by the challenge.

I wrote a short story about a love affair across the *apartheid* colour bar that ended tragically. When it came to shooting the stills, I was extremely fortunate that Dorothy Makhene and Marty Lehman agreed to play the star-crossed lovers. They were ideally cast and gave me very convincingly poignant performances.

It took a few weeks to put the portfolio together and I knew when I sent it off that it would take a while before the school got back to me so I made plans accordingly and assumed I would only be going off to London the following year. In the meantime, television had finally come to South Africa and I managed to get a job working for a small Afrikaans production company making documentaries for the SABC. The programs we made were rather banal and ideologically right wing but I was getting industry experience while waiting to go to film school.

Everything seemed rosy and I had great expectations. All of us in the Russian class (except poor Antoine) had graduated with good degrees and we were optimistically making plans for the next phase of our lives.

New relationships were forming and older unions were being crystallized and consolidated. The theatre bunch had all moved into the house on Park Road, Belgravia. David and Celeste upstairs, Marty and Ruth on the ground floor ecstatic after their summer wedding. Diane and Fat Bill intended to follow suit and were planning to tie the knot in October which was only a month away.

Even Rory was romantically involved. I don't know where he met Rita but they seemed smitten with each other. She was some kind of union organizer, very intense, very committed to the Struggle. I found her a bit hard going. Too self-righteous and serious. She needed to lighten up, I thought.

Cookie was enrolled in an education diploma at Wits to fulfil her obligations to the Transvaal Education Department. Although she had little interest in being a teacher, Cookie knew that the course was only for a year and she approached it with her usual sanguinity.

Her old friend Bob Elliot had spent the holidays travelling around Europe and had met a young French woman who had invited him to her parents' farm. He liked it there and had decided to stay on for a while. See how it all panned out. Obviously I had no knowledge then how important that situation would later be for Cookie. And if I had known, I'm not sure I would have believed it. It would have been inconceivable to me.

13

JAMES

Late in September as the winter started to wane, it suddenly grew very warm, the days marked by blistering sunshine and late afternoon thunderstorms. At least that is the way I remember it. One weekend, Diane and Fat Bill and some friends of theirs that I only vaguely knew planned a little getaway to Sappers Rus near Hartebeespoort Dam. They invited others in the Russian class but only Cookie and I could make the trip.

The drive took about two hours through fairly drab Highveld scenery. Lots of flat grassland, scrubby thorn trees, the odd blue gum. We were bundled into a little bus or Kombi-type vehicle. Three or four rows of seats. Bill was driving, Diane and another woman sitting next to him in the front. Everyone else tightly packed in like sardines. Except for the back row where Cookie and I sat together.

The Kombi had an old eight-track cassette player and Rodriquez's *Cold Fact* was blaring from the speakers. People were chatting in an affable and convivial way over the loud music. They were a pretty lively bunch, very opinionated with provocative and energetic views on most subjects.

At one point there was a robust debate going on about Bill's future. Diane had expressed concern regarding how many times he had been arrested lately. She was worried about him and intimated that they were contemplating leaving the country and going into exile in England. She felt that maybe they could achieve more there, perhaps work with the banned African National Congress or some other anti-*apartheid* group.

In the Kombi there seemed to be a general consensus that, from a pragmatic point of view, this made sense. It was felt that very little could be achieved from the inside of a prison cell. 'Look at Mandela,' a young woman in the second row said. 'He's been totally silenced. A spent force in South African politics,' she argued. 'He will never have a future in this country. One day we'll wake up and he will have died in jail on Robben Island.'

As we moved towards our destination, the vegetation slowly changed from grassland to dense bushy terrain. The veld browner, the bushes more stunted. We passed through some small *dorpies* with their dreary, down-at-heel shops and petrol garages. Bleak villages offering little comfort to the drab, monotonous lives of their inhabitants.

I was a little bored and began browsing through a magazine I had brought with me. *Life,* I think it was, lots of engaging photographs. Cookie asked if she could also look at it. We sat closer. Both of us were wearing shorts and our thighs touched lightly. I could feel a pulse in my neck quivering. The air thick. Everything suddenly heightened, charged.

She had one hand under the magazine vaguely brushing my tummy whenever the Kombi hit a bump in the road. Below us was the Hartebeespoort Dam. We were now on the bridge, the sluice gates open. Through the window I could see the white churning waters. The roar quite deafening. Suddenly an adrenaline kick, a moment of expectation. I felt that we were in some kind of vortex being sucked along ever nearer towards something. But I did not know what.

In the middle of the bridge over the river there is a miniature copy of the Arc de Triomphe and as we drove through it,

Cookie gently took my hand. It was quite electric, as if she was communicating with me in some almost mystical way. Even to this day I'm not sure exactly what it was but it seemed deep and personal, expressing an overwhelming need, a mutual dependence.

I heard myself imperceptibly sighing. Part of me felt greedy and amoral. Slightly afraid. Carnal and dewy-eyed all at once.

It was all very strange. This Kombi full of noisy people prattling on about politics with Cookie and I completely insulated from them, cocooned in our own little world of longing and wordless communication. My manifest lust felt wanton and shameless but even though my heart was pounding, I just let it happen. Like the river rushing below I felt swept along by irresistible, inexorable forces. Taking me ever closer to… somewhere.

This rather surreal state of affairs did not last very long because we soon arrived at our destination, at Sappers Rus. We all clambered out of the Kombi, joking and stretching, surveying the place. We strolled down to the *braai* and pool area. Some of the men started fooling around, wrestling and then someone was thrown in the swimming pool. Soon we were all in, splashing around in our wet clothes. The shock of cold water was good as it brought me down to earth.

Later we changed into dry clothes and I suggested to Cookie that we go for a walk. She took one of the picnic rugs and we headed into the small wooded area that surrounded the camp-site. The trees were mostly conifers, the ground covered with pine straw. We found a secluded spot and I spread out the rug. We lay down. For both of us, I think, there was a sense of heightened expectation. Anticipation.

I remember stroking the dark hairs on her forearm. She was still a little chilled from the swim and had goosebumps. Very tenderly I took her in my arms and kissed her. Then, with the dappled sunlight falling on us, we made glorious love.

That night there was a *braai*. The women prepared the salads while the men cooked the meat. Lots of rare lamb cutlets, succulent *boerewors*, apricot *sosaties*. Apart from Cookie and I who drank only a little, people consumed a great deal of alcohol. It was the first time I had ever seen Diane drunk and, completely sloshed, some of her prejudices emerged. In that toffee-nosed accent of hers, she was denouncing Afrikaans. Calling it a "bastard tongue, a hodgepodge language comprising a mix of kitchen Dutch with Hottentot."

Cookie was livid. She wanted to strangle Diane, come to the defence of her *taal*, her culture. I wanted to tell Diane that the most bastard language of all was English with its appropriation from everywhere else. It's word theft which is exactly what made it rich, gave it that huge, extensive vocabulary. For me, there was something quite bigoted about Diane's attitude in its appeal to linguist purity. The search for what was called "*suiwer*" or "pure" in Afrikaans. Keeping the race sanitized and untainted. This was the kind of jingoist, chauvinistic sloganeering that I truly despised. And I despised it in Diane that night. Nevertheless, both Cookie and I kept silent. I told myself she was just drunk, off her face, forget it. *More is nog 'n dag.* (Tomorrow is another day.)

We all spread our sleeping bags on the concrete floor of a big *rondawel*. Cookie and I zipped ours together making a kind of double bed. Without discussing it in advance but just communicating in some kind of swain's silent secret code, we did not make love that night. I think we both felt too exposed, too vulnerable and that our feelings for each other were still too novel, too private. So we just lay like spoons, clinging to each other. A few of the other couples were not as modest and, despite their efforts to limit the sound effects, there was quite a bit of bonking going on around us.

We woke early in the morning, at dawn. Cookie and I crept quietly outside. The *rondawel* sat on top of a little *koppie* and below us we had a magnificent view over the valley. The light was soft and violet and in the distance we could see the silvery glints coming off the waters of the Hartebeespoort Dam.

We sat on the grass, smoking a cigarette. I felt very calm, very relaxed. Content within myself. And that's when I asked Cookie to come to England with me. I told her that there was nothing more important to me than her love and that I felt we were bonded forever. She said she had heard there were some opportunities for scholarships to teach in England and that she would apply. If she got one, we could go there together.

She told me that all her life, since her father's illness, she had suffered from some kind of low-grade anxiety. An expectancy that whatever she had, whatever belonged to her, could always be taken away. That she was not safe. That she could not be happy because all this could suddenly be obliterated. That hazard was everywhere. But on that morning she told me that she did not feel that way. Instead she said she somehow felt secure. Safe and free from harm. Inviolable.

I know that I felt, what is the word for it, euphoric? Blissful? Like I had just had an epiphany. That I had found a map to some hidden treasure. For once in my life, I was living purely in the moment. In the present. Neither imprisoned by the past nor bound by a longing for the future. Just there. Ever there.

14

Mornings were best for it, Rory found. When there was still very little traffic on the roads, the air fresh with the promise of a new day. He would get up early, always at the same time. Just before five. Coffee and then his stretches. First the calves, then hamstrings and finally his iliotibial band, his weight on one foot, the other crossed in front. Always the same routine. He liked having a regimen. A plan for the day. It made him feel organised, in a groove. Start the day right and everything else would fit into place.

His girlfriend, Rita, would still be asleep. He'd wake her on his return. Maybe they'd have a shower together, make love before getting the boys ready for a picnic. They were hers, two young sons from a previous marriage. Rory liked them, treated them as he would his own children, with love and affection but also with discipline. He believed in restraint, self-control. He thought it was important for the boys to learn it so that they could determine their own fates, control their own destinies.

He slipped on his running shoes. Asics. They gave him the right support and stability for his gait. Enabled him to put in a lot of distance and remain injury free. Outside the sun was rising, a crisp autumn day on the Highveld. The weather perfect for running.

The house where they lived was in the affluent suburb of Saxonwold. Rita had acquired it following a lucrative divorce settlement from her previous husband. Rory liked the place, its spaciousness, the well-maintained lawns and swimming pool.

He walked through the carpeted living room into the large, white-tiled kitchen. Rita's domestic servant kept the home spotlessly clean. The family dog, Prince, a lean Boxer, slept in his basket in the corner. Rory patted him on his way out, promising to feed him soon. Prince rolled over, went back to sleep; it was too early for him.

The route that Rory had plotted allowed him to combine his recreational activities with his underground, clandestine stuff. That way he could kill two birds with one stone. He would run down Cotswold Drive and then make his way around the Zoo Lake, stopping to inspect his post office box in Parkview. From there he would run up Jan Smuts Avenue to the university where he would be able to check on his gym locker. Then back home past the Johannesburg Zoo through Forest Town. That should be about a ten-kilometre run, just what he had in mind. He was looking forward to it. Keenly anticipating the exercise.

Always when he started, his breathing would be erratic, jarring. Then gradually it would settle down and he could get into his stride. Establish a rhythm. Deep shade fell across the pavement, the sun still low in the sky behind him. The jacaranda leaves fanned out like netted ferns, a dark forest green. He loved this part of the city and its graceful, whitewashed homes with curved bow windows and expansive gardens.

Rory was often torn between his censorious Marxist condemnation of the opulence that surrounded him and his own upwardly mobile aspirations. Although intellectually he disapproved of the excesses of capitalism, he nevertheless, at times found himself coveting the wealthy trappings of his neighbours, wishing he had more money, a luxury car. Like that Mercedes over there. That would be good. He could go for that. But then he would reprimand himself and dismiss these thoughts as petty and bourgeois, the product of his origins, the fact that he had grown up poor in the southern suburbs. The wrong side of town. He blamed what he saw as defects in his character on the feelings of deprivation that had characterised his childhood.

That was the problem with capitalism, he thought. *It made people jealous and acquisitive. Grasping and envious. That's why we needed to change it. Socialism will get rid of all this greedy behaviour. People will be much more fairly and equally treated. Equitably rewarded. Everyone will be better off and happier.*

Running past the Zoo Lake, Rory could feel his feet pounding the pavement. He liked the rhythmic sounds he generated through the repetitive movement of his legs and arms. He felt good. Relaxed, at one with the world. There were no cars around when he crossed Donegal Avenue and except for the birdsong it was very quiet, most people still asleep. At the Parkview Post Office, he took a small key from his shorts pocket and opened the box – number 79165. He was surprised to find nothing. Rory had not heard from Kaplan for a while now and he was expecting some communication from his "control". He wondered if everything was all right. Still, he reasoned, getting no word was a good sign. Probably nothing to worry about.

It was a fairly hard climb up Jan Smuts Avenue towards the university but Rory easily scaled the incline, relishing the exertion. His breathing was even, his pace regular and smooth. There were a few more cars on the road by now but no real traffic. Sunday morning and quiet. Just before he got to Jorissen Street, he cut into the university grounds and continued on his way. Running fast now. Reaching his peak.

In the gym, Rory used his key to open the sturdy Yale padlock on the little steel cabinet where he stored his sporting gear. Apart from a pair of socks and a couple of running vests, it was empty. No message from Kaplan. Very strange. He felt a little apprehensive. What was going on? Why had he not heard anything? Was something wrong? It was definitely unusual. Kaplan normally kept him well informed. On a tight leash. This lack of communication was disquieting. Unsettling.

The run home was leisurely and effortless. Rory was feeling energised. The endorphins had kicked in and his mood was buoyed by the chemicals streaming through his veins. But despite the slight euphoria he was getting from his runner's high, Rory, nevertheless, experienced some anxiety. He wasn't sure what was troubling him. It couldn't just be Kaplan's silence. Something else was nagging at him, disturbing him, scratching at his preconscious brain. He couldn't really identify it. Something he couldn't name. The jitters. An edgy feeling.

Rory was at the house now. He opened the garden gate. A loud metallic snap. The sound exaggerated on the quiet street. He walked into the front yard, noticing the boys' playthings scattered on the veranda. A cricket bat and ball, wind-up cars, a Mickey Mouse puppet, a few marbles. Dinky toys. It didn't feel right. Something didn't quite gel.

Everything seemed somehow heightened. His senses elevated and acute. He could hear the birds chirping, a slight hum in his eardrums. Taste salt on his lips. Time seemed to stall, to drag. He felt like he was swimming in aspic. Part of him wanted to turn and run away. Flee. But it seemed irrational, mad. He opened the front door. Walked in. And then the earth turned. His world collapsed in on itself.

Rita was in her pyjamas and dressing gown, sitting on the sofa with her feet up, hugging her knees close to her. She looked haggard and afraid. A mess. Two large, muscular men stood on either side of the living room. Dark suits, their hands clasped in front of them. Deadpan. To her left, diagonally facing her, a man sat in one of the armchairs. He stroked his bald pate, his face flushed with an alcoholic glow, a bulbous Jimmy Durante nose, the obligatory thin moustache. He wore a loose-fitting, nondescript grey suit, white shirt and flashy purple tie. All the driving energy in the room swirled around him. He was calling the shots.

'Rory, so sorry to barge in like this.' His voice honeyed, full of avuncular affection. 'I hate to disturb your Sunday. I know you like your routine. I, too, am a creature of habit. I like to keep things orderly and in place. I should be off to *kerk* now with my wife but, well, duty calls…'

Rory thought he could smell something rank and foul in the room. He wondered about its source.

'*Ag*, sorry man, I'm being rude. Forgetting my manners. And your lady friend has been so kind and hospitable. Made us *lekker* coffee and all.' He leant forward and took a sip from the half-filled cup on the side table to his right. 'I should *sommer* introduce myself. Colonel Piet van Wyk. I'm with the Bureau for State Security.'

Rory had heard about the colonel, knew him by reputation. Van Wyk's nickname was "Klopper" (Knocker) because this was one man you didn't want to come knocking on your door. He had a reputation for being hard-arsed. Ruthless. An obdurate, tenacious sadist.

The colonel explained that he was arresting Rory for "furthering the aims of the African National Congress and the South African Communist Party." He read Rory his rights and added: '*Ja*, you *oukies* think you can get away with anything. Think you can do what you like. But we'll get you. We always get you fuckers!'

Turning to Rita with a formal bow of his head: 'Excuse my language, lady, but that's what they are these commies, *sommer naaiers*. But don't worry, man, we're on to you all. We'll catch you before you can even fart.'

'To be frank, I'm surprised it took you this long,' Rory replied.

'Oh *ja*. I've got something of yours here. Something you might have been looking for.'

From his jacket pocket, van Wyk took out two small items, a small red handkerchief and a handwritten note. Rory could clearly read what was written there. A line of poetry:

"The broken wall, the burning roof and tower
And Agamemnon dead."

Kaplan's message. The signal to flee. To run. The warning he never got.

'It was there waiting for you. Only we got there first,' van Wyk said in a quiet voice. 'Pity about your friend though. Kaplan. He managed to evade us. He got away before we could grab him. Still, we'll catch him. We'll find him. *More is nog 'n dag.* (Tomorrow is another day.) Just like we got you. We've been watching you for some time now. Just had to pick the right time. When it suited us.' Then with a little tilt of his head to his sidekicks: 'Take him!'

The two burly policemen cuffed Rory and then held his upper arms firmly while allowing him to kiss Rita goodbye.

'Look after the boys for me,' he said as they led him out.

Rising from the chair, van Wyk apologised to Rita for the interruption to her schedule and told her how much he regretted having to do this. How he hated involving women in this kind of thing. Men's business. Very distressing, he said.

Rory thought there was something quite grotesque about this outward display of old-world manners and courtesies. The colonel's overt theatricality, his self-conscious performance. The circus ringmaster. It was almost clichéd and laughable. Like some comic book villain. Under different circumstances Rory might have found it amusing, but now it chilled him. Filled him with dread.

What have I got myself into? he thought. *How could I have been such a fool? Playing these silly spy games. This stupid cloak-and-dagger shit! What have I done? I should have been more careful. Trusted my instincts when I got to the house. Or before that when there was no communication from Kaplan. I should have known. I should have realised that something was wrong, awfully wrong.*

Rory's emotions were in turmoil. Imbalanced and out of whack. His fight or flight instincts kicking in and lurching from one extreme to the other. His first response was to panic, to look for an escape, to feel regretful and angry with himself. But soon this switched to defiance and rebellious bravado. He felt contempt for his captors. *Fuck them*, he thought. *I've done the right thing, acted honourably. They're just a bunch of fascists. My fight is honest and true. Pure. Don't surrender the moral high ground.*

This self-righteous anger worked to his advantage. It was the mood that stayed with him, that sustained him. It was the weapon that would enable him to carry himself with dignity, with courage and restraint. Without it he knew he would not be able to endure the interrogations, the torture and the long incarceration that he now realised awaited him. The dark years that lay ahead.

One of the men pulled a walkie-talkie out of his jacket pocket and spoke into it. Rory did not register what was said. His senses were in overload, a deluge of information. Sunlight. Bird noise. A coppery taste on his lips. The clammy hands of the men holding his arms. The sourness of their breaths. A humming in his ears. He felt dizzy and sugar deprived.

A car spun round the corner. Pulled up in front of the house. Rory was quickly shoved into the back seat. A man on either side, pressing against him, hard and bulky. Rory thought of a scrum and beefy rugby forwards. A game he was forced to play. A game he could not win.

The car raced off, heading towards the city. A splatter of light and shade. Slowly, ever so slowly, Rory's jangled nerves started to settle down. The fragmented, confusing sensory bombardment easing off. He felt less awash with those intense physical impressions. Now his conscious mind began to take over, take control as his thought processes become more analytical, more systematic.

How did this happen? he thought. *How did it come to this? Was I betrayed? There must have been some kind of security breach. Or a spy in the network. Some informer who stabbed me in the back. But who could it be? Who knew what I was up to? Who could, or would, possibly finger me? It couldn't have been Kaplan. The colonel said they were hoping to get him but he had slipped away, eluded them. So it had to have been someone in my cell. One of the seven that I distributed banned literature to. But who?*

Rory thought about his cell comrades. Pictured them, one by one in his mind's eye. Considered and evaluated them. At first none of them seemed likely spies. They all appeared genuinely committed to the Struggle. All ideologically sound. No one likely to be swayed by pecuniary gain. And no obvious oddballs or Walter Mitty types. They seemed solid. Dependable.

But what was it that van Wyk had said? Something about watching me for a while? And picking the right time, a time that suited them? So the timing was important.

Rory thought about people in the cell again. What had happened to them lately? What had recently changed in their lives? What was different? Then it came to him. Like a blow to the head. Fat Bill and Diane had just married and left the country. They had ostensibly gone into exile. And were now planning to work with the ANC in England. If one of them was a spy, he or she would no longer have to maintain the contacts they had established here at home, in South Africa. He or she could burn his or her (Rory's mind was racing now. He was quickly dismissing Diane from the equation. Settling on the male gender) bridges behind him. *He would have no further need for me. I would become expendable. The colonel could now reel me in.*

It all fitted. It had to be him. *It had to be Fat Bill,* Rory thought. *He had us all fooled. Fuck you, Billy boy! Fuck you and your new wife too!*

With so little traffic on a Sunday morning, the police had made good time and the car was now racing along Commissioner Street. Rory knew exactly where they were going and he knew he was running out of time fast. He needed to think quickly. It was imperative that he understood exactly what the security police knew. His life might depend upon it. He needed to have a story ready, a story that he could repeat over and over. Even under interrogation. Even while being tortured. Something he could give them. Something that they would accept as true. But something that would not give the whole game away. Something that could save him.

Rory's mind was buzzing, his thoughts jumping from one idea to the next. If Fat Bill had turned him in, if Fat Bill was the spy then the security police only knew as much or as little as he did. So, what did Fat Bill know? That was the key to it.

Well, one thing was certain. Fat Bill did not know about the gun running. Rory felt sure that Bill only knew about distributing the banned literature. That was a relief. The distinction was crucial. It could mean the difference between life and death. Rory understood that if he was prosecuted for circulating communist propaganda, he could expect a fairly substantial prison sentence, maybe as much as ten years. But gun running was something else entirely. That was treason. That was heavy. That carried the death penalty.

Rory told himself that whatever happened he had to make sure that he only confessed to the banned literature. He had to keep silent about everything else. *Whatever you do, don't tell them about the gun running*, he thought. *Then you'll be fine. Then you'll survive.*

As the car turned into the infamous John Vorster Square Police Station, he held that thought at the forefront of his mind.

15

COOKIE

That year was mostly good for James and me. We were madly in love, feeling giddy about each other, obsessed as only lovers can be and full of optimism. I should have known that it could not last and that dark days were ahead, but at the time, everything seemed rosy.

James's application to film school was successful and he was planning on leaving for London in early November. He would spend some time settling in, finding a flat, getting acquainted with his new city before the course started in early January. I had applied for a foreign exchange teaching program in the UK and was waiting hopefully to hear about it so that I could join him a little later.

In the meantime, Diane and Bill had married and were already ensconced in England. After almost continuous badgering and harassment by the security police, Diane's father had persuaded Bill to take the fateful step into exile. Diane felt very equivocal about the move; on the one hand she acknowledged that it was probably for the best but she also knew that the stability of her old life was now under threat. She could no longer cling to the security and protection that her vast friendship networks had provided. They were no more. So too, the sanctuary that her parents offered her as an only child would now be eroded.

Unlike Diane, I was really looking forward to moving to England. There was very little to hold me in South Africa and when my foreign exchange application was approved, I did not hesitate and caught the first plane out of there.

James met me at Heathrow. Although we had only been apart for a few months, we were both excited to see each other and were visibly moved. I remember weeping silently as he held me in his arms. My plane had arrived very early in the morning and there was only light traffic going into London. James had recently bought a second-hand, old Rover 90 and we rambled along leisurely, chatting amiably. I was in such an emotional bubble that I hardly noticed the countryside whizzing past us.

Soon we were in Fulham where James rented a small flat on the New King's Road overlooking Parson's Green. It was a really lovely area with tall trees and terrace houses. Through the foreign exchange program, I had been given a year's work experience whereby I was to teach at Dartford Grammar School for Girls. There was about a week before the school term started for either of us so James offered to show me around London.

We went to all the usual tourist spots – the Tower of London, Speakers' Corner, the British Museum, Westminster Abbey, Kew Gardens. Looking back now I am surprised that we managed to pack so much into such a short period of time. We used public transport, catching the Tube or buses everywhere and I soon began to get an overview of the vast networks that made up this great city.

I loved visiting all the galleries and seeing, in the flesh so to speak, all those wonderful paintings that I had read about. The Courtauld Gallery was particularly fine with its magnificent Impressionist and Post-Impressionist works. And at the Tate I was astonished to find those sublime landscapes by Turner and Constable.

All too soon though the touring was over and with the start of school term my stint as teacher began. I must say in retrospect those were some of my happiest days. The pupils were conscientious, studious and friendly and I really enjoyed teaching. Likewise, my colleagues were helpful, supportive and collegial. The only downside was not seeing James every day. We would meet on weekends when almost every Friday afternoon I would catch the train from Kent. I would get into London at around six in the evening and then join James at one of the pubs near the film school in Covent Garden, either the White Swan or the Lamb & Flag.

James always liked to sit near the back. I remember so many times having to squeeze my way through the patrons to find him sitting on a bar stool engaged in lively conversation with one of his classmates. Holding forth, elucidating on the art of cinema.

How I loved those times! He would always greet me in the warmest possible way. You know his smile – all sparkling eyes and teeth and those cheeks! He was never afraid to show affection. It was one of the things I adored about him.

We would have a few drinks with his school chums where the conversation would always be around films. Occasionally we would discuss philosophy and politics but then the conversation would invariably come back to movies. James was so passionate about cinema. If you asked him which was more important, life or films, I'm sure he would have said films.

Later we would say goodbye to his friends and find a little Chinese restaurant in Soho where we would have a romantic meal on our own. Those quiet, intimate moments together were so special, so magical. And so fleeting.

Saturday mornings would be spent lazing around, reading the newspapers and having a late breakfast. Then we would unfailingly go to the cinema. James took me to see so many films. Films I would never otherwise have seen. Mostly the "classics". From the canon. His favourite films – *The Searchers, Citizen Kane, 400 Blows, Rules of the Game, Alphaville* and plenty more. Some weird Japanese stuff – *Ugetsu Monogatari* and *Sansho the Bailiff.* He loved Mizoguchi's movies with all those long takes, the moving camera, the gorgeous lighting. Also some more contemporary films like *The Conformist* and *Obsession*. Oh, and naturally, Hitchcock and Preminger – *Vertigo* and *Advise and Consent*.

Of course it wasn't all lounging around in darkened cinemas, James was working very hard – going to lectures, working on productions, writing his own scripts, learning his craft. Occasionally he would go on location and be shooting at all hours of the day and night. Still it was a magical time.

But I must admit that during that first winter in England, I really struggled with the cold. It seemed to get in your bones and you could not escape it. James's flat was warm and cosy but I found it bleak outside. I could not get used to seeing so little sun. It was such a great contrast with Africa where you felt overwhelmed by the sunlight.

In the middle of March, I thought the winter would never end. Then suddenly in early April it all changed. The sun finally emerged and we experienced a glorious spring. It was mid-term break and although I had a mountain of marking, I was able to spend the week in London with James. To celebrate the splendid weather and the Easter holidays, Diane and Fat Bill invited us to a lunchtime *braai* at their flat in Hampstead. We arrived late and when we got there the place was packed. People were spilling out of the lounge's French doors onto the garden where Fat Bill was tossing huge marinated steaks on a glowing charcoal barbeque.

Both Bill and Diane greeted us warmly but then soon excused themselves to attend to their guests. James and I mingled making small talk and meeting people. Many were expats, racially diverse South Africans – blacks, whites, coloureds all expressing some nostalgic longing for the homeland. Some were associated with the African National Congress which, at that time, was still banned in South Africa. I spoke at length to Bernie Lebese, a prominent figure in the movement who I thought was amazing. He was open and friendly, surprisingly free of rancour. He spoke optimistically of his hopes for a new, non-racial society. I liked him immensely and immediately, but at the time I didn't realise what a significant role he would later play in my future.

I remember that the following evening, James and I had booked seats at the Roundhouse Theatre in Chalk Farm. We saw *The Ik* which was a Royal Shakespeare Company production directed by one of our theatrical heroes, Peter Brook. It was a rather dark piece that examined some of the social practices of the Ik people, who lived in Uganda near the Kenyan border. Because of severe famine in the area, the tribe survived by adopting extreme individualistic practices.

There are many horrific incidents like the starving of children and the elderly in the play but it attempts to question universal human values. Despite the melancholic and gloomy subject matter, James and I were enthralled by Brook's staging technique and we happily spent the homeward Tube ride dissecting the play.

When we got back to the flat, we were both feeling elated and passionate and pretty soon we began to make love. Without going into any details, suffice it to say that in our haste we neglected our usual contraception practice.

Thinking about it now, after all these years, I am once again struck by how such small incidental issues can generate such profound change in our lives.

16

COOKIE

I don't know what to call them – events, incidents, occurrences. In any case, there were a number of rather strange circumstances that took place and forever altered the direction my life would take. The first of these transpired a short while after I slowly came to the realization that I was pregnant.

Occasionally I had been experiencing these nauseous feelings in the morning and I had missed my period, which was very unusual for me. This was near the end of the school term and I was down in Kent. I went to see a local GP who confirmed my pregnancy and recommended that I also consult a gynaecologist. As I was planning to visit James that weekend, the doctor was able to book an appointment for me with a specialist in London.

On Friday I caught the train but did not go to the West End as James was working on a night shoot for a short film. Instead I took the Tube and went directly to the flat in Fulham. It was a lovely warm, balmy night and I relaxed in the bath before going to bed early. James had told me he expected the shoot to finish at around 3am and we had agreed that I wouldn't wait up for him. I hadn't told him my "big news" yet but was planning on doing it that night. But, of course, that never happened as I'll try to explain.

On Saturday when I awoke, James was still drowsy. I told him I had somewhere to go and that we'd talk later. He was so out of it that I don't think any of this even registered and pretty soon he fell back into a deep sleep.

I remember that morning vividly. It was slightly overcast but warm, the sun occasionally peeking through the clouds. I decided to spoil myself and hailed a cab on New King's Road. The traffic was light and I relaxed in the back watching the world go by. For the first time in quite a while I was upbeat and optimistic, almost light-headed. I had heard pregnancy could sometimes make you feel like that. Supernatant I think the word is. Like you were floating.

My appointment was at the Royal College of Obstetricians and Gynaecologists in Regent's Park. It's really a very attractive part of the city with wide, expansive circular avenues and tall, well-established trees. It's not too far from the zoo and as I got out of the cab I could hear the sound of a lion roaring. Quite an absurd and incongruous thing to hear in the middle of London. It made me think immediately of Africa and of home.

And then something equally strange and bizarre happened. The surgery front door opened and Diane Wilkins, or rather Diane Saunders as she now was, walked out. That brief instant, as time expanded to arrest her elegant movements, will always remain etched in my memory. For one magical fleeting moment the sun burst through the clouds and caught her blonde hair from behind producing a radiant halo of light. To me, she looked ecstatic and overjoyed. Delicate and heavenly, like a Botticellian angel.

I was caught by surprise, a little off balance. Then I waved to her and called out her name. We embraced warmly, kissed each other on the lips as South Africans tend to do. But then somehow we became English and neither of us asked the other what we were doing there. We were unusually reserved. Friendly without being forthcoming. But I knew why she was there. Her whole demeanour gave it away. It was so obvious. She was clearly euphoric and blissfully pregnant.

We exchanged pleasantries and then she invited James and me to come to dinner that night. I immediately accepted even though we had planned to stay at home. It was a spontaneous response on my part. There is no way I could have known how eventful that dinner party would be. How could I possibly have predicted that it would set us on an antagonistic course and that it would forever change all of our lives?

I called James to tell him about the change of plans. Being easy-going and mellow, he didn't mind in the least. The only problem was that he still had a shoot in the afternoon and early evening.

'We're filming in Swiss Cottage so it'll probably be best for me to come straight to Bill and Diane's and see you there. I'll try not to be too late,' he promised.

When I got to their Hampstead flat, people were milling around in the lounge, drinking and socializing. It was quite a large group made up of South African expats and English couples. Some, taking advantage of the fine weather, had spilled out onto the veranda and into the garden. Everybody seemed to get on well, the conversation witty and congenial. I didn't want to drink much so I nursed a glass of wine to be sociable. Soon after, Bill proposed a toast informing us all that Diane was pregnant. He made the announcement quite formally and I distinctly remember him saying she was "with child". I decided to keep silent about my own situation even though Diane was smiling meaningfully at me from across the room. As if she knew some secret.

In those days there wasn't a lot of emphasis on not drinking when you were pregnant and I noticed Diane was knocking back quite a few. Bill was also getting quite sloshed and kept prattling on about the responsibilities of fatherhood. People passed heavily laden plates of finger food and snacks around and I was pleased that it was not a formal, sit-down dinner as I didn't feel like indulging in meaningful conversation and preferred to drift around making small talk.

Fortunately, James arrived soon after, smiling and happy. I was really pleased to see him. He hugged me and I leaned into him relishing his warmth and solidity. I felt good – loved and appreciated. Once again I think my hormones were taking over and inducing tranquil and contented feelings.

We circulated, happy to drift from one group to another. At one stage I found myself in the kitchen helping Diane serve food. We were alone in there and she looked at me quizzically clearly expecting me to say something about my own parturient situation but I remained silent and reticent. After all, despite our years together at university in the Russian class, we weren't really that close. Besides, I was determined not to inform anyone until I had discussed it with James. My aim was to tell him that night but, of course, the universe had other plans.

It was much later in the evening that I stumbled upon that fateful document that would so profoundly change all of our lives. I had just gone to the toilet and was heading back to the lounge but I must have got disorientated because I found myself in the study. Bill's study. Where he kept all his written communications. You must remember that this was before the advent of personal computers which are so ubiquitous now. Then everything was either handwritten or dashed off on a typewriter. And to make copies you had to use carbon paper which was placed behind the original. There were no such things as hard drives or memory sticks. It was all so material, so tactile. So real.

Bill's desk was off to the side of the room lit by a small green office lamp. In the centre was a manual Remington Rand typewriter, its ribbon black and taut. A ream of white paper on the left and on the right a grocery list penned in Bill's flamboyant copperplate handwriting. A blue Parker pen on a very tidy desk. The room had simple and spartan furnishings but it was nevertheless, warm, cosy and inviting. There was a well-filled wine rack on one wall and on the other side floor to ceiling shelving stacked with books.

I didn't mean to probe. Honestly, that really was not my intention. I was just curious as to what books he had been reading and I noticed a few were in the Cyrillic alphabet. One of them I recognized as Turgenev's *On the Eve*. This was a book that I had never read by one of my favourite Russian authors. I took it out of the shelf with the intention of reading a few of the opening lines. But as I did so, I noticed something stuffed behind it. A bundle of papers concealed from view, carefully hidden. Curiosity got the better of me. I pulled them out and, so God help me, began to read.

At first I wasn't sure what I had in my hands until I began to skim through the documents. Soon it became apparent that these were reports from Fat Bill to a superior, someone named Colonel Piet van Wyk. I could not believe what I was looking at. Laid out before me were detailed accounts of espionage, spying activities that Bill had carried out on behalf of the *apartheid* regime. These were communiqués with his master, his case officer, his "control".

The material contained information about how Bill had infiltrated the African National Congress (ANC) and the sensitive intelligence he had obtained. There were terms and nomenclature in there that, at the time, I did not know the meaning of. Phrases like "false flag operations" and "*ruse de guerre*". The word "stratagem" appeared often. He wrote about "assets" and "bang and burn" operations. I should point out that this dossier was all written in Afrikaans, a language that very few people in England could read and understand. But, of course, I could.

Very soon I became acutely conscious of time passing and I was beginning to be afraid that maybe my absence would be noted or that someone could walk in on me at any moment. So I thought I should put the documents back in place and leave everything as it had been. But then, my eye latched onto a name that I recognized. It seemed to leap out at me.

Antoine Pienaar. My dear friend. And then another word jumped out from the labyrinth and threw me into complete turmoil. *Vermoor*. The Afrikaans word for "assassinate". By now my hands were shaking and I was in deep distress. It was apparent from what I read that Bill had ordered or been responsible for Antoine's death. I felt literally sick. I thought I was going to vomit but I forced myself to read on.

I flipped through the pages quickly committing what I could to memory. I could not believe the extent of Bill's depravity and the sheer expanse of his vile influence. He had been able to isolate the right people by penetrating left-wing organizations and feeding the information to the security police. He had betrayed so many people – colleagues and fellow students that I knew and loved. People like Rory Callaghan and so many others. Friends that had been arrested and tortured. It was heinous and unthinkable. Monstrous.

The door was closed but I was getting extremely nervous and so I replaced all the typed pages just as I thought I had found them. Then I put the Turgenev back in the bookshelf. My hands were shaking but I took an eyeliner out of my purse and began applying some make-up, looking at myself in a mirror on one wall. It was fortuitous that I did so because just then Fat Bill opened the door and entered the study.

'Oh sorry,' he said. 'Just needed a refill.'

Then he walked unsteadily over to the wine rack and took out a bottle. I tried to act normal and keep my expression impassive but my nerves were jangling. I mumbled something about feeling sick. This was true as my stomach was churning over.

'Must go to the lavatory,' I muttered and lurched out of the room.

I badly needed to retch. I ran back to the loo and puked my guts out in the toilet bowl. Obviously morning sickness contributed but the nausea was mostly from anguish and heartache. I could not believe what I had discovered. It was intolerable, truly dreadful and beyond redemption.

When I got back to the lounge I quickly found James. I must have looked pale because he immediately asked what was wrong. I told him that I was not feeling well and that we should leave. We made our apologies to Diane and said goodbye. Fortunately, Bill was nowhere to be seen because I know I could not have faced him without giving something away but with Diane I was able to keep my expression neutral. She was sympathetic and said she hoped I would feel better soon. Then James and I left.

In James's old Rover on the way home, I told him everything that I had read in Bill's secret chronicle. Naturally he was deeply shocked and disturbed by the turn of events despite the fact that in the past he had harboured suspicions about Bill.

'What are you going to do?' he asked me.

My hands were still shaking uncontrollably when I answered: 'I can't just let this go. I can't let him get away with this. Not now that I know he was responsible for Antoine. I must tell someone about it.'

'But who?' James asked.

'There's that nice guy from the ANC that we met. Bernie Lebese. He would know what to do with this kind of information. Maybe I should speak to him. Go and see him,' I said.

'It could be dangerous. You know the security police may have their Islington office under surveillance. I'm worried about you. It's not safe.'

'I don't really have a choice. All Bill's betrayals. I can't condone that.'

'Maybe you could phone Bernie. Tell him you need to see him. Meet him in some café. A public place. Somewhere free from harm.'

'That's what I'll do. Make it sound casual and social. A friendly get-together.'

'There's one thing I don't get though,' James said. 'Right up to now Fat Bill's been so careful. He's managed to fool everyone. No one seems to have suspected him of being a spy or of working for the security police. He's infiltrated all those leftie groups. It's all been quite elaborate. And skilfully worked out. Yet now he was extremely careless. It was just sloppy him leaving that material where you could read it.'

'Well it *was* hidden away. He probably assumed no one would look behind some old Russian book. And it was in Afrikaans.'

'I guess,' said James. 'But I was wondering if it was just arrogance, just a belief that he could get away with anything, that God was on his side or if somehow it was more than that.'

'How do you mean?'

'Well maybe unconsciously he wanted to be found out. Maybe it was some kind of parapraxis, a Freudian slip. Some motive hidden to even him.'

It was an interesting idea but we did not explore it further. In a strange way it reminded me that I still had not told James about my pregnancy. God knows I wanted to but with these new developments, with all the intrigue around Fat Bill, I somehow felt the time was not right. I felt that it could wait until there was a more appropriate moment.

And so two days later I contacted Bernie Lebese and arranged to meet him for coffee. Little did I know then that Bill would manage to slip through their fingers and evade the plans Bernie and the ANC hatched for him. He was too smart to take the bait and go to Russia so, as a last resort, they felt compelled to give the story to the press. And what a story! All of Bill's espionage activities including his infiltration of the ANC made front-page news in both the English and South African newspapers. He was an overnight celebrity. Fat Bill Saunders, the master spy who was now being forced to come in from the cold. I guess the ANC felt that when their main plan did not work, this was a consolation prize and that it was something of a coup for them. But it could not have been worse for me.

17

FAT BILL

Fat Bill was angry. Not just angry, fucking furious! Pissed off with everything and everybody! His plans were in tatters. All his hard work for nothing. His cover blown for good. Just because of that stupid bitch. She had ruined it for him. But he would show her. Just you wait and see. She'd get her comeuppance. He'd give it to her. Fix her for good.

There was a storm blowing across Hampstead Heath. Thick clouds building up on the horizon, the sky as dark and bleak as his mood. Fat Bill turned up the collar of his coat to protect his ears from the cold. It was supposed to be summer but the weather was still dreadful. *Godawful pommie climate*, he thought. *Won't have to put up with it for much longer. I'll be back in the sunshine soon. Once I've sorted her out. Once I've given her what for. She'll regret it. I'll make sure she's singing the blues. Fucking cow!*

He'd been drinking and it was contributing to his infuriated state of mind. Fuelling his rage. At lunchtime, in the Spaniard's Inn, his favourite pub, Bill had downed quite a few large whiskies in quick succession. It had made him feel both maudlin and aggro. Adrenalin pumping through his veins. He was up for it. Taking a piss in the toilet, he thought some guy was looking at him *skeef* so he popped him one. A fast chop to the kidneys. A well-timed head-butt. Broke the prick's nose. Shoved his face down the toilet bowl and flushed. Served him right. Bloody *moffie*.

Now Bill was stomping home to the flat on Ferncroft Avenue, taking a shortcut across the heath. On his right he passed Leg of Mutton Pond where just a few months before he had seen some ducks trapped in the ice, their webbed feet frozen overnight. They had to be rescued by a few intrepid greenie volunteers who hacked them free. *Stupid wankers, interfering with nature. Should have let them freeze to death*, he thought.

When he got to the flat, Fat Bill poured himself another scotch. He was pleased that Diane was out somewhere and he had the place to himself. It gave him time for what had to be done. Let him plan ahead. Get up some Dutch courage and steel himself to the task at hand.

Four o'clock in the afternoon and sunset still hours away, Bill had never got used to daylight saving. What time would that be in Pretoria? Two hours later. Just gone six in the evening. A good time for Bill to call his "control", the infamous Colonel Piet "Klopper" van Wyk. He would be home now, settling down in his rocking chair, turning on the television to watch the early news. A *dop* in his hand, the first Cane and Coke of the evening. Spook and diesel. Bill could see it all in his mind's eye. The colonel, he knew, was a man of habit. A man renowned for sticking to his routine. A regular civil servant. A reliable guy. Someone you could trust. Someone you could depend upon in a crisis. When you were deep in the shit. Like now.

Fat Bill dialled van Wyk's special private number, the safe and secure line. He let the phone ring three times. Then he replaced the receiver. He waited for a full minute before calling again. The colonel picked up straight away.

'Billy boy! Howzit my china?'

'No, well fine, sir,' Fat Bill replied, his voice fawning and obsequious. 'And how are you, sir? Keeping well, I hope? How is your lovely wife?'

'We're all good here, my boy. I was just watching the news. Checking out those socialist idiots screwing up the world.' Bill smiled to himself. You could always count on "Klopper" van Wyk. The man was a machine. So predictable. 'Now what can I do for you?' the colonel asked, cutting to the chase.

'Well, sir, unfortunately things are not so good here,' Bill said. 'I'm afraid I have some bad news. Some really bad news.'

'*Ja*, what's that *boykie*? What's the problem?' His voice soft, sympathetic.

'Just this, Colonel, early this morning I was summoned to a meeting at the ANC headquarters. In Penton Street? In Islington?'

'I know where their office is, sonny.' The tone still amicable, concerned, no sign of impatience.

Fat Bill cleared his throat, 'It was a strange meeting. Unsettling. That's why I wanted to run it by you. See what your thoughts were. Ask your advice.'

'*Ja*, go ahead, Billy boy.'

'Yes, sir. First off, I was surprised by all the people there. Usually I only meet with one or two underlings. But this time, there were six of them. All the main *manne*. The important fat cats – Dumise Mhlada, Philip Stein, Jimmy Musona, Siphiwe Tshabala, Bernie Lebese and last but not least, the man himself, Uncle Isaac Spiegel, just recently arrived from Mozambique.'

'*Oom* Spiegel. What the fuck was he doing there?' the colonel said, suddenly more attentive.

'*Ja*, I asked myself the same question. And what the fuck were all those other *oukies* doing there? So anyway, they were very friendly, beaming away at me. And they all seemed to know about me. What I've been doing for them, how I've been helping the cause, the Struggle, that kind of thing. Called me *tovarich*. Comrade. Even asked about my wife. Knew her name. So that started making me suspicious. Alert. Why the fuck would Spiegel know who I was married to? Then he starts flattering me. Giving me the old Spiegel spiel. Telling me how he appreciated all the sacrifices I've made, asking me if I'd settled in in England, did I miss my family, that sort of stuff. Says that my work is so good, that I'm really making progress. Then I really knew he was horse-shitting. I've been making mistakes. On purpose. Just so they would think I was some kind of incompetent twit. So, to say I was doing a good job was complete nonsense. Rubbish. There was something else going on. Spiegel obviously had something else in mind. Some other agenda…'

'Sounds just like *Oom* Spiegel,' observed the colonel, 'always trying to con someone. Always the dirty tricks with him. So, go on. What did he really want? What was he after?'

'Well, he goes on with the praise for a while. Telling me what a good comrade I am. Then he gets down to it. I'm doing such great work that they want to reward me. Give me a real boost, he says. Move me up the ranks. But first they need to train me. Teach me what I need to know. Give me the right background. The correct profile. So they're going to send me to Moscow for further instructions. To learn special espionage capability. Sharpen up my skill set.'

'So what did you do? What did you say?' van Wyk asked.

'Naturally I acted excited. Like this was what I had been hoping for. I pretended to be grateful. I told Spiegel about how fluent I was in Russian. How I had studied it at university. And that's when they made their big mistake. Bernie Lebese joined in the conversation. He said that they knew about my Russian proficiency and "my intimate relationship with those other Irregular Verbs, Pienaar and Callaghan". He said that's why they had thought of me. Why they had decided to give me this big break. And that's when I knew. That's when I realised that they had broken my cover.'

'Hmm. What happened then?'

'I made some stupid comment about how I had always dreamed of one day going to visit the Soviet Union. I rabbited on about my commitment to international socialism, the proletariat and all that crap.'

'What did *Oom* Spiegel do? How did he react?'

'He just smiled and nodded. Real friendly like. He was grinning at me all the time through those big yellow teeth of his. But I could tell. I could see he didn't believe a thing I was saying. He was just bullshitting me. Just like I was bullshitting him. I knew that he knew but I don't know if he knew that I knew that he knew.'

The colonel had been listening to this carefully. Taking it all in, analysing and assessing it. Thinking it through. He stroked his bald pate with his left hand, then he asked: 'So what did you say? How did you play it?'

Fat Bill smiled. 'I decided to keep my cards close to my chest. I told Spiegel that it sounded fantastic. That I loved the idea but that I would have to talk it over with my wife first. That I'd have to discuss it with Diane. And that's how the meeting ended. Then we all shook hands. Everyone was smiling, *tovarich* this and comrade that. Spiegel flashing his grotty teeth, patting me on the back, telling me the weather in Moscow was not as bad as people said. Then I left. Decided to phone you for advice and came home.'

'So let me get this clear,' van Wyk said. 'From what you have told me about this meeting, you seem to think two things. Firstly, that your cover has been broken and secondly that the ANC want to send you to Moscow ostensibly for further training but in actuality, so that they can get their Soviet masters to interrogate you and break you. If you are in Russia, you will be so far outside our sphere of influence that we cannot possibly protect you. You will be totally vulnerable. They will be able to do anything they want to you... Am I representing this accurately? Is this the way you see it? Is this what you think is happening?'

'That's correct, sir. That's exactly how I see it,' Fat Bill replied.

'It certainly seems likely, Billy boy. That is exactly what they would try to do if your cover was broken. Get you out of the country. Into the Soviet Union. Then squeeze you like a ripe kumquat. Squeeze you dry. Squeeze all the fucking juice out of you. Then feed your pulp to the Muscovy ducks in Gorky Park. But how do you think they broke your cover?'

'It was that bitch. Cookie Fucking le Roux. It was all her fucking doing.' Normally Fat Bill would try to keep his emotions in check when speaking to the colonel but now his anger spilled over. The bile in his gut rising to his mouth, souring his breath. 'She played me. Couldn't mind her own fucking business. She had to stick her nose into stuff that didn't concern her. The stupid cunt!'

'Yes, Billy,' said the colonel, his voice soothing, gentle, understanding, 'but how did this happen?'

Bill helped himself to a big sip of Scotch and tried to calm down. Get a hold of himself. Appear rational and reasonable. 'Of course this is all speculation on my part, sir. Maybe I'm putting one and one together and getting three, but it all makes sense.'

'Explain it to me, my boy.'

'Well, remember that party I had? Two weeks ago? I told you about it. It was supposed to be a small, intimate affair but it ballooned out and there was quite a large crowd, eating and drinking. The idea was to keep socialising. Maintain the profile.'

'*Ja*, go on.'

'There were a few dozen people. Mostly English lefties and South African expats including James Morrison and Cookie le Roux from my Russian class. So we had quite a bit to drink. Everybody was happy. The conversation lively. We touched on politics but in a dilettantish way. Spoke of the theatre, cinema. That kind of thing. I didn't notice her but my wife told me later that Cookie had been feeling sick and had gone to the loo.'

Bill knew he needed to be careful here. Play it smart. Tell van Wyk what happened but make sure the colonel didn't get the idea that Bill had in any way been negligent. That it was, somehow, his fault. That he had screwed up. No, Fat Bill needed to ensure that he came out of this smelling of roses.

'People had been drinking quite a bit and I needed to get another bottle of red wine. I kept my supply in the study and when I walked in Cookie was there fixing her make-up, putting on eyeliner. She gave me that look. You know, when you've been caught out doing something you shouldn't. She blushed and mumbled something about drinking too much. But she was quite sober. Unlike the rest of us, she had hardly had anything to drink. She was very pale though and stumbled off to the toilet. Anyway, I didn't think anything of it until the next day... I was in the study again and then I got this weird feeling in my bones. A kind of premonition. I went over to the bookcase where I keep all of our classified correspondence. It's usually concealed in a recess behind a special Russian book. I checked the hiding place and found everything was intact. But, I usually place the documents face down and this time they were face up. I got a clear sense that reports had been moved. Moved and read. By Cookie.'

The colonel sighed, rubbed his bald pate again. 'But that's not so bad, Billy boy. How much of it could she have read in that time? Anyway, most of it would have been unintelligible to her. Cryptic. Some of it was even in code. I don't think it could have harmed us too much.'

'With all due respect, sir, you don't know her. She's not like everybody else. She's got this little trick with her memory. Reads something once, actually doesn't even have to read it. Just look at it, give it a passing glance. And then it's in her head. She's memorized it word for word. The stupid cunt has always had this spectacular recall. A photographic memory.'

'Hmm. But you don't know for sure, do you? And even if she did memorize the document, you don't know if she would have done anything with it, do you?'

'That's right, sir. I don't know for sure. But it makes sense. If she went to the ANC with this she would have been able to repeat it back to them, relay the whole document to them. Just that phrase Lebese used, the one about the "irregular verbs" and mentioning Pienaar and Callaghan. That was in the document. That was in the report I telexed you. There's nowhere else they could have got that information. It had to be her. She fucked us!'

Van Wyk sighed again. 'Let me think about this a bit, Billy boy.'

Both men were silent for a while. Bill had another sip of Scotch. In the background he could hear some traffic noise coming from the Finchley Road.

'Okay, then. This is what we have to do. We have to assume that your cover has been broken. That the veil has been ripped away. But even if it hasn't, even if they know nothing, we cannot allow you to go to Moscow. That's just too bloody dangerous! That's not even an option. So there's nothing more you can achieve there. We can no longer use you as a strategic agent in London. You should come home. Back to Pretoria. You've done an excellent job there. And there's plenty more you can achieve here. I'm reeling you in.'

Fat Bill sighed. 'Thank you, sir. I won't let you down… And the girl, Colonel, what about her? What do we do about Cookie le Roux?'

'That's your call, Billy boy. If you think the cunt tried to fuck us, then she's dead meat. Do with her what you will.'

And that was it. There was no more to say. Overall, it had gone pretty well, Fat Bill thought. As good as could be expected. But that was the easy part, dealing with the colonel. The hard job lay ahead. He dreaded even thinking about it. But it had to be done. He would have to tell Diane.

18

DIANE

I suppose my first response was surprise. Confusion. Shock. I didn't know what he was talking about. He spoke of undercover work, false flag operations, taking the initiative against the enemy, the Cold War, doing what was necessary, the preservation of our culture and lifestyle, the superiority of our race and a whole range of other things. I could not take it all in. I was being bombarded with information, facts and figures. None of it was making sense. This could not be. What on earth was Bill talking about? All these justifications and rationalisations. This song and dance about patriotism. It was just smoke and mirrors. An evasion of the truth. A refusal to say the one thing that we both knew was central here. The one word that mattered. Betrayal.

The betrayal of one's friends. The Judas kiss.

But perhaps I'm getting a little ahead of myself, maybe I should go back and explain how this all came about. Well, not all of it, because I was kept in the dark most of the time. Secrets abounded, there was actually very little that I knew and most of it I only found out later, when it was reported in the press or when it was necessary for me to be told. After all, I was an outsider and would always remain one. I was never given access to what Bill's friends called *die binne kring*, the inner circle.

So let me tell you what I remember from those days. I promise that no matter how fallible or flawed my memory might be, I'll disclose all those things that I can still recall, those events that remain, that are still fresh. I think I should also limit my account to what affected me, confine my story to what I felt and so on. In that way I can at least attempt to be accurate. Even then I'm not sure that any of it will really help explain my decision. Perhaps none of it will seem authentic. Perhaps I'm just fooling myself, trying to vindicate my choice and exonerate my guilt by trying to explain something that can't be explained. A course of action that most of the time doesn't even make sense to me.

So, to recap – about a year before all this happened, Bill and I had decided to leave South Africa. Well, we were partly persuaded to do so by family and friends. My father was particularly insistent as he anticipated that Bill would, almost certainly, end up in prison for a long time. (If only he had known!) I was also worried about him – thought he was exposing himself to far too much danger. (If only I had known!) In any event, we ended up taking everyone's advice and moved to London.

When we landed at Heathrow, I felt quite down and depressed. It was the first time I'd travelled abroad and been so far away from my family. I'd always been very dependent upon my parents and I knew I was going to be homesick. Everything felt quite final, this big break from the past, from our country. We were in exile now and we had no way of knowing if we could ever come back. At least that was what it felt like to me. I found it quite scary as if we'd leapt across this crack in the ice and all I could do was look back and see the crevasse widening.

Bill said we should think of it as a holiday and pretend that it was the honeymoon we hadn't had because he had been in jail. He assured me that it was only temporary, that *apartheid* could not last forever and that we'd be back home before we knew it. Some honeymoon! On the flight over, my period started. I had forgotten to bring tampons so the air hostess had to find some for me. I felt bruised and tetchy. Even more grumpy and crotchety than usual at that time of the month. And the famous London weather was not helping. When we landed it was cold and rainy, the skies a gloomy grey.

It had been a long flight and we still had to get from the airport to where we were going to stay in Hampstead. Bill and I had no idea how to get there and we had been told that cabs were wildly expensive for such a long ride. We managed to catch a bus to somewhere in South Kensington, I think maybe Gloucester Road, I'm not sure anymore. Anyway, the scenery from Heathrow along that route is particularly dreary and bleak with all those dinky toy houses one on top of another. Everything was unfamiliar and foreign, so alien. I felt really dispirited and unhappy.

It was about 9:30 in the morning and rush hour when we finally got a cab to Hampstead. The traffic at that time was horrendous as there was some kind of industrial unrest or workers' strike in the Edgware Road so we had to take a detour which made the trip even longer. I was sullen and impatient. This was not the kind of arrival I had been hoping for. But unfortunately after that everything seemed to get even more chaotic and stressful.

At the flat we planned to rent, the key was not under the flowerpot as promised so Bill had to walk down the Finchley Road to find a public phone booth and call the landlord who was naturally out of the office and not contactable for hours. Bill ran out of small change and had to find a bank but they would not cash his traveller's cheque without identification. So he had to come back to the flat to get his passport. That's where he found me sitting on the pavement with our suitcases, cold and weepy. It was turning into a nightmare!

Finally, Bill managed to track down the estate agents who had a spare key. Their office was in the Hampstead village which was a bit of a trek and he only got back much later. By that stage I had had enough! I was tired and angry. My stomach cramps had kicked in and I was freezing cold. I just wanted to have a bath and crawl up in bed but once again we were thwarted! The geyser had been turned off and as English plumbing systems were different from what we were used to it took us a while to figure out how to turn it on. So it was another three hours before we had hot water.

I know I'm making a big deal of it, this ghastly introduction to my new city but in a way it coloured or defined my whole stay in London. Over the entire time we were there I never managed to feel completely comfortable and I never really settled in or felt entirely at home. I did, however, make a number of good friends once I started working. All my life I've been popular, always been surrounded by people who seemed to like me. Don't ask me why that is as I'm not particularly charismatic or anything. Not like Bill. I think it's because I don't judge people. I just accept them for what they are and know that everybody's different. Everybody's got their reasons. Even me.

The job I got was working as a dental nurse at a practice in Swiss Cottage. I was quite lucky to get it even though the dentist, Dr Trevor Wilson, was my dad's friend and was very happy to employ me. There was, however, a problem with me getting a work visa. Fortunately, Dr Wilson had a large number of South Africans and Russian Jews as patients. He was able to argue to the authorities that he needed a nurse who was fluent in both Afrikaans and Russian to assist him with understanding his patients' needs. Isn't it strange how such incidental skills can come to one's aid in the most unpredictable ways?

It was a large practice employing a number of dentists and nurses. Most were young, about the same age as me and the general vibe around the place was very chummy. Some of the dentists were South African and I soon established a number of easy friendships. There was a great deal of socialising which involved party-going and pub crawls.

Right from the start Bill and I were invited to numerous dinners and soon we were able to establish a sizable network of friends which consisted mostly of colleagues from the dental practice but also expats who had moved to London. Some of the latter

115

were political refugees and exiles (as we saw ourselves) but also ordinary people who had come to the UK to expand their career opportunities or simply for adventure. We even managed to hook up with our old friends Cookie and James from our Russian class who were over there for further study.

It didn't take Bill much time to find work as he had a long list of left-wing contacts and through one of them he met Solveig Martensen. She was a leggy blonde just this side of forty who ran a Norwegian Government-sponsored education project called the Frydenlund Institute. The institute worked closely with the African National Congress to sponsor and provide bursaries for promising young black South African exiles.

Soon (all too soon if you ask me) Solveig offered Bill a job as her personal assistant. The position involved quite a bit of travel to Oslo, Paris and Amsterdam. They often flew together and were booked into the same hotels. Very cosy. I have to admit that I behaved badly, got jealous and accused Bill of having an affair with her. He denied it vehemently but that didn't make me feel any better. No matter how much he protested his innocence, the green-eyed monster stayed with me. For the first time in my life, I felt insecure, uncertain and out on a limb. Although I had all these casual friendships, there wasn't really anyone I could confide in and it made me feel quite vulnerable and exposed.

Bill, on the other hand, was in his element. Happy as old Larry. He was exactly where he wanted to be, doing things according to plan. His position at the Frydenlund Institute brought him into direct contact with the ANC and he established working relationships with many of their education officers. He visited their offices at Penton Street in Islington and he was often briefed by some of their senior people including Siphiwe Tshabala. Like any good spy or conman, he made sure they trusted him. They never doubted his motives or commitment to the Struggle. He was affable and mercurial. Doing what Bill always did, making progress, making inroads.

And during all this time he seemed oblivious to my anxieties and self-doubts, unaware of the crisis of confidence I was experiencing. He just kept doing his own thing, his eyes fixed on the prize, the goal ahead of him. If I try to picture Bill at that time the image that comes to me, the one I see most clearly, is that of a boxer bobbing and weaving in the ring, skilfully evading his opponent through carefully timed jabs and feints. Fat Bill, the pugilist, the consummate prize fighter.

This situation went on for some months. Bill blindly carrying out his agenda and me feeling insecure. It could not go on like that. I felt I had to make some changes. I was feeling too fragile and I needed something I could hold on to, something that seemed permanent. Something of my own. And that's when I decided to stop taking the pill.

In retrospect I'm not sure it was the right choice because instead of giving me independence, some kind of autonomy from Bill, it actually bound me closer to him, made me more subordinate and more under his control. Even less my own person. Once I became pregnant I was tied to him forever. It was irrevocable.

It didn't happen at once though. The falling pregnant part, that is. (I still wonder about that phrase – how does one "fall"?) It was quite a few months of being off the pill before I missed my period. And then I still wasn't certain. I waited a bit longer before I went to see my GP. She confirmed my pregnancy and recommended that I also consult a gynaecologist, so I phoned and made an appointment.

I remember that Saturday vividly. It was a warm day but overcast. The practice was at the Royal College of Obstetricians and Gynaecologists in Regent's Park.

After my consultation was over, something strange occurred. As I walked out the surgery front door, I almost literally bumped into Cookie le Roux. She was looking, as usual, calm and graceful but I was caught by surprise, a little off balance. We embraced warmly, but she seemed somewhat reserved. Clearly she was there for the same reason as me and it was obvious that she was pregnant but she said nothing about it. We chatted awhile and then I invited her to come to dinner that night. We were holding a party and I thought it would be great if she and James could join us.

At the time I thought the party went quite well. Cookie looked gorgeous and had arrived on her own. She said James would be joining her later. I noticed she wasn't drinking much but everybody else was knocking them back, including Bill and me.

It must have been fairly late in the evening when Cookie finally stumbled upon that fateful document of Bill's. I always wondered how on earth he was foolish enough to leave it where someone could read it but he must have been getting careless. Or maybe it was simply hubris. He was always so smug.

In any event, when she came back in the lounge, Cookie gave no sign that anything had changed. There was no apparent eureka moment, no revelatory gestures and no clear mood change. As far as I remember, her demeanour remained the same. But soon after that she and James excused themselves, saying that Cookie felt unwell. Then they left the party.

Of course I was in the dark about any of this. At that time, I knew nothing of Bill's activities. And I certainly did not know what Cookie had discovered. I had no reason to suspect Bill, no reason to imagine he was anything other than what he pretended to be. I'm sure most people won't believe this, or comprehend it. But it's true. He was a really good spy. Everyone was fooled by him. Even me. And I'm his wife.

But then, once his cover was blown, he had to tell me. At the time Bill wasn't completely certain but we later found out that Cookie had definitely reported her findings to the ANC. For her, the decisive moment, the key element that had persuaded her to take the information to them, was Antoine's death. That was crucial to her resolve. Once she knew about that, nothing could hold her back.

Later, when Bill managed to slip through their fingers, when he evaded what they had planned for him and did not take up the offer to go to Russia, Isaac Spiegel went to the press with the story and made it public knowledge. All of Bill's espionage activities including his infiltration of the ANC made front-page news. He was an overnight celebrity. The spy who came in from the cold.

But that night, the night he told me, I wasn't just surprised. I was also afraid. Not only of Bill but of myself and my judgement. How could I possibly be so wrong about someone? How could I have misread him so badly? What was wrong with my perspicacity? Was my intuition and discernment so flawed? Somehow I could not believe that he had managed to lie to me for so long. What on earth was wrong with me? It was scary.

Admittedly he was pretty forthcoming and communicative. He told me the whole sorry saga – how he had been recruited in the police, the plans they had worked out, how he infiltrated the Left, etc. It was all quite elaborate. Of course he acknowledged that he could not have done it without my help, without all the contacts I was able to give him. That made me feel sick. Clearly in the beginning I was nothing more than a pawn to him, a means to an end.

And all those betrayals. Our colleagues that had been arrested and tortured over the years. I had to take some responsibility for that because without my help he would not have been able to do it. Isolate the right people, penetrate the leftie organisations and feed the information to the security police. Closing in on not just acquaintances but dear friends. People like Rory. And then Antoine. How could I condone that? How could I be a part of that? I felt nauseous and excused myself to vomit in the toilet. Obviously morning sickness was part of it but I could not stand it. It was intolerable, truly dreadful and beyond redemption.

And then he offered me a choice. I could go my own way which meant staying in London and working at the dental clinic. Or I could go back home with him, back to South Africa and Johannesburg, family and friends.

I tried to imagine what that signified and all that it entailed. Bill would no longer be working clandestinely, he would be in the open, unashamedly a police captain committed to maintaining the status quo and the *apartheid* state, brazenly supporting everything that I abhorred and had fought against. His new friends (and presumably his *real* ones, the ones he was unlikely to betray) would be mostly Afrikaner politicians, bureaucrats and security policemen like himself. We would have to socialise with them and their wives. *Braais met die Boere. Sosaties* and chops sizzling over the hot charcoal while the *ouks* talked rugby and sipped on ice-cold Castle lagers. The women on the other side of the lawn sitting round the tables laden with salads, home-made pickles and cream cakes, their babies on their laps, shouting commands to the black servants. I would be entertaining all my old enemies. It was like a vision from Hell!

But when Bill gave me the choice, it was not like there was a choice. There was so much menace in his voice, his whole visage dark and threatening. I had never seen him like that. I did not feel I could cross him. He strutted across the room pouring himself another Scotch with complete assurance never doubting for a moment what I would do. He knew that with the baby, with my child kicking in my belly I would have to go with him. And so I did.

19

COOKIE

Even after the press ran the story about Fat Bill Saunders, the "master spy", I still hadn't told James that I was pregnant. I know you will find that strange and I can't really explain it except to say it did not feel right to talk of such intimate things when all this other stuff was going down.

Amongst other things, I was being harassed by reporters who wanted me to give them an exclusive interview. God knows where they got my name and phone number from! Anyway they were quite persistent so James and I decided to take advantage of the splendid weather and take a short sightseeing trip to the English south and west. It was the school holidays and we both felt we deserved a break.

We took the old Rover and headed out of London. The first place we visited was Stonehenge. I'm not sure why, perhaps because we had such high expectations of the place, but we were a little disappointed. It didn't quite live up to what we had anticipated.

Avebury, on the other hand, was most impressive. I guess it was the scale of the site, how huge it is, the size of the stones. The general sense of reckoning about the place. Impending destiny and the time of day. The sun just rising. Masses of grey clouds gathering above the horizon. A feeling that the sky was low above our heads. All of that and more.

There did not seem to be anyone else there, at least no other tourists. We came across a postman riding his bicycle through the village, delivering mail and we asked him for directions to the museum. It would only open in about twenty minutes, he told us. The postman had that English eccentric quality about him and he had the look – thin, lined face, little twitching moustache, flushed cheeks, a knowing smile. I recognized him immediately as he had just stepped out of a Dickens novel – Wemmick or some such caricature.

James and I walked around the vast henge for a while taking photographs. When we got to the museum, the curator let us in and lo and behold, it was the very same postman we had talked to earlier, the postman's attire now abandoned and replaced by a National Trust uniform, his cap at a jaunty angle. He told us that he doubled up, doing both jobs as the village was so small. Sometimes, he said, he kidded tourists by pretending to have a twin brother. It all seemed in keeping with the place. Avebury's strange "vibe".

We stayed for ages and only left when it was getting dark. Just outside Salisbury, we stopped at a small B & B for the night. For some reason that I'm not sure of, I guess out of fun or mischievousness, we pretended to be English. James put on his best "public schoolboy accent" and I spoke cockney rhyming slang and all. Nick, the landlord, seemed to be completely taken in as did the staff at the restaurant where we ate. The "Compasses Inn", Nick's special recommendation. A fourteenth-century free-house reeking with atmosphere. I even remember our order. James had a pepper steak with parsley mash and a Drambuie sauce while I ordered lamb served with minted peas and a redcurrant jus. We had a lovely Spanish Rioja to wash it all down. This was followed by a crème brûlée dessert which we shared.

Later, after we had made love, I thought of telling James my "big news", telling him that I had just found out I was pregnant.

But for some reason (that I am now unsure of), I wanted to wait until we were back in London at the Fulham flat, so I kept silent about it. To this day I am ambivalent about whether it was the right choice or not. Certainly if I had told him then, things would have taken a different turn. My life would have been otherwise. But it was not to be.

At breakfast in the morning, the landlord served us eggs with his own home-made pork sausages. Still affecting a plummy accent, James complimented Nick on the sausages calling them "bloody good!" When Nick retired to go to the kitchen, James turned to me and said in Afrikaans: '*Hulle is net soos Eskort wors,*' ('they are just like Eskort sausages') referring to sausages that are famous in South Africa.

It must have been my hormones going crazy but I suddenly got all weepy and burst into tears.

'What's wrong, darling? Are you alright?' James asked in a concerned voice.

'I'm just a little homesick, that's all. Talking Afrikaans always reminds me of my father.'

James leaned over, hugged me and gently kissed my forehead.

'Don't worry,' he said, 'we'll be home soon.'

From the perspective of time, after all these years and after all that's happened I'm amazed at just how ironically mistaken he was. But at the time his words comforted me.

Over the next few days we managed to do quite a bit of sightseeing going to Bath, Bristol, Cheltenham and finally Oxford where the weather turned nasty. The rain was pouring down from a black and angry sky so we ended up going to a movie. James found a revival house and we cuddled up in the back row watching *The Godfather 2* (again!).

Back in London we climbed the stairs up to the Fulham flat. James turned the key in the lock and we carried in our luggage. It all seemed exactly as we had left it except for one thing. In the lounge, at the centre of the coffee table, a hard-covered book had been carefully placed. We saw it the moment we entered the room. There was something theatrical about its placement. As far as I could tell, nothing else had been moved or touched.

As I reached over to pick up the book, James shouted out: 'Don't touch!' but his warning had come too late. When I think now about all those letter bombs Fat Bill sent to people, I realize how utterly stupid my actions were. But this was not a bomb. It was a message. A threat.

The book was in Russian (of course!). A beautiful copy of Boris Pasternak's *Doctor Zhivago*. On the title page there was an inscription in Bill's overblown copperplate handwriting. It read:

Dear Cookie,

I hope you had a good holiday. Personally I find the Cotswolds overrated. I looked after the flat while you were gone. Don't worry, wherever you go, I'll always be waiting for you. Take care!

Yours eternally,
Bill

The message was quite plain, quite clear. *Wherever you go, I will seek you out. You are in my sights.*

Never before and never since have I been so acutely aware of being in the presence of pure evil. It had permeated the entire flat. There was a polar chill in the room. Steam was coming from our breaths and both James and I were shaking, but not from the cold. We felt defiled. Tainted.

One page had been dog-eared, marking a place. With my hands trembling, I opened the book. A section had been underlined. Here is a translation of what I read:

Lara: Wouldn't it have been lovely if we'd met before?
Zhivago: Before we did? Yes.

Lara: We'd have got married, had a house and children. If we'd had children, Yuri, would you like a boy or girl?
Zhivago: I think we may go mad if we think about all that.
Lara: I shall always think about it.

Fat Bill's threat was now quite explicit. Somehow he had found out about my pregnancy (probably from Diane) and he was warning me that whatever I was carrying in my belly, boy or girl, he or she was not safe. He was coming for me and, more ominously, my child.

I cannot describe just how palpable the fear I felt was. Real terror. Not so much for me but for my loved ones, for James and for our baby.

James said: 'It's obviously meant to intimidate us. But what does it mean?'

'I don't know,' I replied.

But I knew. I knew.

Both of us struggled to go to sleep. James held me in his arms and kept telling me that it would be alright. That he would look after me. That I should not worry.

But I could not get that line from *The Godfather 2* out of my head. It comes in the movie when Michael Corleone wants to have Hyman Roth assassinated. Tom Hagen says: 'It would be like trying to kill the president, there's no way we can get to him.'

And Michael Corleone, the Godfather, replies: 'If anything in this life is certain, if history has taught us anything, it is that you can kill anyone.'

If history has taught us anything. If history has taught us anything...
You can kill anyone. You can kill anyone...

The lines kept going round and round in my head.

There were a few things I knew, a few facts that I was certain of. I knew Bill wanted to kill me and my child. And I knew he could do it. I also knew that James was powerless to stop Fat Bill. He could not protect me. It also became clear to me that as long as

James was with me, as long as we were together, his life too would be in danger.

I had to come up with a plan. I had to find a way to keep us all safe. All three of us. Late that night it became apparent to me that I would have to go away, to a place where no one knew me and where no one could find me. Where I could start afresh with a new identity. But I would have to do it alone.

It must have been at least three in the morning before I fell into a fitful sleep. I dreamed my father was a milkman. He was driving one of those electric milk floats. It was somewhere in London, probably the Chelsea Embankment. Cheyne Walk I think as I could see the Thames behind him. It was snowing heavily and strong gusts of wind had bent the trees over. Suddenly he was standing directly before me. He had a container in his hand with bottles of milk. He picked up a bottle, bashed it against a wall and drank from the jagged neck. Milk and blood were spurting in great waves from his mouth, running down his chin onto his white coat. The coat had *Tara Hospital* embroidered on his chest. His eyes were dreadful, bloodshot and bulging. He lisped and spoke to me: '*Jy gooi die Rooitaal goed.*'

I tried to answer him but my mouth felt like it had sand in it. He said it again: '*Jy gooi die Rooitaal goed.*' The literal translation is "You throw the Red language well" but the expression means "You speak English like a native". He turned on his heel, kind of limped away and then hurled himself into the river. He sank like a rock.

I woke suddenly. I was hot and sweaty. James was still asleep. I kissed his forehead and went into the bathroom. I looked at myself in the mirror, studying my face. I'm not sure what I saw there but I felt calm, serene. Cool-headed. It had come to me. I now knew what I had to do and where I had to go.

20

COOKIE

The bus only took me as far as the village of Ille-sur-Têt. The instructions I'd been given were to wait outside a little bistro until someone arrived to pick me up. The sun was high in the sky, the air dry and dusty so I sought refuge from the heat deciding to rest on a small stone bench partly screened by a patch of mottled shade. Once there I lit a cigarette and inhaled deeply. It seemed to help ward off the nausea I'd been experiencing all morning.

I was starting to feel better, more relaxed than I had been on the journey which, given my emotional state, was extremely stressful. Occasionally I had found myself weeping uncontrollably and sometimes my left arm shook in deep, scary spasms. Nevertheless, I was surprised at how well I had coped on my own and overall I discovered a personal courage which both surprised and gratified me.

Back in Fulham I had waited until James left for film school before I began to pack a small suitcase of essentials. Then I wrote him a farewell note. In it I made no mention of my pregnancy but rather tried to explain that I was leaving because of the danger I felt we would both be in if I stayed. I told him that it was for the best, that I loved him and would love him forever and that our separation would tear my soul apart. I tried desperately to spell out that I was acting magnanimously but, in retrospect, my actions must have seemed self-serving and narcissistic, my explanations empty and hopelessly inadequate. I really could not tell him how conflicted and crushed I truly felt.

At Charing Cross Station, I caught a train to Dover and then the ferry to Calais where I spent the night. The little *pension* near the station was quite comfortable but I struggled to sleep haunted as I was by thoughts of James and concerns for his safety. Most of the night was spent in turmoil about the decision I had made and I constantly questioned whether it was the right choice. My sleep, when it finally came, was fitful and dreamless.

I took the train to Paris the next morning and made my way from the Gare du Nord to the Latin Quarter where I checked into a hotel off the Boulevard Saint Michel. It was from there that I phoned my old friend Bob Elliot and explained my situation. He was most sympathetic and immediately offered me refuge and a place to stay and hide out.

'You can stay as long as you like. Emilie will be delighted to meet you. I've told her all about you,' he insisted.

'But are you sure you have space?' I asked.

'Of course. It's a massive farmhouse with plenty of bedrooms. We always have guests.'

'What about food? I'm pretty broke.'

'No problem. We all share everything. Anyway, if you're up to it you can help with the farm work. Pick grapes, plant veggies, milk the cows. That kind of thing. It's a kind of commune.'

'Sounds ideal. Just what I need right now.'

Bob then explained how I was to get there.

'Take the train from Gare Montparnasse heading south to Bordeaux. You'll have to get off there and change to another train that goes via Toulouse to Narbonne and Perpignan, right on the other side of the country not too far from the Mediterranean coast. From Perpignan you need to catch a bus to our nearest village, Ille-sur-Têt. Are you writing this all down?' he asked.

'No,' I laughed, 'it's all in my head.'

'Oh *ja*, I'd forgotten about that memory of yours. Is it still the same?'

'*Ja*, still getting me in trouble,' I joked feeling some of the tension in my neck muscles easing.

'There's a little bistro in the town square just near the terminus. It's called *La Vie en Rose*. I'll meet you just outside it on Thursday when the bus gets in. About 4:30.'

Even this late in the afternoon it was still blisteringly hot despite the fact that in the distance I could see powdery snow covering the peaks of the Pyrenees. I was looking forward to the prospect of warm sun on my skin, something I had missed living in England.

When I first got off the bus, the town square had been quiet and empty but now people were slowly drifting back after their siestas. There was a gentle murmuring of conversation, a convivial atmosphere, the ebb and flow of village life. I glanced at my watch. 4:55. Bob was late but I was not concerned. He'd be along shortly, I trusted him, knew he was dependable. And soon, there he was strolling across the square, his head held high, his back straight, an easy smile on his face. *God, he's so laid back*, I thought. *Nothing fazes him. Wish I was like that. We could be in a war zone and he'd still be the same, taking it all in his stride.*

'Good to see you,' Bob said, kissing my cheek and swinging my knapsack on his back. 'How was the trip?'

'Fine. Fine. Your directions were faultless.'

'Let's go this way,' he said leading me from the square. 'My truck's just around the corner.'

It was an old grey Citroën H Van and quite perfect. I could not have imagined him driving anything else. The side panels were dented and the engine coughed and spluttered, spitting out dark black smoke when Bob started it up. But somehow it felt splendid, the ideal vehicle with which to begin a new life.

It was so ironic to find myself there, in the Languedoc-

Roussillon region, where my ancestor, Jacques le Roux had come from. This is where he grew up, and from here he was forced to leave and seek refuge from persecution first in Holland and then later in South Africa. He had to desert his homeland and live in a foreign land to escape oppression and massacre. And now I was doing the same but only in reverse. It seemed like destiny was leading me back here. To France.

The road was only paved for a short distance before it gave way to gravel and the truck bounced around as the Citroën's shock absorbers were pretty worn. Nevertheless, I felt quite comfortable as Bob drove slowly in deference to my health which he immediately enquired about.

'It's been fine. I haven't really noticed anything different yet except maybe the occasional nausea. Morning sickness,' I told him.

We chatted amicably in that easy, relaxed, familiar manner that we had always had with each other. Bob told me about the farm which his girlfriend, Emilie, had inherited from her parents after they had both been killed in a car accident some years earlier. The countryside near Ille-sur-Têt was mainly a wine-producing area, he said, pointing out the terraced vineyards clinging to the rocky hillsides on both sides of the road which twisted and turned around secluded coves and rocky outcrops.

The landscape was very reminiscent of the Cape where I had holidayed as a young girl. My father's sister was married to a wine farmer in the Franschhoek district and I had fond memories of visits to their rambling homestead where I had played with my many cousins. The large French cypress trees, scrubby bushes and parched soil brought back pleasant childhood recollections.

The farmhouse, however, bore little resemblance to those evocative gabled Cape Dutch houses and was instead distinctively French with its tiled roof, lime-plastered walls and wood-shuttered windows. It was a double-storeyed building, rectangular in shape covered by a large blooming bougainvillea which clung to the front wall, climbing past the solid wooden door to the roof, its bright purple bracts showering the entrance with colour.

Inside it was surprisingly cool but airy and light built around a central atrium which housed a sparkling blue swimming pool. Bob left my single suitcase at the front door and led me straight to the courtyard where we found Emilie sunbathing.

Right from the start, she and I hit it off like a house on fire. Emilie was warm and welcoming, hospitable and easy-going. She welcomed me into her home like a long-lost friend and I immediately felt accepted.

Emilie slipped a loose fitting robe over her bikini and showed me around the house. Then she led me to where I was to stay. The room was light-filled, whitewashed and very homely. There was a single bed, a small wardrobe and a writing desk. It was lovely and I could not have wished for more.

During my stay, there were always plenty of other people around. Some were semi-permanent members of the commune and others itinerant labourers who worked on the farm. Like them, I picked fruit, planted vegetables and took turns at cooking. In some ways it was quite idyllic. For the first time in my life there was no pressure on me to work hard, study, make a living. I could just do as I wished without demands. I no longer had to put myself under stress and I enjoyed working in the fields with the sun on my skin. Physically I felt strong and healthy. Every day I could feel my baby growing inside me and whatever hormonal changes I was experiencing made me feel energised and invigorated.

At the same time though my heart was breaking. There was a great emptiness in my soul where James should have been. I felt torn asunder, ripped apart by the great loss of my one true love, the father of the child growing in my belly. Many nights I cried myself to sleep, weeping terribly.

I missed everything about him. His chubby cheeks, his lovely smile, his strong hands. But most of all I missed our intense conversations, his passion for the cinema and politics, his direct honesty. Often I just could not imagine my life without him. But I knew I had to. I knew the threat from Fat Bill was real and ineluctable.

I also knew that I couldn't stay at the farm in France indefinitely. I had to make plans for the future, a future not only for me but my baby. It was imperative that I find somewhere safe where no one knew us and where we could blend in without drawing attention to ourselves. But where could that be? South Africa was impossible. It was much too dangerous. I considered Europe, somewhere on the continent, but I did not have the appropriate identification papers for legal residence or asylum. Besides, even though I had some good language skills, I would never be able to pass myself off as a native or local and I would certainly stick out like a sore thumb.

I thought long and hard about it for some months. Then I remembered that dream I had about my father wherein he told me: '*Jy gooi die Rooitaal goed*'. It was like a revelation. Everything suddenly became clear and I realised that the only place where I could safely integrate and invisibly merge into the community would ironically be England. The more I considered it, the more convinced I became. Fat Bill would never think of looking for me in England. He would never, in his wildest dreams, imagine I would return there. And so I decided to become inconspicuous and English. I resolved to go back to London.

Once I had made up my mind, I felt relieved. But there was still a major problem as I lacked the relevant documentation to live and work in England. And that's where Bob came into his own proving just how ingenious and resourceful he could be.

All the time that Bob was at the farm he did not just grow grapes and other fruits. He also cultivated a crop very close to his heart. One large section of the property was fenced off and used exclusively to produce and harvest marijuana. The ripened crops were gathered and stored in a large barn for drying. Then the dope would be loaded up in the Citroën H Van and Bob would drive it down to Marseille where he sold the cannabis to some very unsavoury characters in the French *Milieu*. Many of them were members of the Corsican Mafia who distributed illegal drugs throughout Europe.

So, after I told Bob that it was my intention to return to England, he promised to sound out his contacts in order to explore the possibility of acquiring the appropriate documentation for me. As it turned out, for a quite reasonable fee, Bob's *Milieu* associates would be able to procure a forged passport.

But first I had to make some adjustments to my appearance. I cut my long dark hair into a short and sassy Louise Brooks style bob. Then I bleached it blonde. If I say so myself, it made me look quite striking and very different. The change felt good, like I could start all over.

Bob got his Nikon and took some passport-size photos of me which he took to Marseille. When he returned a few days later he handed me an authentic looking but fraudulent English passport. I opened it and discovered that my new name was Carol Basinger. As I looked at my new identity, I felt a strange dislocation almost like the world had somehow subtly shifted on its axis. There before me was my *doppelgänger*, the person I was about to become, the singular and unfamiliar psyche I would now have to adopt before I could start my new life.

I immediately set about becoming her, becoming Carol Basinger. It was vital that I transform myself into her and adopt an *alter ego*. So I would sit in my room alone and try to talk in what I considered to be an estuary accent. I started by making grammatical shifts like using double negatives and changing "isn't" to "ain't". I would read aloud from a book and practise glottal stops pronouncing words like "little" as "li'le" or "Scottish" as "Sco'sh". "H's" at the beginning of words would be dropped as would "g's" from the ends. Rhyming slang followed. I was already quite adept at this from my performing days at university but soon, with lots of practice, I managed to perfect it. Even a Londoner would have been fooled.

At the same time, I worked on my movement, changing all my usual gestures and body language. I adopted a much more stylised way of walking with my head held high and my shoulders square. I tried to let all the rigidity and tension out of my muscles and concentrated on simply gliding across space. In my head I imagined myself floating along like a female version of Yul Brynner. It did not take long before this seemed natural.

Late in my pregnancy, I decided it was time to leave France and head back to England. Bob lent me some money to help me get settled. In London I managed to rent a small flat just off the Walworth Road near Elephant & Castle. My landlady entirely accepted my credentials and readily assumed that I was English, giving me sympathetic advice on childbearing and recommending a local NHS doctor.

It was tough and scary being on my own but I really had no other choice. I had to preserve the security my new identity provided. At night I often struggled to sleep and missed James terribly. I wished he could be with me and help me through it but obviously that could not happen.

Some weeks later I began to get signs of change. I started experiencing regular contractions originating in the lower back and then moving to the front of the abdomen. When they steadily increased in strength, I realised that my time had come. I caught a cab to the hospital and within a few hours I delivered a daughter. I called her Sarah. She was born at St Thomas' Hospital which is officially recognised as being within hearing distance of Bow Bells, making her a genuine cockney.

THE 1980'S

21

RORY

The jacarandas were in full bloom when Rory left the imposing gates of Pretoria Central Prison. Marty and Ruth had come to fetch him and were standing in the bright sunshine leaning on the bonnet of their red Toyota. They smiled, waved and then Ruth ran towards Rory throwing her arms around him. For a moment Marty held back but then he too embraced his friend. It had been some years since they had all seen each other and the occasion was acutely charged, Rory visibly moved by this sincere and caring act of friendship.

'Thanks for coming to get me, guys. I really did not know who else to ask,' Rory somehow managed to say.

'No problem,' said Ruth. 'We wanted to be here. It was important for us.'

During the early part of his incarceration, Rory was allowed one visitor a month and his girlfriend, Rita, had regularly come to see him. But then over time her visits dropped off and she came to the prison less frequently until one day she told him that she would not be coming around anymore. Rita said she could not sustain this kind of relationship and it was time to break it off. In any event, she told Rory she had met someone else. It made sense, he really could not expect anything else. He recognised that Rita had her own life to live but nevertheless, it was a stab to the heart.

Sometime later he received an even deeper blow. Rory's dear grandfather was having serious health problems. He had been diagnosed with pancreatic cancer and was in great pain. Then word came through that the old man had lost the fight and passed away. Rory was devastated. He applied, on compassionate grounds, for permission to attend the funeral but his request was denied. The authorities were not particularly sympathetic to political prisoners.

Now, on their way back to Johannesburg, Marty drove past the Voortrekker Monument. This austere granite edifice ostensibly celebrated the famous Battle of Blood River of 1838 in which a small number of white settlers defeated a large Zulu army. It had, however, become a potent symbolic commemoration of *Afrikanerdom* and by extension, the *apartheid* regime.

Marty was doing his usual thing of bombarding Rory with a barrage of questions: 'So what was the food like? Were the prison guards real bastards? Did you make any new friends in jail? What did you do for exercise? Did you get access to books?, etc., etc.' Rory smiled to himself thinking how little his friend had changed when his own life was now so different. He was finally liberated from prison but nothing about him felt free especially when confronted by a building which, to him, seemed so emblematic of oppression.

'You're going to find a lot of things have changed,' Ruth said turning around to face Rory on the back seat. 'Some dramatic but others more subtle.'

'Like what?'

'Like the Struggle… It's not being driven by white intellectuals any more. Oh sure, there are still whites who are committed and make their voice heard but they seem much more in the background, irrelevant to the direction the resistance is taking. It's all happening in the black townships now. The post '76 Soweto youth are now at the vanguard, driving the movement, the protests. And they're so organised. They put together massive crowds and they are not afraid. They confront the police head-on even when they are being shot at. They use the *toyi toyi* as a weapon and as a kind of dance of death. It's both impressive and scary to see.'

'Well that's to be expected,' said Rory. 'After all, it's really their struggle and the proletariat would eventually supplant any bourgeois intellectuals.'

'Yes, that's the theory. And it's all good. I support all that. It's just that...'

'Just what?'

'Well, I don't know. There's stuff that bothers me,' Ruth said. 'For example, there are some people who are espousing a kind of reverse racism. They don't want anything to do with whites. I've seen young men at protests wearing T-shirts that say: "One settler, one bullet."'

'*Ja*, it's pretty disturbing,' Marty said. 'A lot of them have bought into the Black Consciousness movement.'

'Yes, I came across quite a lot of that in prison,' Rory remarked. 'But I think it's a passing phase. I think the real movement will still be driven by a commitment to non-racial principles. They are the founding tenets of the Freedom Charter.'

Despite his years of hardship in prison, Rory remained an optimist and he was still committed to Marxian principles. He was still a believer and he wasn't the only one. At Pretoria Central Prison nearly all the political prisoners were left-wing radicals and they were all white. The segregationist dogma of *apartheid* extended all the way to the penal system. This meant that white prisoners of conscience were housed at Pretoria and blacks or "coloureds" and Indians were incarcerated on Robben Island.

There were, of course, black people in Pretoria Central but they were almost all common criminals and many of them had been convicted of capital offences. The condemned prisoners were confined to a section called "The Pot" where they waited for their death sentences to be carried out. The gallows were strained to capacity and the hangman kept very busy. Sometimes multiple hangings were effected with as many as seven men being executed at the same time. For an entire week before the condemned met their fates they would sing traditional songs dancing and pounding their feet on the ground in the open courtyard. Many a night Rory and his fellow captives would listen as the mournful voices and hopeless rhythms of the doomed men echoed through the cells.

The politicos stuck together, seldom fraternising with the other prisoners. They exchanged books, ran workshops and conducted seminars wherein they discussed in granular detail Althusser's radical epistemology. Most of them remained committed to their communist roots and planned to work with trade unions upon their release back into the wider community.

Rory, however, felt differently. If prison had taught him anything, it was that he never wanted to return. And, although his ideals and principles were still intact, he was now committed to keeping out of trouble and staying under the security police's radar. He was determined to leave the Struggle to others and live a quiet, hassle-free life.

In the meantime, he needed a job and a place to live. Marty and Ruth had kindly offered him a place to stay in the big house they shared with David and Celeste at Park Road, Belgravia. The room they gave Rory was in the attic. It was large and airy with a fine window overlooking the lawn and the massive oak tree that dominated the garden. One of the most challenging aspects of prison life was the lack of contact with the natural environment and Rory now had access to a glorious view of Johannesburg's eastern suburbs. On many a morning he would look out the window, drink in the bright orange sunrise and relish the pristine beauty of the world before going on his customary run.

After his long confinement, everything seemed new, vibrant and alive. When he started running again Rory had to take it easy gradually building up to full fitness. Later he was able to extend his distances, taking the back roads through Rhodes Park and then onto the green fairways of Kensington Golf Club. On these runs

Rory was keenly awake to the sheer radiance of the world, the trees, the sunshine, the birdsong.

On that first Sunday at Park Road, Marty, Ruth, David and Celeste hosted a welcoming home party for Rory. A great number of people were there to celebrate his liberation including friends from university days and the Melville Theatre Group. James represented the old Russian class but Rory noted the not insignificant absence of Fat Bill and Diane, poor Antoine and, of course, Cookie.

Everyone sat in the shade under the huge oak while Marty and David threw succulent chops and steaks on the *braai*. The mood was relaxed and cheerful, all Rory's friends happy to see him, to know that he was back with them, safe and seemingly okay. The day was bright and luminous.

Sometime later Rory found himself standing over the dying embers of the fire with James. He had heard from Ruth that his friend had suffered terribly from the loss or disappearance of Cookie and was drinking heavily. Rory could see from his demeanour that something had changed; James seemed gaunt and withered, battered by exigency and circumstance. Rory knew the look. He had seen it in many of his cell mates. He had seen it in himself.

'I hear you're looking for work,' James remarked. 'I might be able to help you.'

'How's that?'

'Well right now I'm freelancing as a cameraman. A stringer for the BBC and CNN. They send me out to cover news stories for them. Mostly rioting in the townships. I need someone to record sound for me.'

'That sounds great but I don't know anything about sound recording.'

'It's not that complicated. Usually it just involves holding a microphone and pointing it in the right direction. With a little bit of training I'm sure you could manage very easily. Are you interested?'

'Absolutely! It's exactly the kind of thing I'd love to do. An adventure!' said Rory excitedly.

'Fantastic!' said James. 'Let's meet tomorrow and I'll show you the ropes.'

James was as good as his word and the next day he gave Rory some basic training and left him a couple of technical manuals to read. He also provided him with a Nagra tape recorder and a few microphones. Over the next few weeks Rory methodically practised with the equipment until he felt confidently proficient. James would often visit in the evenings to assist Rory and refine his training. Rory made excellent progress and was soon ready for his first film shoot.

James phoned him early one morning.

'Just got a call from CNN. We need to cover a funeral. I'll pick you up in twenty minutes.'

Rory dressed hastily and waited outside with his equipment until James arrived in a battered microbus. They quickly loaded the sound gear into the back and were off, James driving fast.

'Here, put this on,' he said handing Rory a CNN vest to slip over his tee shirt. 'This will give us some protection if things get nasty. The mob don't like the SABC filming them because they know that it will be used for propaganda. But they want their message to be seen abroad so it's important they know who we represent.'

'Is this dangerous?' Rory asked.

'Well sometimes a lot of shit goes down but usually the violence is against the police or people they believe to be informants. Like I said they don't dig the local newsreel guys but they've never attacked anyone working for an overseas media outlet. So we should be cool. Are you afraid?'

'Not at all,' said Rory. Which was true. He was extraordinarily calm. 'Just want to know what to expect.'

'The important thing to remember,' James said, 'is that you stick with me at all times. Whatever happens just stay with me. And keep your eyes out for what's going on around us. I'm looking down the camera's viewfinder so I can't see anything to the side or behind. If you spot something that looks interesting, that advances the story we're after, just nudge me in the ribs and point me in the direction where the action is. Same thing if you think we're in danger. Got it?'

'Sure. No problem.'

The funeral was for a young man from Dobsonville. He had died while held in solitary confinement at John Vorster Square. The police claimed he had slipped and fallen down a flight of stairs, hitting his head so badly that the lacerations were fatal. Of course no one believed this and a large crowd was following the funeral procession and planned to use the event to protest against the government and to draw international attention to the use of torture in South African jails.

Up ahead the road was blocked by a huge crowd of people singing and dancing. They were all slowly making their way to the cemetery and there was no way past them. James turned off onto a side road and gunning the engine made a detour around the massive throng of ululating mourners. The microbus bucked and bounced on the sand road corrugations as James made a series of twists and deviations before arriving directly in front of the swarming bodies.

'Okay. That's it,' he shouted. 'We're on foot from here.'

Rory and James jumped out and began unpacking and preparing their gear from the back. By now the pack had caught up with them but everyone just swept past, unconcerned as they could see the CNN logo on the panels of the microbus.

When they were ready the film crew joined the mass of swirling bodies and let the momentum of the crowd sweep them along. They were the only whites in a sea of swirling black figures. James was shooting handheld, highly skilled and proficient, the camera seemed to be an extension of his body, his movements fluid and mobile. Rory pointed the microphone in the general direction that everyone was moving. In his headphones he could hear quite clearly the anguished grief-stricken lamentations of the people, the keening doleful and heartbreaking.

They had to cover some distance before getting to the cemetery gates and Rory was pleased that he was so fit. Soon they arrived at an open grave where a space had been prepared for the family and the most important mourners who sat on chairs holding framed photographs of the deceased.

A black priest performed the service reading from a large bible. He spoke in Tswana, a language that Rory did not know well but every now and then he was able to pick up the odd word. James filmed from a respectful distance until the service was over and the body lowered into the grave. The priest then yielded the stage to the cadres. A few firebrands stood up and made speeches. Some spoke in English knowingly addressing an international audience. At this point James moved in closer sometimes filming from a low angle. The crowd started to become very animated shouting out radical slogans and singing freedom songs. Then at some undefined moment, everyone turned and began moving out of the cemetery *toyi-toyiing* down the parched, dusty streets.

James and Rory followed them swept along by the mob's righteous anger until they were back at the microbus.

'Okay, that's enough for today. I've got to get this material off to the network right away,' James said.

While they were packing up the gear, he turned to Rory: 'Well done! Excellent! You seemed to handle everything really wonderfully.'

Rory beamed: '*Ja,* thanks. It was very interesting. I've never been to one of those before.'

In the next few weeks Rory accompanied James on a number of shoots – bus strikes, street protests and of course more burials. All were in the designated black townships but then on 13 February 1982 they covered a funeral in the city of Johannesburg. It was a very poignant and heartrending experience that profoundly affected Rory's thinking. The world seemed to shift on its axis and he was once again plunged into a perilous and uncertain future.

The deceased was twenty-eight-year-old Neil Aggett, the first white man to have died in police detention since 1963. A romantic idealist, deeply committed to the Struggle, Aggett was a medical doctor who also worked as an unpaid union organiser for the Transvaal Food and Canning Workers' Union. He and his partner Dr Liz Floyd were detained by the security police and held in custody without trial. Both were interrogated. For more than seventy days Aggett was tortured and subject to battery, waterboarding and electric shocks. His interrogators used threats against his partner in an attempt to manipulate him. A fellow prisoner saw him being half carried and dragged back to his cell. Then, unable to withstand further torment Aggett committed suicide by hanging himself with a scarf.

The funeral service was held at St Mary's Anglican Cathedral in Wanderers Street, Johannesburg and presided over by Archbishop Desmond Tutu. Approximately 15,000 people attended and because the cathedral could not accommodate all of them, the crowd spilled out onto the streets. Despite a large police presence, the congregation sang revolutionary songs with gusto.

James and Rory filmed in the cathedral and when the service was over, jumped in their microbus to follow the chanting mass of people on their way to West Park Cemetery. A large number of people marched on foot while others crammed into buses. The buses were so full that some comrades stood on the roofs balancing precariously and Rory was surprised that no one fell to the ground.

The massive horde turned off Kingsway and snaked down D. F. Malan Drive. People were dancing the *toyi toyi* and ululating passionately. James noticed that many were openly carrying the banned African National Congress flag and it was the first time he had witnessed such a flagrant and defiant symbolic display of insignia. He found the whole experience both magnificent and terrifying.

Rory drove the microbus while James shot handheld. Occasionally they would stop and set up the camera on a tripod enabling James to use the zoom and vary the size of shots from big close-ups to extreme wide shots emphasizing the epic character of the event.

At the graveside there were polemical speeches. One comrade spoke about Aggett's interrogation and torture and Rory thought of his own ordeal at the hands of the security police. He could still feel the wet towel over his face, his suffocations and the intense pain when jolts of electricity were applied to his testicles. Fortunately, he had been able to give them something. He confessed to the banned literature but he was able to hold back on the gun running. The police thought he had been broken and so they ceased grilling him. Aggett, on the other hand, had not been so lucky.

The whole experience of being there, at that funeral at that time, left Rory profoundly unsettled. Once again he felt the mysterious turning of the earth, the migration of giant forces beyond his control. He felt breathless. It was as if the scales were falling from his eyes and he was experiencing a life-changing epiphany. He knew then that he could not continue remaining a passive observer of the Struggle. He knew he would once more have to enter the fray. He did not then know what form his action would take, he just knew that he could no longer sit on the sidelines.

It was sunset when James and Rory finally drove home. As they were passing the Melville *koppies* Rory could see a flock of birds wheeling in the sky. They seemed to him to be an ominous portent of danger. He felt the uncertain future drifting just beyond his grasp, buoyant and unmoored.

22

SARAH

I've always wanted to find out about my father. I never knew him, you see, or anything about him until I was much older. Growing up he was never around and I had to learn to deal with my illegitimate status.

I still remember the first time someone called me a stupid bastard. It was at another kid's birthday party and I was only about five years old. The events leading up to it are a blur but the taunt, the insult and the hurt still remain with me.

When I came home, wearing my pink fairy dress and clinging to my tattered panda bear, I asked my mother what it meant, to be called that. A bastard.

Well, she flipped. She was absolutely livid. She wanted to thrash the boy who had insulted me. And, as is her wont, she didn't think about the consequences, certainly did not think about the effect it might have on me. She just grabbed the phone and called the mother of the child whose birthday it was. Then she gave it to her and shat on the poor woman from a dizzy height.

Of course she wasn't English (even though everyone including me thought she was) and lacked their restraint. She certainly had little patience for their famous reserve. Most people found her to be very direct as she was outspoken and blunt to the point of being rude. Throughout my childhood she embarrassed me on many occasions.

Don't get me wrong. I adore my mum. She brought me up on her own and I know I was the most precious thing in her life. But she could be difficult at times. She was so forceful and strong-willed. Formidable. And she never stopped to think about the fallout from her actions. She just wanted to protect me and ensure that no one ever called me a bastard again.

Most people think that only men can be bastards but that's not true. There have been lots of famous female bastards like Marilyn Monroe and Eva Peron. But it's still one of the oldest and worst insults in the English language despite the fact that the person being insulted is guiltless and the guilt lies elsewhere. These days when you call someone a bastard, it's just a swear word like arsehole or dickhead and its true meaning is often ignored. But I'm a real bastard. An illegitimate child. My parents were never married and for most of my life I knew nothing about their time together. For so long I knew nothing about their relationship and what they felt for each other. And I certainly did not know my father at all. I knew so little about my past because my mother refused to ever talk about it. Until now that is.

It's not like I didn't ask her. There were many, many times when I was a child that I nagged her to tell me about my father. But that was always a taboo subject, one she was just not prepared to discuss.

I remember when I was about eight or nine years old, we had this fabulous teacher at school – Mr Jeffries. He was different from all the other teachers. He was very tall and his thin frame accentuated his height. He wore tight corduroy trousers in striking colours – mustard yellows, flaming reds, emerald greens, you name it. Conservative blacks and greys just did not feature in his wardrobe and his shirts were striped or polka-dotted in bright, vivid hues. Mr Jeffries had an ivory cigarette holder that held some kind of brown, sweet-smelling cigarettes and he always looked you in the eyes when he spoke to you.

Of course what we children loved about Mr Jeffries was not his camp and eccentric style but rather his stimulating and thought-provoking classes. He was the most wonderful and inspirational teacher you could ever imagine. Instead of history, he taught us myths and legends from all around the world and instead of PE (which all the other kids did) he had us skipping around the playground learning traditional folk dancing. One whole lesson was just dedicated to finding out the meaning of the word "oomph".

Because he seemed to know and care about his pupils, it was the goal of every child in the school to get a place in Mr Jeffries's class. Here he taught us to value art and encouraged us to recreate the paintings of Botticelli, Rubens, Caravaggio and Picasso. Through him we were first exposed to opera and at the end of term he took a rabble of excited South London school children to the Royal Opera House in Covent Garden to see *Tosca*.

Mr Jeffries knew I loved to write stories and at every parents' evening he would say to my mother (with a great deal of oomph!): 'There are books in this girl, you must encourage her to let them out.'

A few years ago, I learned from a neighbour that Mr Jeffries had died of bowel cancer. When she spitefully insinuated that his illness might have had something to do with his sexuality, I wanted to tear her tongue out. But I held on to my anger and just told her that I thought Mr Jeffries was a very great man who had shown children in a deprived London inner city suburb that it was okay to be who they wanted to be. To this day I still feel the loss of him and wish I could thank him for being the man he was.

Anyway, one of the assignments Mr Jeffries gave us was to draw up a family tree by tracing our forebears. Obviously this was not the kind of homework I could do on my own, so I asked my mother to help me. I had spread out all my papers on the dining room table and my mother sat patiently next to me encouraging me to trace back my ancestors and to fill in links on the big spreadsheet in front of us. A few weeks before she had written, on my behalf, to the Huguenot Society of South Africa to get the research we needed to compile my family tree. The relevant documents had just arrived in the post and we were sifting through them for the information we needed.

One side of the tree was by now pretty complete and I could trace my ancestors right back to the seventeenth-century. In France at that time, Protestant Huguenots were being persecuted by the Catholic government and my forebear, Jacques le Roux, sought refuge in Holland where he was offered free passage to the Dutch Colony in the Cape of Good Hope.

It seemed that the Dutch East India Company was looking for people with viticultural skills who could make wine and brandy. The Cape was a stop-off point on the long voyage from the Netherlands to the company's colonial and trading interests in Asia. Ships sailing along that route needed to replenish their provisions of fresh fruit, vegetables and wine. Colonists were needed to harvest crops and produce potable wine and spirits.

Apparently my ancestor, good old Jacques le Roux, had the right experience and aptitude and was given passage on the *Voorschoten*, the first ship bringing French Huguenots to the Cape in 1688. He was accompanied by his new bride, the former Marie-Jeanne Naude. The records indicate that they had been married for less than a week and that Jacques was born in Nimes, near Montpellier in the south of France in 1663. There are no equivalent documentary archives available on Marie-Jeanne and I was unable to find out where and when she was born.

I had a similar lacuna or discontinuity on the other side of my family tree. There was a great big gaping hole on my father's side. The void was glaringly obvious. Everywhere there was an offspring, there were two parents – a father and a mother. Except for me. Even my mother commented.

'Now, what about your father? I don't know too much about his family, but we need to fill something in.'

This was unfamiliar territory for me. All my life she had never mentioned him.

'You do know you have a father, don't you?' she asked.

Although I was not completely *au fait* with the facts of life, I did know that two parents were required, so I just nodded my assent. Mentioning paternity like this was completely out of character for my mother. Usually the subject was off limits and each time I had broached it in the past, she had simply shut the discussion down. Now she seemed to be initiating it.

'Like me he also comes from South Africa,' she said.

Then she told me his name and I wrote in the space for my father "James Morris". To this day, I don't know if she intentionally misled me or whether I heard her incorrectly or if she even saw what I wrote but from that moment on, I mistakenly believed my father's name was "James Morris" not "James Morrison".

She told me that he was a 'very nice man' and that they had loved each other dearly.

'But it was impossible for us to be together. Things in South Africa just got out of hand. It was too dangerous, too complex...'

She went over to the window and looked out on the cold London streets. For a while she was very quiet. Even then when I was so young, I could feel the emotional charge in the room. I sensed that something of inestimable importance was about to happen.

She spoke softly, almost to herself: 'It's probably time now. It might be safe. It might be okay. Things are changing...'

Then she turned and looked me directly in the eyes: 'I have a friend in Johannesburg. I'll write to her. See if she knows where your father is. See if it's okay to try and contact him. I'll write tomorrow. Don't worry, I'll arrange things. I'll try and sort this out.'

I don't know exactly what I felt but it was as if all the air had been sucked from the room. The gas fire was hissing slightly but otherwise it was very quiet. I remember that I didn't want to say anything, the moment was too raw.

Then my mother's face changed. She seemed to be coming

back into the room, back into the present, away from the dark place she had just visited. She smiled at me and told me to clear up my things and get ready for bed.

In my bedroom, when I was in my pyjamas, we knelt in front of the bed and I said my usual prayers as we did every night. But everything was not the same, not "as usual". Instead there had been some kind of shift – some minor agency in the universe had ever so delicately altered.

Usually as a child I accepted the information I was given. Occasionally I might have enquired about factual things but I never questioned an adult on their behavioural choices. I respected the hierarchy of age but at this moment I somehow broke from my conditioning because there were too many things that didn't make sense to me.

While my mother was tucking me into bed I asked: 'Mum, why has my dad got a different name from us?'

'Because we were never married,' she replied.

'And Mum, when we were doing the family tree, those people who sent us the information... from South Africa. They thought your name was Marie le Roux. That's what you must have told them. But your name is Carol Basinger...'

She sighed and once more I felt the charged emotions in the room.

'That's what my name used to be. A long time ago. A very long time ago... now go to sleep, my darling girl.'

Then she kissed me on the cheek and turned off the light but left the door slightly ajar. I could see her in the lounge. She had switched the overhead light off but there was a rosy glow from the gas fire. She poured herself a drink which was not like her at all. I watched as she stared into the fire in a way that unnerved me.

I know she wrote the letter and sent it off the next day because I went to the post office with her. But I don't know if she ever got a reply or if she did, what it might have said. Unless prompted by me, she never mentioned my father again.

23

FAT BILL

Throughout the time that Rory had been languishing in prison, Fat Bill was busy consolidating his position in the security police and eliminating all his enemies or perceived enemies.

He had an office at the Randburg Police Station and would drive his Mercedes there from his home in Sandton. Although the traffic could sometimes be heavy, he enjoyed the commute as it gave him a chance to think on his own. Strategize and plan his next moves. In the car he would play his favourite operas as loudly as he could. He was particularly keen on Verdi's *Nabucco* and he had recently acquired a rare recording of it featuring Luciano Pavarotti. On this particular morning Bill had it blasting from the car speakers while he stroked his pencil-thin moustache and unselfconsciously sang along to the *Hebrew Slaves Chorus*.

When he entered the police station, a couple of patrolmen immediately jumped to attention and saluted. Bill vaguely acknowledged their fawning and walked straight to his office. Most of the constabulary were somewhat in awe of him and were not sure how to behave. They found him mercurial and capricious, somewhat unpredictable. But, in reality, Fat Bill was quite methodical and deliberate about his undertakings.

Today he had decided to draw up a hit list of people he considered to be most dangerous to the state. The government's public enemies. Those people that Bill thought needed to be marked for elimination. An assassination file.

He fed paper and carbon paper into his typewriter. Like a good bureaucrat he would make three copies, to make it official. He knew that he would have to run this by Colonel "Klopper" van Wyk and others in "*die binne kring*", the inner circle, for approval but sometime later this would become unnecessary. Soon Bill would be given the flexibility to call his own shots, to act off his own bat. This was in keeping with his superiors' desire to keep their hands clean. They wanted to make sure that if the tables turned against them, if the shit ever hit the fan they had plausible deniability. They wanted to be able to claim they knew nothing. And so they gave Fat Bill his own license to kill.

He began by typing out a number of headings – a classification system enabling him to pigeonhole people into groups. This was quite a large and comprehensive pecking order that included amongst others the following:

Communists
Black Activists
White Liberals
Student Activists
Trade Unionists
Afrikaans Intellectuals
Clergymen
Academics
Exiles
Foreigners

Bill had a special box which he allocated to Artists. He sub-divided this group into Writers, Musicians, Theatre People and Film-makers.

In each category there was a hierarchy, a ranking system by

which the most celebrated or notorious adversaries were placed at the top and the least dangerous found at the bottom. Over the years, Fat Bill would constantly revise this pyramid of knavery, shifting the names around, deleting some and replacing them with others. This would depend upon who had been eliminated and on his personal assessment of who still represented the greatest threat. Sometimes though he made these decisions on a whim or his own personal animosity towards the individual concerned. He had a great deal of independence to execute opponents at his own discretion. There were no restraints and certainly no checks and balances.

The column headed "Communists" was the most exhaustive and included names like: Cedric Cohen, Jack Mohlala, Brigit Britten and "Spanner" van der Merwe. Naturally, the name heading the list was none other than "Oom" Isaac Spiegel.

The "Black Activists" column was also very comprehensive and contained, amongst others, Bambata wa Luruli, Duma Mokoena and Precious Selinda. Fat Bill thought long and hard about whom he would include in the "Writers" section. Some names were straightforward and obvious like Nadine Gordimer and Andre Brink but he also added Ruth Jacobson at number five. At the top of the "Theatre People" list was Churchill Khumalo followed by Malcolm Purkey and another of Fat Bill's former Russian class associates, David Kastner in sixth position.

In some cases, next to someone's name Bill would type in bold face and capital letters the acronym **TWEP** standing for "Terminate with Extreme Prejudice". Isaac Spiegel was one person so emphasized.

Overall most of the names that appeared on the list were not surprising. It could be argued that many of these people were self-evidently enemies of the state and had condemned themselves through either their speech or their actions. They had sealed their own fate.

But one name stood out from the rest and its inclusion seemed odd, anomalous. Under the heading "Foreigners", Fat Bill had written Leif Halvorsen, Norway's prime minister. This seemed a strange choice despite the fact that Halvorsen was an outspoken critic of the *apartheid* regime, calling it "an especially gruesome system". He had supported United Nations proposals to impose economic and cultural boycotts against South Africa but then so many other international leaders had done the same.

But perhaps this was not such an incongruous choice if one remembered that Fat Bill had met Leif Halvorsen on a number of occasions when he was working for the Frydenlund Institute. Solveig Martensen had introduced them and the two men had taken an instant dislike to each other. From the outset, Halvorsen distrusted Fat Bill and was instinctively wary of him, his caution spontaneous and visceral.

On the other hand, Halvorsen represented everything that Fat Bill abhorred. The man was a socialist, an honest politician who spoke up for truth, justice and the Rule of Law. Besides, his relationship with Solveig seemed a little too close and intimate. Perhaps they were more than colleagues and friends? Fat Bill certainly felt a profound resentment towards Halvorsen. To him, it was not just business, it was deeply personal.

Next to the name Leif Halvorsen, Bill wrote **TWEP.**

It took almost two months of meticulous planning for Fat Bill to set up his first assassination. Because he viewed the initial one as a kind of trial run, a rehearsal for more ambitious future hits, he decided to kick things off with a rather humble, less illustrious target. A small fish. Working from his list, Fat Bill selected Norman Stern who taught political science at Wits. Stern was a left-leaning academic who was active on a number of committees that Bill suspected were fronts for the banned African National Congress.

Fat Bill had no qualms about picking a Jew for his first victim. He had a clear anti-Semitic streak and thought that Jews, given their relatively small population had disproportionately high wealth and influence in the country.

On Colonel van Wyk's recommendation, Bill chose two potential assassins. "Chopper" van der Byl and Koos Steenkamp were both men that van Wyk trusted and had used in the past. They were battle-hardened veterans of the Angola War and highly trained enforcers. Neither man had anything approaching a conscience. In fact, they enjoyed killing especially if it meant getting a R20,000 bonus per strike which would bolster the cash needed to support the rather expensive cocaine habits each man had acquired.

There was also a larger team at Fat Bill's disposal to assist with logistics. These were security police recruits well aware of their mission and *modus operandi*. They were all sworn to secrecy and committed to clandestine operations. Many were experienced torturers and interrogators who had honed their expertise over many years. Others had even more sinister histories. But all of them answered directly to Fat Bill Saunders.

The team began by casing out Stern's home and observing his normal everyday activities. He lived in an unpretentious one-storey house on Dunbar Street in the ethnically diverse suburb of Yeoville. Bill and his team were able to secure a high-rise apartment on Mons Road which enabled them to daily view Stern through binoculars and telescopes. There were also operatives on constant stake-out in cars and on foot observing Stern's every move and relaying the information back via walkie-talkie.

The team noted that Stern regularly played golf early every Saturday morning. Just after 7am he would leave his house carrying his clubs over his shoulder. Then he would place his golf bag on the pavement while opening his garage with a key. Stern would then deposit the bag in the boot of his car and drive off to play his customary game at the Observatory Golf Club.

Fat Bill decided that would be the ideal time and place, just as Stern was lifting his golf bag and dropping it in the boot. The academic would be concentrating on the job at hand and would be unconscious of his surroundings, oblivious to what was going on around him. It would be the moment he was most exposed and vulnerable.

Two weeks later it went down. At seven in the morning the sun was still low in the sky. A turtle dove foraged on the pavement, its soft, drawn-out call sounding like a lament. A short way up the road, two of Bill's operatives crouched down in the front seat of a *bakkie*. From there they had a clear, unrestricted view of Stern's front door and garage. They waited tensely, anticipating the mayhem that would soon ensue. The day was fine, full of both promise and dread.

Despite their callous indifference to Stern's fate, the men experienced a potent apprehension when the front door opened. Only once Stern had turned the garage door key did they spring into action. The passenger hastily spat a command into his walkie-talkie: '*Vat hom!* Take him! Now!' At the same time, the driver started the *bakkie*.

Just then, a Honda motorcycle roared around the corner and headed straight for Stern. Van der Byl was driving and Steenkamp rode pillion, a pump-action shotgun on his shoulder pointed directly at the young academic. Confused, Stern began to move slowly, his flight mechanism kicking in. There was a monstrous blast and Stern's guts exploded out of his back in an ugly scarlet mess. Steenkamp managed to get off one more round, this one blowing half of the young man's face away.

Van der Byl gunned the Honda's engine, the *bakkie* now speeding alongside of it, blocking out the potential for identification from neighbours. Somewhere a woman screamed. Then both vehicles spun round the corner into Bezuidenhout Street. It was done.

The *bakkie* kept going, the back wheels skidding as it turned into Louis Botha Avenue. Meanwhile the motorcycle made a detour into Mons Road, turned sharply and tumbled down the ramp into the underground parking garage of an apartment block. Van der Byl and Steenkamp pulled up fast and dumped the Honda into the back of a waiting Toyota HiAce panel van. They jumped in the back and banged the doors shut. The van reversed in the garage, drove out into the street and was gone.

Later that night, Fat Bill was just finishing his dinner. Diane had prepared him his favourite meal, beef wellington which he had washed down with a good Pinotage. He was feeling marvellous, very happy with the way today's venture had gone. The planning was meticulous and the execution shipshape. Excellent. He thought he deserved a reward for his achievement. A little pampering. Something to lift his spirits even higher. Besides there was that itch that needed scratching, the one Diane could not reach.

He told her that he needed to go into the office to sort out a minor problem. 'Don't wait up,' he said. 'I'm not sure how long it will take.'

Then Bill drove his Mercedes into Hillbrow and parked close to the entrance of the Adelphi. Inside the pub, everything was just the way he liked it. The lights soft and low, the music melancholy, the men horny. He felt wanton and libidinous, almost giddy.

Very obtrusively he dropped his car keys on the bar top and loudly ordered a single malt Scotch. The drink went down fast and he ordered another before he began to appraise the talent. It didn't take long before he was hitting on a red-haired twink with a small basket. Things were looking up.

Soon Fat Bill and Ginger found themselves at the Banket Street flat. The young man ascended the first flight of stairs while Bill lingered behind ogling the cute jiggering buns. He felt all those familiar feelings. A slight headiness, his tongue thickening, his speech slurring, his penis swelling and hardening. *This is going to be fun,* Bill thought.

24

JAMES

One evening, after a particularly gruesome experience filming in Soweto, James brought Rory home to Park Road. Ruth invited him in for a drink and they were all in the lounge upstairs. It was June, dark and cold, the middle of a bitter Highveld winter. The gas heater hissed in the background as they sipped their chilled white wine and watched the early television news. The story that James and Rory had been covering earlier in the day came on.

'Is this your footage?' David asked.

'No. This is SABC stuff. The crowd won't let them get in too close. You can see they're filming with a long lens. But we're right in there, almost on top of the action. I'm shooting with a wide angle. Our footage will be much more graphic,' James said pointing at the screen. 'There, you can just see Rory now right on the edge of frame.'

'Was it scary?' Ruth asked.

'Frightening and horrific!' Rory said. 'But not for James.'

'How's that?' Celeste wanted to know.

'Well,' James replied. 'It's very different for me. Rory can see everything that's going on. The whole event just as it unfolds, the movement of the crowd, the intensity of the action. He can feel the mood of the people, their anger, their hate. But I experience nothing of this. I have a little window I'm looking through. I can only see what the camera sees. Nothing outside of that. And I'm concentrating on getting the image right, composing the shot. Worrying about the exposure. Changing angles and shot size. What's actually going on, that doesn't concern me. The process of filming seems somehow to filter out the real world. I'm dealing with an image not an event. It's only when I turn the camera off that I can see the carnage. Then it becomes hard to deal with.'

On the screen the mob is running, chasing after a young woman. They grab hold of her, bring her to ground like an animal.

'What's happening now?' Ruth asked.

'They think she's a police informer. A traitor. Maybe you don't want to watch this part,' James said.

'No, I think I need to see this,' Ruth insisted.

They all watched aghast as a man dragged the young woman along by the hair. Some in the pack punched her in the face and chest. A man kicked her in the ribs. She fell to the ground but they pulled her along. Then someone placed a rubber car tyre around her neck. The crowd secured it in place with barbed wire bent around her torso. The woman screamed in fear. A man poured petrol over her twisting, writhing body. She begged and pleaded. A young comrade spat in her face. Then the tyre was set alight. She was engulfed in flames. It took a long time for her to die. It was a very painful death.

Everyone in the room was very distressed. Ruth wept. Celeste seemed to recover sooner than the others as she was a medical doctor who witnessed violent death every day working at Baragwanath Hospital.

Then the state president P. W. Botha appeared on the television screen. 'As you can see,' he said, 'there are criminal elements trying to destabilize the country. To make it ungovernable. We cannot allow this state of affairs to continue. We have to take drastic measures to restore law and order. Consequently, I am now declaring a State of Emergency.'

He then proceeded to spell out exactly what this entailed and that it would give the police extraordinary powers to arrest and detain anyone and hold them indefinitely in solitary confinement. Furthermore, political funerals were restricted, curfews imposed, indoor gatherings outlawed and television news crews banned from filming in areas where there was political unrest.

These incidents became the genesis for the Melville Theatre Group's new play *Ungovernable*. Unlike earlier work, the new play tackled the current situation head-on. There was no attempt to hide its intent through allegory or oblique references; instead it faced the chaos and unrest in the townships with a disarming fidelity. At the same time, however, it could not be described as a work of realism. The play was highly stylized and theatrical. To this end, David Kastner collaborated with an extremely talented puppet-maker, Dan de Waal, who built a large number of life-size marionettes. Actors operated and moved these puppets not from above but by actually inhabiting their frames or shells and pulling on artificial limbs.

The central character, played by Churchill Khumalo, was a committed revolutionary bent on making the *apartheid* state "ungovernable". The strikes, boycotts and resistance were all observed by a newsreel cameraman who recorded the unfolding anarchy with a restrained detachment. He functioned as a kind of traditional chorus adopting a cinematic voice-over technique that added a cool overlay to the dramatic action. Naturally, James participated in the play's workshop process and was able to help David with the play's development by drawing extensively from his personal experiences filming in the townships.

Marty Lehman played the part of the cameraman, inhabiting the puppet torso, gliding across the stage and delivering his poetic stream of consciousness lines in a most lyrical fashion. He also made an immense contribution to the art direction, drawing a series of eerie and grotesque charcoal sketches that formed the backdrop to the play's action.

Ruth, on the other hand, was busy completing her second novel and was unable to commit as much time and energy to the project as usual. She was also somewhat disaffected and estranged by certain tensions that had been developing in the theatre group. The trouble began where so many of these kinds of problems begin, in the bedroom. Churchill Khumalo, a notorious womaniser and bedswerver was carrying out an affair with Beth Levy and when Beth's husband, Charles, found out, all hell broke loose. This incident seemed to unleash a whole series of formerly hidden indiscretions and petty jealousies that some in the group had harboured for a while. Long-kept secrets were suddenly disclosed and all manner of imprudent follies crawled out of the woodwork.

David took it upon himself to try and heal the rifts. It was a daunting task as there were broken hearts to mend, bruised egos to repair and oodles of sheer bitchiness to put aside. It was at times like this that he remembered Sartre's famous observation that "Hell is other people". David had to call on all his diplomatic and negotiating skills to soothe tempers, mend fences and restore trust but because of his personal commitment to the group he was able to bring about some kind of normalcy. He also knew that for some people the Melville Theatre Group was their only home. They needed its stability for their own sanity.

Unlike David, Ruth found the tensions in the group much too tedious and bothersome. So, rather than engaging with the fray, she decided to contribute less to the theatre and concentrate instead on her own writing and creative work. She had already made some progress along these lines. A year before she had completed a novel, *Sunset in Exile*, which told the story of a young man who finds life in South Africa under *apartheid* so oppressive that his conscience forces him to seek a new life abroad. The book was a lyrical, magical account of the loneliness of exile and ultimately a tragic love story. Its delicacy and haunting beauty were, in some ways, influenced by and reminiscent of early Turgenev. Not unexpectedly, it had sold quite well and received excellent press reviews.

Ruth's novel was but one component of a wave of creativity that was sweeping across the country at that time. South Africa in the 1980s was undergoing a cultural revolution, a kind of Prague Spring, wherein so many of the arts were flourishing. There was a burgeoning musical transformation that synthesized western and African traditions. This movement was spearheaded by groups like Jaluka and others but crashed onto the international scene with the release of Paul Simon's *Graceland* album.

A number of highly influential and award-winning novels were being written, published and widely read. The work of Coetzee, Gordimer and Brink elevated local literature and brought national themes and obsessions to a wider readership. In the theatre, radical and innovative plays were being performed all over the country and audiences were vocal and engaged. Despite the inner turmoil, the Melville Theatre Group was a significant contributor to this movement and the new play *Ungovernable* was destined to be an influential and seminal work of that period.

James often felt frustrated by the fact that the only art form that did not seem to be going anywhere at this time in South Africa was the cinema. A number of films were being made but none of them had any real merit. This was partly due to the fact that most of the major production companies were in the hands of government lackeys or *broederbond* members who made very conventional films that celebrated *apartheid* and the status quo.

He had written a couple of high-quality screenplays that he had tried to produce but James was unable to find the necessary finance to get the projects off the ground. Investors were just not interested in bankrolling challenging and contentious subjects.

One thing was certain, he did not want to be a newsreel cameraman all his life. But after President Botha's State of

Emergency proposal even that seemed under threat. James realised he would have to take stock of his life and consider his prospects very carefully.

25

I never thought I would ever get over Cookie. That first week was the worst. Nothing seemed real. I thought there must be some mistake and that at any moment she would simply walk back through the door. Over and over again I read her note wondering if I had missed something, if I had not correctly understood it. Maybe there was some secret message in there that would reveal where she had gone and why she had left me. But no matter how many times I scrutinized the note, I remained confused, baffled by her motives. Shattered and lost.

Everything in the flat reminded me of her. I could picture her brushing her teeth in the mirror, reading the newspaper in the lounge, lying in bed with her orange floral pyjamas. She was ubiquitous, everywhere and nowhere. I felt emphatically alone.

For weeks I was haunted by a recurring dream, a nightmare. I had bought a ticket to a movie that I had wanted to see for a long time. Somehow I knew that it was a masterpiece, the kind of film that would profoundly affect the way I thought about the cinema, about the world. And yet when I went to the door, the usher would not let me in. I waved my ticket in his face but he blocked my path. Behind that door I knew something of priceless importance was happening. If only I could get in I would discover what it was. On the screen an erudite drama was unfolding, dynamic and vital. I needed to see it. I waved my ticket above my head. But no one would let me in. And then I would wake up shaken and unnerved.

At night I would look across Parsons Green at the lights along the way to the Tube station. There was a fish and chip shop that stayed open until late, a newsagent and the pub. That was it but I would stare at them for hours. I couldn't sleep so I started drinking Scotch. A lot of Scotch. It helped me to pass the time.

In the mornings I would reluctantly drag myself off to film school. I was finding the classes harrowing. Everything reminded me of Cookie. On the Tube I would sometimes catch a glimpse of a young woman with long, dark hair and my heart would rock in my chest. I was an emotional wreck.

All I knew was that it had something to do with Fat Bill and the message he had left Cookie in the Pasternak book, *Dr Zhivago*, as well as the fact that she had exposed him as a spy to the ANC and the subsequent coverage in the British press. I would have thought that once his identity was out in the open, she would have felt safer but for some reason that I didn't know about, that was not the case. She felt more exposed, more under threat. And so I began to blame myself. To chastise myself for not being stronger, for not being more protective of her. For being unable to persuade her that I would look after her no matter what.

London is a fine city, superlative and unparalleled in so many ways but if you are there alone it can be desolate and bleak. For months I felt ripped apart and morose, hollowed out. My only saving grace was to throw myself into my work at film school. I volunteered for all kinds of projects and offered my services as a cinematographer to anyone who had a halfway decent script. Because I was conscientious and committed, I was highly sought after.

One film I shot was called *Fables of Enchantment and Regret*. It was a kind of modern Oedipal story full of dream-like and surreal imagery, very challenging from a photographic perspective. The director was an Australian, Tim Stephenson, nicknamed "Stevo". He and I just clicked, we saw eye to eye on aesthetic matters. The movie was highly ambitious but I believe I was able to fashion the appropriate imagery to complement Stevo's visionary *mise-en-scène*.

Playing the female lead was a very attractive young ballerina, Kate Taft. Somehow, throughout the shoot, she and I seemed always to be thrown together. In the beginning Kate was having a little difficulty with her performance in some of the nude scenes. During one of the breaks I gave her some advice based on my experience as an actor in the theatre group. It certainly helped and after that she was much more relaxed and her performance less wooden. We soon became friends and, inevitably, lovers.

The affair didn't last very long. Although we enjoyed each other's company, we weren't exactly simpatico soul mates. It was light, pleasurable and a little steamy. That was all but I'm extremely grateful to her. She helped me get out of the rut of self-pity I was stuck in. I was able to move on, start living again and jettison that vacuous feeling.

But I still felt restless and unsettled. Anchorless and drifting. I started travelling to different areas of London, different suburbs. I still don't know what I thought I would find there. Maybe some semblance or trace of Cookie, I'm not sure. I would catch a Tube heading off in an unfamiliar direction and then get off at a random stop and just wander around. Sometimes I would pop into a pub for a drink and watch the locals. Occasionally I would pick up a young woman and have a one-night stand. Looking back at it now, it all seems a little effete and self-indulgent but my heart was wounded, callow and green.

All too soon my course at film school was over and it was time to go back to South Africa. Despite being reluctant to leave England, I, nevertheless, had ambitious goals for the future. There were powerful stories I wanted to tell on film, compelling movies I wanted to make. In many ways I believed that the political climate in my country was a breeding ground for singular and exceptional fiction in which we had unique tales to tell.

I thought, naïvely as it turned out, that I could contribute to and participate in a cinematic renaissance, a new dawn of South African film-making. Drawing from the example of the *Nouvelle Vague* or French New Wave film-makers, I believed that it was possible to make low-budget movies that radically engaged with the social and political upheavals of the time. I wanted to make iconoclastic films that not only told relevant, personal stories but that also experimented with narrative form, visual style and editing.

Sadly, it was not to be. When I returned to my homeland I wrote a number of promising screenplays which I attempted to produce. Finding the finance for any of these ventures proved impossible. Local studios and production companies were only interested in promoting the status quo and making very conventional melodramas that celebrated commonplace puritanical values. The industry was notoriously controlled by pro-*apartheid* producers who benefitted from government subsidies that rewarded jingoist narratives.

Over time I grew frustrated and disillusioned. Fortunately, I was able to find employment as a stringer shooting newsreels for CNN and the BBC. But after the State of Emergency was declared, even that dried up when the government decided to crack down on the coverage of political events.

In the meantime, Ruth had just completed her second novel, *A Battalion of Spies*. We, all her friends, were invited to the launch held at a bookshop in Hyde Park. I was extremely proud of her and delighted to receive an early signed copy of the first edition.

The novel is set in a fictional country, Murcuro, which is a fusion of South Africa and some imaginary Eastern European state. Murcuro is a dictatorship run by a former spy and assassin who puts down a series of popular insurrections by the most brutal means. Franz Theunissen is a man who has built his career on falsehoods, cover-ups, murder and betrayal. He is prepared to manipulate any ideological position to further his own narcissistic ends.

Many early commentators saw the novel as an allegorical work that brilliantly reflected the current South African scenario, but I thought the book went much further and that its critique was both deeper and broader. It seemed to me to be a condemnation of ideology itself and a profound and chilling account of life under totalitarianism. A truly ominous, haunting and prophetic work.

There were some, in our inner circle, who were quick to point out distinct parallels and similarities between the central character, Franz Theunissen, and our own local miscreant, Fat Bill Saunders. It's very likely that Ruth drew heavily on her personal observations of Bill but the character she created in Theunissen is complex and fully-rounded not just some shallow caricature.

In any event, the general consensus from all readers was that Ruth had written a masterpiece, a novel of great complexity and insight. Her publishers certainly believed it to be an important literary work and had entered it in a number of competitions. Their faith in the book was confirmed when the novel *A Battalion of Spies* was shortlisted for the prestigious Booker Prize.

We had a big party at the Park Road house to celebrate her success. It was a glorious night. Ruth's parents, Sadie and Benjamin, were there as were most of the members of the Melville Theatre Group and other close associates and colleagues. Everyone was elated, the mood jubilant. Marty made a very moving speech in which he spoke about his love for Ruth, their blissful life together, Ruth's prodigious talent and her dedication to her craft. I felt privileged to be a friend.

It was very late when I finally arrived home. At the time I was living in a small flat in Rosebank and when I opened the front door the phone was ringing. I stumbled through the lounge in the dark and picked up the receiver.

'Hello,' I said.

'G'day, James, is that you?' I recognised the voice straight away.

'Stevo! You old bastard! It's two o'clock in the bloody morning!' I always started to talk Strine when I was with him.

'Well I reckoned that's the best time to get hold of you. I tried calling earlier but the phone just rang,' Stevo replied.

'I was out at a party.'

'Bet there were plenty of sheilas, if I know you.' A shared chuckle.

'So what's happening? What can I do for you?' I asked.

'Look, I'll keep it short and sweet, mate. I've just got the funding to direct a feature. The movie's based on a script I wrote. A post-apocalyptic story about this travelling theatre company that moves from one nomadic settlement to the next performing Brecht plays. It's set some time in the near future just after a virus or fever has killed off most of humankind. All of technology has broken down. A few cars but there is a shortage of petrol which becomes the new currency replacing money. There are a bunch of weirdos and bogans fighting for supremacy in the desert. Anyway, to cut a long story short, I need a good cinematographer. Someone I can trust. So I immediately thought of you.'

'That sounds fantastic! Congratulations!' I said. 'And you want me to shoot it for you?'

'I do. If you're interested,' Stevo replied.

'Absolutely! I'd be honoured. That'd be marvellous.'

We then spent some time discussing practicalities. Principal photography was scheduled to commence in three months but I would have to apply for a visa. Stevo filled me in on how to go about doing this. He then promised to send me a copy of the screenplay as soon as possible. Finally, we made plans to communicate regularly so that we could both be on the same page regarding the film's aesthetic. I thanked him and we signed off.

I was over the moon. This offer could not have come at a more opportune time. A time when I was starting to get pretty despondent about my career. I thought of this as a tremendously lucky break. Over the last few years, the Australian film industry had blossomed and the country was making provocative and inspirational movies. Government agencies had spent a great deal mentoring new talent and nurturing young artists. Fine directors like Peter Weir, Gillian Armstrong, Phillip Noyce, Jane Campion and others had emerged to make astonishing films. I saw this as my big chance. My time to show the world what I was capable of. I could not fuck it up.

The next morning, I called Rory and told him about the offer I had just been given. We had already had some discussions about how to proceed now that the newsreel shoots were drying up.

'I'm really sorry about this. I don't want to leave you in the lurch like this. It's just that this is an opportunity of a lifetime,' I told him.

'Not a problem,' said Rory. 'I'm very happy for you. I hope it goes really well. In any event, I've also been doing some soul searching and I've decided to get back involved in the Struggle. To commit myself to change in the country. And so I've spoken to some people at the UDF and they are going to give me a job working with trade unions. So it will all work out for the best.'

This was a relief for me as I did not want to let him down in any way. Recently I had decided that it was time to make some changes in my life. I felt like I had been given a reprieve, a second shot at life and I needed to make the best of my lucky break.

So I decided to cut down considerably on my drinking, only having the occasional glass of wine with a special meal. I also wanted to work on getting fit and healthy in preparation for the Australian shoot. Rory gave me some tips on running; the best shoes to buy, stretching exercises, slowly building up fitness, wind sprints, etc. After about a month of this I felt confident enough to join him on his early morning jogs and we began a regime of running together. I found it exhilarating. My rhythmic strides generated a kind of meditative state and I felt both at peace and liberated. Free. I was keenly anticipating my trip abroad and the new life that I felt was waiting for me.

A couple of months later I set off on my journey, my Australian adventure. I bid a tender farewell to my family and close friends but little did I know then that one of my dearest I would never see again. Once more I find myself wishing that I had some foreknowledge, some premonition of what was about to happen. But I knew nothing and even if I had, I'm not sure what I could have done to change the terrible course of events.

At the airport I passed effortlessly through security and customs. While waiting for the flight I began reading the newspaper in the transit lounge. The usual boring, parochial stories about the misadventures of local celebrities. But then on about page five I came across a rather curious report. Just the day before, the Norwegian Prime Minister, Leif Halvorsen had been assassinated.

Apparently Halvorsen and his wife had been at the theatre attending, ironically, a production of Ibsen's *An Enemy of the People*. He had dismissed his bodyguards (who needs them in Oslo?) and they were on their way home, walking across a busy thoroughfare. Suddenly an armed man stepped in their path and shot the prime minister twice. A bullet to the head and another in the chest. The news reporter described it as "a very professional hit that had the police baffled."

The article then went on to note that earlier that week Halvorsen had given a major speech to the Stortinget or Norwegian Parliament about the evils of *apartheid* which he said "had to be abolished as it could not be reformed." The report merely noted this in passing. There was no suggestion of a connection between the speech and the assassination. No cause and effect relationship was implied.

Reading the report, I also did not assume that the two incidents were linked in any way. It just seemed odd to me. Norway was just such a civilized and safe place, virtually a symbol of the ideal enlightened society. An assassination on the streets of its capital city seemed bizarre and ludicrous.

What on earth is going on? I asked myself as I boarded the aeroplane. *Has the world gone completely mad?*

26

SARAH

Are you my dad? Are you the one? Can it be you? These are the questions I would silently think to myself as I searched for my father in the faces of strangers. Anyone who was blonde and blue-eyed was a likely candidate. My mother had told me often enough that I resembled him. That we had the same colouring – the identical sun-bleached platinum hair and ultramarine eyes.

Of course he had to be the right age too. In his early thirties I figured. So when I found someone who had all the appropriate credentials, all the right ingredients, I would stare at him shamelessly, curiously inspecting his features for signs of my own. *Is it you? Can you see that I am looking for you? Can you feel in your heart that it is me? That I am here?* I would secretly and wordlessly ask.

I felt sure that if I did find him, if I did find my father, if our paths did cross in those labyrinthine London streets, then he would know me immediately and I would know him. That we would somehow recognise each other. That we were psychically bonded.

Once, when I was about seven years old, my mother and I were catching a train to the coast on our way to France. I saw this man sitting in the carriage a few seats away from us. He smiled at my mum. They exchanged glances. I was very young but I was still acutely aware of the electricity flowing between them. I remember that there was a distinct volatility in the air, an inexplicable *aliveness*. The moment unformed and callow. Giddy. The man had all the right elements – blonde hair, steel blue eyes. He and my mother seemed to recognise something in each other. I can't even guess what it was – a hunger, a need, a connection, a feeling. Some kind of speechless reciprocal communication in their primeval brains. Maybe they fancied each other, I don't know. But all I could think of was that he must be the one. He must be my father!

Immediately I stared him down, giving him the test, willing him to mystically speak to me. To give me a sign. *Show me that you are the one! Be the one!* I prayed. *I call on you. I invoke you!* (God only knows where I learned that word.)

The man must have noticed how intensely I was looking at him. I'm sure it would have seemed odd to him. Perhaps he thought I was deranged, mentally unstable or just overly possessive of my mother. In any event, his eyes shifted from my mother to me. Then he looked away. But soon he lifted his eyes back to me. I kept up the intent stare. Once again he avoided my gaze and turned his attention to the window where the English landscape was slipping away from us. A few minutes later he left our carriage and moved to another.

It seemed to me that these kinds of things were always happening until my mother told me that my father lived in South Africa and that he did not even know about my existence, did not know he had a daughter on the other side of the world. Then I began to understand that it was incredibly unlikely that our paths would cross, that we would meet by chance. I soon realised that the only way I was going to get to know him was if someone contacted my father and told him about me.

So I started to nag my mother about finding him. Begging her. She had written that one letter to a friend in South Africa but nothing had come of it. My mum had not even told me if she had got a reply. I had invested my youthful dreams and longings upon the outcome of that letter but it had all been in vain. My aspirations had been thwarted, my hopes dashed once again. I felt cheated, duped.

Almost every day I asked her to contact him. Tell him about me. But she refused. I suppose a stranger, an outsider might think I was pestering or maybe even harassing her but that's not the way I saw it. In my mind, from my point of view, I thought I had a right to know my father. I wanted to meet him, see what he was like, see what he thought of me, if he loved me. All the other kids at school knew both their parents, why couldn't I?

So I kept nagging.

By this time, my mum had a boyfriend, Reg, who used to visit and sleep over often. He's a Geordie and was a keen supporter of Newcastle United. Once, when we were having our tea, he was going on about some game that his team had just won. I rudely interrupted and asked my mother: 'Does my dad like football?'

She tried to fob me off. 'Not that I know of.'

'Does he support a team?'

'No, they only have rugby in South Africa. No one cares about football.'

Even though I could tell she was getting impatient with me, I kept on.

'Does he play rugby?'

'He used to. When he was in the army. But I don't think he still does.'

'What did he do in the army? Did he kill anyone?'

And so on. *Ad nauseam*. One question leading to another, until she would just ignore me. Change the subject or give me the silent treatment.

I know I have a stubborn streak in me and I doggedly pursued this line of inquiry whenever I got the chance. Even the most innocent remark could start me off. Like my mother trying to get me to eat more nutritiously.

'Eat your peas. You need to eat more veggies.'

'Does my dad like peas?' Playing with my food, moving it around on my plate with my fork.

'Yes, I'm sure he does. I'm sure he loves peas. If he was here he'd tell you that and tell you to eat your peas.'

'But he's not here. Why isn't he here? Why don't you contact him?'

'I've already told you. It's not the right time. It's too dangerous.'

'But why? I don't understand why.'

'I told you. It didn't work out with us. We had to be apart.'

'But other children know their dad. Even when their parents are divorced the dad comes around.'

This would always really frustrate my mum. Get her riled up and angry.

'Yes, but he's not around. He's in another country.'

'But you could contact him. You know you could write to him. Or phone him. Why don't you phone him?'

Now that I know the truth, now that I know what really transpired, I realise it must have been painful for her. All these questions. This endless badgering. But I could not help myself. I desperately wanted to know my father.

It eventually got to the point where Reg took me aside and asked me to quit. He said that I was distressing my mother and that I was making her ill with all these requests to contact my father. He told me it had to stop.

But that did not end my quest. It didn't finish there and I devised a new plan, a plan that did not depend upon the cooperation of my mother. I decided that I would find my father myself.

And so, one day in the school summer holidays, I got up early in the morning and braided my long, blonde hair. I dressed in my denim jeans and a light coloured blouse. In my purse, I made sure I had enough money for a bus ride to and from the West End.

When I went downstairs, my mother and Reg were finishing

their breakfast. They offered to make some for me but I opted for cereal. I was anxious and wanted to leave as soon as I could. Make it quick and simple, I thought.

I told my mum I was meeting some school friends in Leicester Square and then going on to see a movie. Although I hated lying to her, I didn't feel that I had any other choice. I knew that if I told her where I was going and what I planned to do, she would try to stop me.

On the Walworth Road I caught the number 12 bus. It was one of those big, red, iconic double-decker Routemasters that tourists still expect to find in London but which have now been replaced by Bendy buses. I sat upstairs looking out the window as we passed Elephant & Castle and then crossed Westminster Bridge. It was an overcast day and the Thames looked grey and muddy from where I sat. My heart was pounding, I was getting closer to my destination but I was still upbeat and expectant.

When we stopped just before Trafalgar Square I jumped off leaving from the open rear platform of the bus. I walked past Nelson's Column and the lion statues heading east towards the Strand. It was the early nineties, the last days of *apartheid* and there was a huge demonstration outside South Africa House. I had not taken this into account when I planned my trip and I was a little intimidated by all the protestors. Nevertheless, I stumbled through the crowd mumbling apologies on my way. The building is fairly imposing and grandiose having been (as I found out many years later) designed by Sir Herbert Baker. Going up the stairs, I felt very small and insignificant but tried to appear older and more self-confident. The crowd, with their placards and principles, frightened and badgered me, hurling abuse my way.

Inside the embassy it was dark and cavernous, badly lit. I thought they might be trying to save money on electricity. I made my way to the reception desk serviced by a young woman in her early twenties. She was heavily made-up and wore a very short mini skirt and sported large, gaudy, sparkling earrings.

'Can I help you?' she snarled while chewing gum.

'Um, I'm trying to find someone,' I nervously mumbled. 'A South African national.'

'Is it? You looking for someone in the embassy?' she asked. I could barely understand her thick guttural, almost incomprehensible accent. She seemed like an alien. I wondered if my father also spoke like this.

'No, no. He lives in South Africa. I need to contact him.'

'Is it? How you going to do that?' The vowels flat, the tone disinterested.

'Maybe you have some phone books here? I want to get his number.'

'*Ja*, we've got plenty of those. Where does he live?'

'I'm not sure.' I hadn't even thought about this. 'Maybe Johannesburg?'

'What about Cape Town? Port Elizabeth? Pretoria? Durbs by the sea?' she was teasing me now, taking the piss.

I was becoming confused, uncertain.

'Um, maybe we could try all of those,' I stammered.

'*Jislaaik jong!*' I had no idea what that meant. 'Okay, *skattie*. I'll *sommer* go get them for you.'

She seemed to glide away, her backside swaying from side to side voluptuously as she disappeared into one of the adjoining rooms. Her whole demeanour was overtly sexual and once again I felt myself in some kind of unfamiliar, alternate universe.

Soon she was back with a pile of phone books in her arms. She sat me down at one of the small tables and gave me a pen and paper.

'Good luck!' she said.

I started on the Johannesburg directory. It was quite intimidating to find more than twenty people with the surname "Morris" and first initial "J". I thought most people in South Africa had Dutch names and I was expecting my task to be much simpler. Nevertheless, I carefully wrote down all the phone numbers. *But how could I make all these overseas calls?* I thought. *It's going to be much too expensive. Besides my mother would never let me.*

Cape Town was even worse. There must have been over thirty "J. Morris's" in the phone book. I started writing them all down but I was becoming quite despondent. The whole process seemed impossible, a futile enterprise. What was I thinking? Why had I come up with this crazy idea? *You're mad*, I thought.

Of course, the entire exercise was completely in vain, pointless, as I was still under the illusion that my father's name was "Morris" not "Morrison". If only I had known! Not that it would have made any difference. There's likely to have been just as many "Morrisons" if not more. I still could not have phoned them all. And, even if I could, what would I say? 'My name is Sarah. I'm looking for my father. Are you him?' Crazy! I would never be able to do it. I would never have the courage. What if I found him and he didn't want to know me? I would be devastated. Rejection was the one thing I would not be able to deal with. And who knew what he would say. He probably had another family, other children. Why would he want me in his life?

As I sat in that gloomy embassy reception hall, I began to realise what a stupid plan I had come up with. *You idiot!* I told myself. *This never could have worked. You're just wasting your time! You silly, silly girl! Mad fool!*

I didn't even bother with the other cities. Durban, Pietermaritzburg, etc. I was feeling much too disheartened. Like all my other attempts to contact my father, this was proving to be just as ineffective. Fruitless. Maybe it was not meant to be. Maybe the gods of the universe wanted it to be so. Maybe it was my destiny to always be a bastard.

I went back to the desk with all the phone books and thanked the receptionist.

'That's okay, *skattie*,' she said. 'Hope you found what you were looking for.'

I just nodded as I was too choked up to speak, too angry with myself, too tearful.

Outside the embassy, the protestors were still shouting abuse and waving their banners. I pulled my shoulders in, trying to make myself small and invisible. 'Racist scum!' someone shouted at me. The crowd was pressing against my body, making it difficult to get through. A man screamed in my face: 'Bigot! *Apartheid* bitch! Go home where you belong!'

By now the tears were gushing down my face. I was sobbing and struggling to speak or breathe. I stumbled on, pushing past the self-righteous mob, trying to make a path, trying to find my way through. With all the jostling, the piece of paper that I had written the phone numbers on fell from my hand. The demonstrators were chanting now. A woman gestured with her fist and cried out: '*Amandla!*' The crowd responded shouting, '*Awethu!*'

Everyone seemed buoyed by their communal bonding, their camaraderie, but for me it was frightening, a group mindset. The protestors' fury was terrifying, especially when their anger was directed my way. I was relieved to finally escape and leave the frenzy in the square.

In the bus I cried all the way home. I felt mortified by the whole experience, humiliated and bitter. My mouth tasted of iron ore and I wanted to vomit but more than that I felt a panicky desperation, an overwhelming melancholic hopelessness. At the time I would not have been able to describe my mood, I would not have been able to give it a name. I would not have known what to call it. But I know now. Despair.

I did not tell my family what had happened and where I had been. In fact, until today I have never told anyone about it, about my trip to Trafalgar Square. The entire episode was much too painful to revisit. I have kept it hidden in a secret corner of my heart.

27

The movie was called *Nullarbor Fever*. In the script there were two time periods – Before the virus or fever struck down and virtually destroyed humankind and After. The Before scenes were all shot in Melbourne and the After scenes were filmed in and around Eucla in Western Australia.

Eucla is really in the middle of nowhere. A small town on the Eyre Highway somewhere between Adelaide and Perth, Eucla has an official population of eighty-six and lies at the start of the Nullarbor Plain, a vast, empty, inhospitable, treeless (hence the name) desert area. There's not much there; a small hotel, a restaurant, a museum and the world's longest golf course. Driving by car from Perth to Adelaide or the other way around is an almost mandatory experience for Aussies. It's a distance of about 2,700km and there are virtually no settlements along the way except for the iconic roadhouses selling petrol, sandwiches, coffee and vehicle stickers that say: "I have crossed the Nullarbor."

Principal photography started in Eucla because it was easier to schedule the After scenes first. The population of the town more than doubled when our cast and crew arrived. Some of us stayed in the Eucla Motor Hotel but the rest were temporarily housed in

183

caravans and tents. For the two months that we were there the small hamlet buzzed and rocked.

The shoot was physically demanding because of the heat so we mostly worked early in the morning and late in the afternoon. This was great for me as the light was more suitable at these times and consequently the picture's photographic quality was appreciably enhanced. Overall, the Australian crew was disciplined and hard-working so the whole experience was rewarding and enjoyable.

Although there were essentially two major time periods, the story was told in a non-linear fashion with flashbacks to the past or present and flash-forwards to the future. After the fictional virus devastated society, nomadic groups fought each other for limited resources. In particular, they wrangled over petrol reserves. (Some years later I learnt that this major premise in the film is flawed as petrol goes stale and has a short storage life.)

I thought Stevo was a fine director. Not only was he able to get credible performances from all the actors but his use of *mise-en-scène* was innovative and poetic. Many of the scenes had a surreal aesthetic but he wed his fairly outrageous imagery to a clear narrative line that the audience could follow and empathise with. The film was partly about the necessity of art, or more particularly, how the theatre can save us.

Stevo was very influenced by Theo Angelopoulos's *The Travelling Players* as well as the films of Miklos Jancso. Both of these directors were noted for their use of long takes incorporating complex camera movements. This posed a number of problems for me and made the cinematographic elements very challenging.

On one occasion, towards the end of the Eucla shoot, the first assistant director ran over to me in a panic.

'Stevo wants to do a "walk thing". It's not in the script at all, mate. What the hell are we going to do?' he asked.

'Okay,' I said. 'Just what is a "walk thing"?'

'It's like that scene in *The Wild Bunch* where William Holden and Ernest Borgnine and those other guys, I forget their names, go walking through the town to confront that Mexican general. After they've been rooting those prostitutes...'

'Oh, *ja*,' I said. 'Stevo's been dying to do that routine all the way through film school. That "walk thing". Might as well do it now,' I said.

And so we did. The "walk thing" involved lots of camera tracking and the use of long focal length lenses which made focus pulling a nightmare. But in the end we carried it off and the sequence worked beautifully for the movie.

After Eucla, Melbourne was like being on a different planet. To me it was a revelation. I loved the city with its rickety old trams, narrow lanes, superb restaurants and vibrant music scene. We did most of our filming in and around the central business district with a few scenes shot in the inner suburb of Hawthorn along Glenferrie Road.

Every night we would watch rushes at our cutting rooms in St Kilda. That's where I met Karen. She was employed as a sound editor and I was surprised to find another former South African working on the production.

Karen had originally come to Australia on a student exchange program. After matriculating in Johannesburg, she took a gap year in Melbourne living with a host family and attending a local high school. It seemed like quite a plucky escapade for a young girl to do but as I learned more about her, I soon realised just how gutsy and fearless she was.

When the exchange program was over she returned to Johannesburg to complete a degree at Wits. By that time, an unruly wave of criminality and lawlessness was sweeping over the city. Burglary, rape and murder were becoming commonplace and the citizenry responded by blockading themselves behind high walls, electric fences and employing armed response security personnel.

To someone as free-spirited and adventurous as Karen, this was impossibly restrictive. It felt to her like people were imprisoning themselves in their own homes. There were a number of incidents where friends of hers had either been attacked or had their cars hijacked at gunpoint. Johannesburg was becoming dangerous and unsafe.

Karen began to nostalgically call to mind her secure and unfettered life in Melbourne. Like so many other people, she started to think about emigration. She talked it over with her parents and they fully supported her desire to move abroad. For them, the future seemed uncertain. The government was responding to the unrest in the country by ruthlessly cracking down on dissidents. It looked like South Africa was spiralling towards a bloody civil war. As much as it pained them to encourage their daughter to emigrate, they did so believing it would be the best course of action for Karen to take.

And so she moved to Melbourne which is where I found her. She was ten years younger than me but it never seemed like it. Karen was one of those people that are born mature and that even as a young child would seem grown-up, an adult. There was nothing frivolous about her, she was eminently practical and competent at everything she tackled. That is not to suggest she lacked a sense of humour, quite the contrary. She had an infectious laugh and used her innate narrative gifts to tell hilariously funny anecdotes. But she was, I guess, serious-minded. She wanted to move through life in a straight line with no detours. And if you wanted to be on that path with her, you had to be forthright and honest. Committed. No bullshit.

She lived in a sunny two-bedroomed flat on Dickens Street right opposite the St Kilda Botanical Gardens. We would often meet after work for dinner at one of our favourite restaurants in Acland Street and then catch a tram back to her place. On warm nights we sometimes bought ice cream from an Italian *gelateria* and slowly walked home going past Luna Park and then on through the quiet, leafy streets.

By then, principal photography on the film had been completed and there remained just a few pick-up scenes to shoot so I had time on my hands. I allowed myself to fall into the routines and rhythms of Karen's life. Every Saturday morning, she would take her notebook, pencils and paints to meet up with a group of like-minded urban sketchers. Karen's drawing book was filled with a record of the buildings and places she had visited. Her milieu.

I invariably accompanied her on these jaunts to seek out architecturally unusual sites. While she sketched I would read or sit and observe her. Karen on her portable chair with her soft auburn curls just visible under her floppy brown hat. I loved to watch how she wrinkled up her freckled nose, closed her left eye and held up one finger to get a visual perspective on the building she was drawing.

Afterwards we would grab a light lunch and then either visit an art gallery or browse through a bookshop. Just to be together was enough. In the evening one of us would cook a meal. Karen's were usually more elaborate than mine but we both enjoyed making varied tasty dinners. Then it was usually early to bed. I have never met anyone who liked to sleep as much as Karen. I would often lie awake, stroking her freckled shoulders while she dozed away, dreaming of God knows what. I would lie there in the dark listening to the forlorn sounds of the trams gliding down Carlisle Street, the windows rattling, the breaks squealing on the tracks and I would wonder where this journey I was on would lead me.

At the time I had been having talks with a well-connected producer who was interested in hiring me to shoot another feature film Down Under. I was considering my options and knew that I would soon have to make a decision about cementing my relationship with Karen. I would have to decide whether to move permanently to Australia or return to South Africa. But then fate intervened and the decision was virtually taken out of my hands.

The phone rang and then time stood still. It was David calling from Johannesburg. As I listened to him, it felt like a giant boulder was being dropped on my heart.

28

JAMES

'James, sorry to call you so late. It must be about midnight there,' David said.

'No problem. I was awake.'

In the background I could hear Celeste asking him if he had got through to me. I dreaded what was coming.

'Listen, I've got some bad news. Really bad news. Are you sitting down?' David asked. I could hear he was really troubled. Wretched and all torn up.

'What's happened? Tell me.' My voice agitated.

'It's Marty… He's dead.'

'Oh no! Oh no!' My immediate response was disbelief. 'That can't be.' But I knew it must true. 'What happened?'

'It's kind of a weird and fucked-up story but I'll try and tell you how it went down. You know that Ruth has been on this book tour, promoting her novel. Well she was in the UK, in London, doing television interviews, bookstore readings and signings, etc. All the usual crap publishers want you to do to sell more books. Anyway, at the end of one hectic day, just yesterday actually, she phoned Marty from her hotel room. To catch up and chat with him. They talked for a while. Mostly small talk, what he'd been doing, what the weather was like and so on. Then he told her that a parcel had arrived in the post for her. Addressed to Ms Ruth Jacobson and sent from the Booker Prize Advisory Committee. He asked her what he should do about it. And then…' David broke off for a moment. Too emotional to go on.

'Take your time,' I said.

'It's okay,' David said, his voice thick, clearly rattled. 'I'm okay now…' After a short while he was able to resume. 'So Marty said "There's this parcel here from the Booker Prize people. What shall I do with it?" and Ruth said: "Open it. I want to see if I won." So Marty tore the envelope open. But it must have been a letter bomb. And then it went off. A huge explosion. The blast tore him apart. Blew Marty to smithereens. The discharge taking out half the dining room wall. Bricks all over the place.'

David broke down again, unable to continue. My body was shaking. My nerves all jangled. Nothing seemed real. It took a while before David was able to continue. Once he had composed himself, I asked him about funeral arrangements.

'As you know, in our faith we like to bury the dead as soon as we can. But in this instance the police are not releasing the body. Not that there is much of a body. The dining room is littered with blood and pieces of human flesh. It's a gruesome sight. Truly awful. The police have declared it a crime scene. There's a forensic team in there looking for clues and evidence. But I don't think they'll find much that can lead to a conviction. In any event I think we all know who was responsible…'

Fat Bill. I knew that's who David was thinking of. But he didn't say as much. He seemed reticent and I wondered if he thought the phone was being bugged. That was certainly feasible and it would not surprise me. I wondered if he was afraid. I had never known David to be scared of anything before but the game had changed. Now there were no rules.

'Are you still at the house?' I asked.

'No. The place is a mess. A twisted wreck. There's a hole in the front wall as big as a truck and the building is unstable. In any event, we're all too distraught to stay there. Ruth has just flown back from London and is staying at her parents' house. Celeste and I are bunking down with her folks. As you can imagine, everyone is in a state. It's chaotic.'

I commiserated with him and asked him how Ruth was holding up.

'Should I call her?'

'Not now. Give it a couple of days. She's heavily medicated and deeply tormented. She keeps blaming herself. Saying it's all her fault. That she should not have asked Marty to open the package. It's no use telling her that if she had been the one to tear the envelope, then she would now be dead. She just keeps punishing herself.'

There was not much more to say. We agreed to keep in touch on a daily basis and that I would fly home as soon as a date had been set for the funeral.

It was only once I had replaced the receiver that I began to cry. I wept uncontrollably. Karen tried to calm me but I was heartsick and inconsolable.

Marty was my dearest friend. No one had ever been so good to me. He was always patient and supportive even when I did the most awful things. All those bad years when I was drinking too much and having reckless affairs, he was never judgemental or critical, just sympathetic. I owed him everything. Marty opened up the cinematic world to me and gave me the confidence to follow through on my dreams. He was a gentle soul and I knew then that I would mourn his loss acutely. To this day, I still miss him terribly.

I remembered a time in the past when Marty and Ruth had come to visit me in London. I was still studying at film school but Cookie had disappeared and I was in despair. It was Christmas Eve when it unexpectedly began to snow. Remarkably, Ruth had never experienced snow before so this was a magical night for her. On a whim I suggested driving to Buckingham Palace which I imagined would be an enchanting sight in the storm.

The air was crisp, the snow crunching under our feet. Christmas lights and decorations colourfully sparkling and mysteriously shimmering as we piled into my old Rover 90 and glided down New King's Road heading towards the palace via the Chelsea Embankment. I could see moisture droplets glistening in Ruth's long mousy-brown hair. She looked ethereal and sublime. Like an angel. We were all in good spirits, Marty as talkative as ever.

Buckingham Palace was spellbinding, the snow beginning to come down in heavy flurries. We drove past it a few times, marvelling at its splendour. On a bend in the road, I turned rather sharply into Birdcage Walk and suddenly the car started to skid. I turned the wheel to avoid the curb but that only made it worse. The car veered left then skewed right and we ploughed into the pavement. The tyre made a huge thumping noise and burst as the Rover groaned to a halt.

While I changed the tyre, Marty and Ruth lay on the pavement staring up at the sky, the snow coming down in sheets. We had had a few drinks at home and they were a bit tipsy. In hindsight, I probably should not have been driving. Anyway they were thrilled by the storm and revelled in the blast of snow. They responded by making up lines of poetry to describe the wondrous event. Marty would start with a line and then Ruth supply an answering line. Like a musical call and response.

Marty: 'It's great to be in the snow.'

Ruth: 'But it looks different from below.'

Marty: 'It's cold and we need to go.'

Ruth: 'Only if James drives slow', etc., etc.

They kept this up while I was changing the spare wheel, getting more and more inventive as they went along. They were delighted by their new game which I found hilarious. We laughed and joked all the way back home to Parson's Green. A truly memorable and exquisite night. I will treasure it forever.

Back in Melbourne, my heartache and anguish was slowly giving way to indignation and fury. It seemed beyond outrageous that this kind of butchery was possible. It was nothing more than state-sponsored terrorism. What kind of barbarism allowed and encouraged the assassination of writers and artists? It was truly heinous.

It was at that moment that I decided I could no longer call South Africa my home. I could not continue living in a society where such violence against the innocents was sanctioned and condoned. From that moment on, I resolved to emigrate to Australia and try to make a new life for myself in a foreign land.

Two days later, David called me again to say that Marty's funeral was scheduled for a week later. With a very heavy heart, I booked a flight to Johannesburg. It was time to say goodbye to my beloved friend.

THE 1990'S

29

SARAH

I have decided to write a journal. The aim will be to record this process of finding my father. I want to tell how it all came about, the events leading up to it and what it has been for me meeting him and his family and everything I have discovered about them. Of course I will also have to touch on the more distant past and describe my life with my mother, growing up and all that.

But it won't be your usual *bildungsroman* as I don't have enough self-confidence to tackle something as ambitious as that. No, there won't be any great expectations and there's unlikely to be an account of my sentimental (or otherwise) education. This will be very different, looser, less structured, not methodical or precise. After all I haven't written anything for ages and ages, not since I was still in high school and that was nothing but a jillion ghastly poems full of adolescent yearning and romantic longing.

No, this will be more like a notebook and I will fill it with whatever comes to mind, random thoughts that occur to me, memories, even dreams (if I have any that are worth writing about) and everyday incidents. Ideas that pop into my head, digressions, anything and everything that occurs to me in fact.

I was thinking of calling it *The Bastard Diaries* as that seems a good name to me. And what about a subtitle too, something like *The Search for the Father I Never Knew.* Yes, I like that as it sounds rather grandiose and epic. It's probably a bit pretentious but then who's going to read it? Not too many people, only me and my friends and whoever I give the journal to. It's not for public consumption at all.

And although it's about me and my feelings, I realize that I will have to, occasionally, talk about larger issues, such as the historical events that were playing out on the world stage. Just to give it context and to explain how it all tied together. How my little story (which I thought was so big and significant, all-encompassing) was connected to the important developments taking place thousands of miles away.

Take, for instance, when Nelson Mandela was freed from prison. Who can forget that iconic picture? He and Winnie surrounded by hundreds of smiling faces, the space around them flattened out by the long focal length lens, the crowd ecstatic, the two central characters with their fists high above their heads in defiance. That image is indelibly and forever stamped on the brains of so many people.

It was obviously a colossal moment for my mother who was glued to the television, weeping copious tears. The newscasters talked about the potential for real change in South Africa, referring constantly to "talks about talks". They called it "a monumental milestone for the disenfranchised majority in the country". I was enthralled by the mythical saga that was unfolding and the effect this incident was having on my mum but I was too young to understand the full import of what was playing out on the screen.

Certainly I was oblivious to the effect that this could have upon me. Its connection to my own life seemed tenuous at best. Indeed, I could not have imagined that any of this would somehow bring me any closer to finding or, God forbid, meeting my father. It was not even on my radar.

But, from that moment on, my mother began to act a bit weirdly. Maybe that's too strong a word for it but her behaviour was definitely a little strange. She was much more secretive. She would lock herself alone in her bedroom for long periods. I could hear her talking in hushed tones to someone on the phone. Once it sounded like she was speaking another language but I couldn't be sure. She never told me what it was about and even though I put my ear to the door, all I could discern were agitated whispers.

As a result, this seemed to put even more pressure on my mother's already fragile relationship with my stepfather, Reg. Actually he wasn't my stepfather then as they hadn't got married yet. But from what I could see, they appeared to be fighting all the time. My mum would often stay out late, sometimes only coming home in the early hours of the morning, and Reg, who hadn't moved in with us yet, had his own place but was visiting less frequently.

Often they would be very cool to each other and on those occasions, I would try to stay out of their way. My mother could really turn on the ice if she was mad at you. Throughout my childhood she would put on the sulks if I had done something wrong. I love her dearly but I can tell you that you didn't want to be on the wrong side of her. She was scary and unnerving. As an old friend of hers once told me many years later: 'Cookie is a tough cookie.'

At other times Mum and Reg would lock themselves in the bedroom and I could hear muffled but angry voices. Sometimes there was shouting but I couldn't make out what they were saying. It was very distressing. I wondered if one of them was perhaps having an affair. Recently I came across this book about human sexuality (something that my mind was frequently turning to at that time) which said that we are all hardwired to be unfaithful. That it's in our genes. That we can't help it and shouldn't feel guilty about it. I wasn't sure about the writer's conclusions but I certainly worried about my mother's and Reg's fidelity. It was stressing me out terribly.

What was even more disconcerting, was that my mum was, at times, drinking very heavily. This was not something she had ever done when I was growing up. So I was worried.

One night, sometime later, we were watching the news and there was an interview with a man, Isaac Spiegel, who had just returned to South Africa. I had no idea who he was but the moment he came on screen, my mum suddenly sat bolt upright. It was obvious, even to me, that this was someone she knew. She listened very attentively to what he had to say. Spiegel said now that Mandela had been released from prison and that the African National Congress had been unbanned, he felt free to return "home" to South Africa. The journalist conducting the interview identified Spiegel as a resistance fighter and a leading figure in *uMkhonto we Sizwe* known in English as *The Spear of the Nation*.

I remembered that in one of Mr Jeffries's classes he had taught us about the Russian Revolution. He said that once the civil war was over, after the Bolsheviks had won, a large number of exiles returned to Russia. One of these was Lenin who would later head the new government. So I assumed that something similar was happening in South Africa and that many émigrés who had lived outside the country were now returning to their homeland. It never occurred to me that perhaps my mother was contemplating doing the same.

There was something very familiar about Isaac Spiegel. He reminded me of an actor I had seen in some old movies. There was the same charisma or animal magnetism, an aura of confidence and sincerity. He looked straight into the camera and seemed to be talking directly to you. I thought he looked principled and trustworthy. But I didn't like his big, ugly, yellow teeth.

His appearance on television had a profound effect on my mother and as soon as the news report was over, she abruptly jumped up, stormed over to her bedroom and shut the door. Soon after I could hear her once again talking on the phone. This time I was sure that she was definitely talking in a language I could not understand.

Some months later, there was another news story involving Isaac Spiegel. This time he was the victim of a botched assassination attempt on his life. He was in Port Elizabeth campaigning for the African National Congress and after the rally had finished, he was getting into his car. As he touched the door handle, there was a somewhat muted explosion and he was thrown into the air. Fortunately for him the bomb was faulty or poorly made and he was not too seriously hurt. He did, however, lose two fingers on his left hand.

This incident put my mother into a feverish state. She pulled at her short, bleached-blonde hair, smashed a fist into the living room door, screamed in frustration and drained a big glass of brandy. Then she was once again shrieking down the telephone.

To make matters worse, I was in what I call my "rebellious teenage years". If my mum made a request or started a conversation, I would give her the silent treatment. And if Reg asked me to do anything, I would be rude and cheeky to him. Often I lied to my mother about where I was going at night. Once I told her I was sleeping at my friend Jill's place but instead we went to a nightclub until three in the morning where we drank loads of cocktails and got high sniffing poppers. Jill and I had nowhere to sleep so we snuck into the ladies' loo at a fancy hotel and slept on the floor until the cleaners chucked us out in the morning.

It was not the happiest time of my life but I suppose the only godsend (if I can call it that) was that I was devouring books voraciously. I read in the library until it closed and then continued at home until all hours of the morning. With all the attention South Africa was getting in the press, I was curious to find out as much as I could about the place. I started reading all the usual stuff – Gordimer, Paton, Brink, Coetzee, etc. The essential canon. But I also found more obscure writers such as Ingrid Jonker, Olga Kirsch and Etienne Leroux. They all wrote in Afrikaans but I was able to find translations. I also read a book by Ruth Jacobson who my mum seemed to know. In addition to novels and poetry, I was intrigued by South African history and tried to find out as much as I could about the past. One book that fascinated me was *Commando* by Deneys Reitz.

If it hadn't been for this book, I probably would not have experienced the rather bizarre and curious incident that transpired. Reitz had written an autobiographical account of his own military exploits in the Boer War and I found myself captivated by that historical period. I wanted to discover more.

By chance I noticed that there was an Australian movie called *Four Horsemen* screening in the West End. The film dealt with Australia's participation in the Boer War which, up until that time, I was ignorant of. I invited a few friends to come with me but no one was interested so I went to the movie alone.

I was amazed to learn that Australia had sent more than 16,000 men to fight in the conflict. What surprised me even more was that all these men fought on the side of the British Government. In the past, convicts had been transported to the penal colony of Australia. Most prisoners had committed petty offences for which they were disproportionately punished and Britain had unceremoniously dumped them on a far-off continent. I would have thought there would have been some animosity towards the Empire. But not at all, instead there was blind allegiance. The way I saw it, the Boer War was the first anti-colonial war fought in Africa and I was astonished to discover that the Aussie Diggers were fighting not for independence but on behalf of the colonial power. It seemed ironic and sad to me.

In any event, when the film finished the credits began slowly rolling down the screen. I was sitting in the dark, indifferently watching when suddenly there was one of those moments. A moment when the arc of the universe seemed to turn in on itself. A synchronous moment. For there on the screen I read: Director of Photography – James Morrison.

I knew it could not be a coincidence. There could be no other James Morrison who was a cinematographer shooting a film about South Africa. It had to be my father. Besides I could intuit it. I had a kind of prescience with every part of my being anticipating him. My heart was bobbing around in my chest. Ahead of me I could discern two converging lines coming closer together. I knew that something monumental was happening, at once disquieting yet somehow soothing.

So now I knew that my father was in Australia. I also knew that it would not be difficult to track him down. I still very much wanted to contact him, talk to him but part of me felt apprehensive and fearful. There was so much I still did not know about what had happened between my parents. I decided that no matter how she reacted, I was going to have it out with my mother. This time she had to tell me the truth. She owed it to me.

Outside the cinema I stood in the middle of Leicester Square. It was late December and the streets were dense with shoppers and revellers. They seemed to be moving in slow motion while my mind raced. The sky was darkening, clouds turning black, the wind high and sharp. The weatherman had predicted a blizzard. I wanted it to envelop me. Carry me away. Under my breath I sang: 'Let it snow. Let it snow. Let it snow.'

30

SARAH

I really had to steel myself in order to talk to my mum. Before I spoke to her I could feel my body taut and quivering but there was only one thought motivating me. It was imperative that she understood how determined I was to find my father.

I told her about watching that movie and my conviction that he was the cinematographer.

'But I don't know why he's in Australia. I thought he lived in South Africa,' I said. 'Anyway, I want to find him and meet him. Get to know him. It's really important to me. You have always stopped me and he has always been a taboo subject but I need to know my father. So I hope you won't stand in my way.'

My mother then did something that I would never have predicted. She put her arms around me and pulled me to her, hugging me gently.

'Of course you need to know your father,' she said. 'I have always wanted that to happen. For both of you.' She was softly crying and I could feel tears welling up in my eyes. 'It's just always been too dangerous. But things have changed. The world has changed. It might be possible to contact him now. But first I have to tell you what happened and why I had to protect you like this.'

Then she told me the entire story. Beginning with her difficult childhood and then her university days and, of course, enrolling in the Russian class and everything that flowed from that. Joining the Melville Theatre Group, her sterling performances, meeting my dad, Antoine's death, moving to London and exposing Fat Bill Saunders as a spy. The whole enchilada as she knew it.

At times I found it difficult to follow the narrative. It appeared both outlandish and fantastical that these things had happened to my mother. They seemed to have befallen someone else. And in a way that was true because part of my mother *was* someone else. A person I did not know. A woman called Cookie.

I felt a similar detachment from my father. As much as my mum told me about him, I still did not know him. He seemed distant and remote. Unreachable to me and beyond my ken. I barely grasped him as a concept, my father, the man who begot me but I still could not get any sense of him as a person. He was floating out there somewhere and I needed to stretch out into the unknown and touch him.

But not yet. Still not yet. My mother persuaded me that we had to wait a little longer. At least until after the elections in South Africa. They were scheduled for late April, 1994. That was about four months away. I didn't know if I could handle the delay but, at least now I understood the rationale for waiting.

'I really expect the ANC to win easily,' my mum assured me. 'Then there will be a new government in control of the police and the army. Fat Bill will no longer have any power over me. He won't be able to hurt the ones I love. I'll be free of him at last. The stranglehold he's had on my life will be gone. And then you can get in contact with your dad.'

She put her arms around me and held me tight. I felt like I did when I was a little girl and it was only her and me. We were close again. The room was warm, the heat pumping out of the radiators. Over her shoulder I could see into the street below. The snow was coming down heavily blanketing the trees and parked cars. It was a huge storm but I felt secure. Within me I carried a sense of anticipation as if I was nearing the end of a long and arduous journey. I knew that I was closing in on my destination but it still seemed somehow far away and elusive.

'Your father is definitely in Australia,' my mother told me. 'I've talked to some of my contacts and apparently he moved there some years ago. He's living in Melbourne. I know you want to get in touch with him and I think you should. I know how important it is for you. But you need to approach this carefully. You need to be prepared for disappointment. He's got his own life now. And he does not even know about your existence. He might not necessarily want you disrupting his new life. It might be too difficult for him. And his new family. If he has one.'

Over the next few months I thought about this often. If my father had a new family, what would they make of me? Would they embrace me or push me away? Maybe they would see me as a threat to the endurance of their intimate relationships. And what about my father? Where would he stand on this? Would he want me in his life or would he just see me as an encumbrance? An unnecessary complication? A burden he could do without?

But dwelling on this was kind of academic and pointless for no matter what anyone else thought, I had to do it. I really had no choice. And so I waited while the world slowly turned.

Then, on 27 April, 1994 my mother, Reg and I watched the miracle of the first South African non-racial democratic election peacefully unfolding on television. In the weeks immediately preceding the vote-casting, this had seemed highly unlikely. There were gunfights on the streets of Johannesburg, political assassinations in Kwazulu Natal and the *Afrikaner Weerstandsbeweging* staged a blundering and abortive *coup* in one of the Bantustans. Even though the plot ended disastrously in bloodshed, the attempted overthrow, nevertheless, served to highlight the precariousness of the situation.

Remarkably then, the election progressed without incident. Everyone patiently stood in long queues waiting to cast their votes.

The day was momentous and historic. My mother wept as she watched it happening. I understood exactly how she felt but my own response was more nuanced. The significance of the events was not lost on me but I was carried along by my own personal concerns. This election meant that I could contact my dad. I could finally get to meet the man I had thought about for so long. I would be a bastard no longer.

Needless to say, the African National Congress won an enormous majority of the votes and was able to form a government with Nelson Mandela taking on the role of president and head of state. Many commentators predicted a new era of peace and prosperity. Of justice and fairness. Of emancipation and equal opportunity. Of tolerance and civility. It was a long time coming but a change, in the words of Sam Cooke, had finally come.

But that change was not going to happen overnight. There were many complex issues that had to be resolved before good governance could begin. Mandela's vision, as my mother explained it to me, was to create a unified country and heal the wounds of the past. How could that be possible when so much pain, sorrow and guilt defined the dreamscape? And what about justice? Surely the blood of the victims of *apartheid* cried out for reparation, for amends, if not for vengeance?

'This is only the beginning,' my mother told me. 'There is still much work to be done before we can contact your dad.' (*Not again* I thought.) 'The new government has agreed to establish a Commission to look into the crimes of the past and determine who must be prosecuted and who must be given amnesty. I don't know if that's going to take the form of court cases like the Nuremberg Tribunals or whether some other process will be put in place. We'll have to see. But in the meantime there are other practical considerations. For example, how is Mandela going to deal with the army? On the one side you have the freedom fighters who fought a war of insurgency and on the other side, you have the regular troops who opposed them in support of *apartheid*. How will the new government integrate those two groups of sworn enemies and convince them to work together?'

My mother was very animated. She was pacing up and down, puffing on a cigarette despite the fact that she had ostensibly given up smoking. 'And the same thing applies to the police. They will have to mix and merge officers from both the old and the new regime. It's going to be complicated and difficult to accomplish. And what will happen to Fat Bill? Will he be assimilated into the new police force or will he be prosecuted? Surely he will have to be tried for crimes against humanity? But we don't know yet what will happen. It's best we wait a little longer. See how it all pans out. I know you feel disappointed and cheated but it's for the best.'

I couldn't really argue with her logic. Of course she was right but I could not help feeling let down, crestfallen. It was not fair. I still had to wait even longer to know my father. It was so disheartening. I had waited all this time and now I had to delay our meeting still further.

At the time I felt beguiled but now, with the benefit of hindsight, I have come to realise just how advantageous that waiting period was to me. In the first place it enabled me to meet Jeff. If I had been in Australia, I would never have gone to that party in Islington where he bowled me over. Once again I am struck by the fact that small events, chance encounters, fortuitous or unforeseeable accidents can have such profound consequences. Someone once told me that in Alcoholics Anonymous meetings they call coincidence your Higher Power acting with anonymity.

In any event, that night, in Islington, it was complete happenstance that I was invited to the party. A couple of girlfriends and I were drinking at a pub in the City. One of my friends, Cathy, met a bloke she fancied and he persuaded all of us to come along to a party he intended going to.

It was a lovely spring night, the air crisp but without any chill. We caught a Tube to the Angel followed by a short walk. The party was in a second-floor flat and the living room was heaving with gyrating, swirling, dancing bodies. I managed to get a glass of white wine and then pushed my way through the crowd towards the large veranda that overlooked Islington Green.

'You look harassed,' a young man said.

'I'm just not good with crowds,' I replied.

And that's how I met Jeff. At the time I thought he was nice looking. (I still do.) Dark shoulder-length hair combed back away from his forehead. Deep blue sincere eyes in a chiselled face. All cheekbones and hard lines in a kind of rough, unfinished way as if the sculptor was in a hurry. Very laid back. I remember he wore a denim shirt, black cords and a charcoal windbreaker. As I said earlier, he bowled me over. It must have been a fast ball because I never saw it coming.

One thing that has always impressed me about Jeff is how empathic he is. No matter what mood I'm in, he always spots it straight away and acts accordingly. In the time we have been together he has helped me to gain confidence and self-assurance. I suppose that I've always had a bit of a chip on my shoulder because of being a bastard and all but these days I'm not as brash as I used to be. I'm more relaxed and serene. Not so uptight.

Being with Jeff has definitely made me more mature. I'm more rounded now and sure of my place in the world. And I'm more patient. Certainly having Jeff around made the waiting game of contacting my father so much easier to endure though I did, occasionally, still chomp at the bit.

But eventually we got the news that we had been waiting for so long. Fat Bill had resigned from the police force and had applied for amnesty under the newly established Truth and Reconciliation Commission. There were no longer any obstacles in my path. I was free to write to my dad.

My mother and I had tracked him down and discovered that he was teaching at the Melbourne Film School. So early in February 1997, with my heart in my mouth, I wrote him that fateful email. It took me some time to figure out what to say. In the end I kept it as simple as I could:

> I'm sorry to bother you but I'm trying to contact the James Morrison who studied at Wits University and the London Film School in the seventies. Is that, by any chance, you?
>
> Regards,
> Sarah Basinger

So now I have heard back from my father and I have a new journey ahead of me. I face a new challenge, one that I feel hopelessly unqualified for. Nothing in my life has prepared me for this. I feel clumsy and inadequate. Out of my depth. I have no way of knowing how I will deal with it or how I will feel. For I am flying to Melbourne, Australia (where my father now lives) to meet him. To that *terra australis incognita*. I am both joyous and anxious. I want him to love me. I want to be the daughter he can be proud of. But I know I have so little control over what will come to pass. All I can do is let it happen. Let it be.

31

FAT BILL

Never one to let the grass grow under his feet, Fat Bill had been making plans for years. He knew that a day of reckoning was coming and he wanted to be prepared for it. *These idiots are not going to catch me napping,* he thought. *No arsehole is going to put me in prison. I was just doing my job and now these cunts will try and prosecute me. That's not going to happen. Fuck them! I'll make sure that I'm safe. Inviolable. I'm going to walk away from this unscathed.*

Throughout the long process of negotiations between the *apartheid* government and the African National Congress, it had been apparent to Fat Bill that once a new government came into power, there would be retribution. The victims of human rights abuses would want justice. They would demand that the perpetrators of violence against humankind be punished. And so they would have him in their sights. They would want to take him down. And he was not going to let that happen. He was not ready for defeat, privation or an ANC jail.

Almost immediately after the elections, one of the first actions the new regime took to address the crimes of the past was the creation of the Truth and Reconciliation Commission (TRC). This body was given the power to grant amnesty, under certain circumstances, to the perpetrators of gross human rights violations such as murder, abduction and torture. In an attempt to recover the truth, anyone applying for amnesty would be required to give testimony in public.

The commission was a controversial body. Many felt that those guilty of gross human rights violations should be charged in a court of law and tried just as Nazi felons had been in the Nuremberg Tribunals. Surely this, they argued, was the only way to deal with such horrific acts against humanity. But that's not what was negotiated. That's not the deal that was entered into by both sides. The ANC could only persuade the previous government and its security forces to cooperate in free elections if they offered amnesty in exchange for the honest truth about the crimes of the past. Fat Bill realized that the process was flawed from the outset. He saw an opportunity to circumvent the system, to pick up the ball and run. To take the gap.

Bill had a very powerful tool at his disposal – blackmail. Years before negotiations and talks even began, he had been amassing incriminating information about his enemies and putting together dossiers that could be used to extort them. This was relatively easy to carry out as he had all the resources of the state security system at his disposal.

In his office at the Randburg Police Station, he asked Jakob "Mamba" Fourie to come and see him.

'Close the door and sit down,' Fat Bill commanded. 'I've got a job for you. A very important job. But this must be done carefully and prudently. I don't want too many people knowing about it.'

'*Ja* sir. I understand. I know when to be discreet.'

'That's why I picked you, Mamba. This is a very special assignment. Not one I would give to a cokehead like Steenkamp. I need someone I can trust.'

'You can depend upon me, sir,' Fourie obsequiously replied.

He was a ferret-faced man, very slender and small-boned. His short dark hair was heavily pomaded and combed forward. He had a nervous twitch in his neck which he struggled to keep under control. This had given rise to his nickname as he often appeared to be jolting forward like a striking snake. Despite this affliction, he was a cool customer who was never known to lose his temper. He kept to himself, a cautious and wary loner. Perfect for the task at hand.

'I want you to go to London. Stay there for as long as it takes but I want you to get the information I need.' Fat Bill smiled sardonically, his face flushed and dissolute. 'Your job is to get as much dirt as you can on the ANC cadre operating out of England. Anything incriminating or compromising on any of them. If one of them likes fucking little boys, I want to know about it. Any bad habits like drugs or alcohol, you let me know. Anything in their past, like shoplifting or assault, whatever. Someone who regularly visits prostitutes, I want his name. And get photos. The more lurid and mortifying the better. Anything kinky or sensational.'

'What resources will I have?' Fourie asked.

'Whatever you need. Money's no object. I have some contacts there. Guys I used in the past. Surveillance experts. They've got all the right gear to ensure you get what you need – taped conversations, intimate photos, video recordings, the lot. I'll put you in touch with them. They're real professionals.'

'I suppose you want a dossier on each subject?'

'Absolutely,' Bill said. 'But only go for the kingpins, not the small fry. See what you can get on Duma Mokoena and Bambata wa Luruli. Also Precious Selinda. I've heard she likes it in the *tokhis*. And you need to concentrate on getting some shit on "Oom" Spiegel. As much dirt on him as you can. He's the head honcho.'

Fat Bill expanded his blackmail schemes even further, grilling another underling, Danie Hofmeyr. He looked like your typical Afrikaans civil servant – thin moustache, bifocal spectacles, short back and sides haircut, trousers high on the waist, polished brown shoes and a grovelling manner.

'Who's our man in Angola?' Fat Bill demanded. 'Who have we got that's infiltrated the ANC camps there?'

'Well sir,' Hofmeyr purred in his oily submissive voice, 'the best man we have in the field is Mossie Ngubane.'

'Mossie! That fucker! Who gives himself a bird's name? Sparrow. What kind of a nickname is that? I heard he was unreliable and an alcoholic.'

'I believe it's his real name, sir. It's on his birth certificate.'

'What about his drinking?' Bill asked.

'I believe it's under control, sir.' Despite his brown-nosing manner, Hofmeyr stood his ground. The man had guts. 'In any event, he's an excellent spy. One of our best. He has ingratiated himself with the camp commander, Tim Goniwe. All reports indicate that he is, as they say, "in like Flynn". He gives us fine grained espionage communiqués. I can personally vouch for him.'

'Well he better be fucken good. And circumspect. Because I have an important role for him. I want him to discover and report back to us, or rather to me personally, on any human rights abuses that might take place in any of the ANC camps. Any torturing of prisoners, any abuse of villagers, any coercion to make people take up arms against their will. Anything that contravenes the Geneva Convention. In fact, anything that might present the ANC in a bad light if it became public knowledge.'

'I'll brief him accordingly, sir.'

'You do that,' Bill said smiling, 'and tell him it's of vital importance. A priority. And say if he does this for me, he can expect a special reward. Naturally the same goes for you. I'll make sure you get a huge bonus.'

It was not only his enemies that Fat Bill got compromising information on. He concocted intimate and incriminating dossiers on all his superior officers as well as senior figures in the *apartheid* regime.

He had a large file on the Minister of Police, Jaap Geldenhuys, that included confidential memos ordering the torture of political prisoners. Major-General Casparus Vorster, Fat Bill ascertained, had a penchant for young, under-age girls and possessed a library of child pornographic photos. Some of these featured Vorster himself indulging in pedophilic sports.

There was an enormous amount of evidence of senior policemen participating in torture. If a black man did not crack under violent interrogation, the police afforded him a degree of respect. But if a female detainee refused to break, this fuelled the torturers' anger. They would have to humiliate her, ensure that the *kaffermeid* knew her place. This usually involved violent rape, coerced oral sex, sodomy and the insertion of foreign objects into the vagina. Fat Bill was able to acquire considerable video evidence of these actions by high-ranking policemen.

He even had a compromising report on his former mentor, Colonel Piet "Klopper" van Wyk. This included documentary evidence implicating the colonel in ordering a certain comrade, Jake Khutwane, to be water-boarded. And then, when Khutwane accidentally died under interrogation, van Wyk ordered his body to be thrown into the crocodile-infested Komati River.

Of course, Fat Bill was himself guilty of similar atrocities. He had participated in torture, ordered assassinations and sent parcel bombs to perceived enemies. In all of these, he had acted with impunity. As a consequence, he knew he would be vulnerable when a new regime came into power. He was also cynical enough to realise that his colleagues would be happy to throw him under the bus if it meant saving themselves. So the dossiers he obtained were an effective insurance policy. A future safeguard for when the bad times finally came. And come they would as surely as the turning of the earth.

Bring it on, he thought. *I'm ready for you fuckers. All of you. Suck my big ugly dick!*

213

32

SARAH

'Gang-gang cockatoos,' said Olivia.

The birds weren't particularly attractive being mostly grey and non-descript looking but they certainly were noisy, their calls shrill and piercing like a rusty gate opening.

'Some people think their cries sound like a cork being pulled from a wine bottle,' she explained.

'In that case, I'll stick to screw tops,' I quipped, irritated by the horrible squawking.

All the time I was in Australia I found the bird noises irksome and occasionally menacing, even eerie. English bird calls, on the other hand, are bucolic and soothing, almost serene. But then, on that first visit, everything sounded louder and more hostile to me than back home. It did, however, smell similar, not as strange as other places I've been. In some cities, especially Asian ones, there is a peculiar odour that seems to hang in the air and pollute the atmosphere. It's not necessarily a foul stench but it is very distinctive and singular. An acrid broiling smell combined with gassy carbon fumes and the redolent whiff of garlic-infused cooking oils. Melbourne was not like that though. It smelled fine. Normal. Just like London in fact.

There were four of us, my father, my father's wife (or do I call Karen my stepmother?), Olivia and me. Oh, and their dog Danny. We were on the beach in Black Rock less than a mile from where they lived. A large flock of these cockatoos had just flown overhead and my half-sister was identifying them.

It was quite uncanny how much Olivia and I resembled each other – the same plump cheeks, broad foreheads, ski-jump noses. Two days before, just after I arrived, we did this whole sister bonding thing of comparing bodies – same height, exactly 168 centimetres barefoot, standing back to back; similar shaped and sized boobs, the left one bigger than the right, our nipples pointing up; each with an ugly patch of *keratosis pilaris* on our upper left arms. Trying on each other's glasses we discovered that we had the same astigmatism, could see very well thank you very much. The only obvious difference was the colour of our hair, Olivia a brunette and me blonde.

I had read about twins who had been separated from birth and then when they met twenty years later, they discovered how much alike they were – parting their hair the same way, a taste for similar foods, weird habits they shared. It was like that with Olivia and me. Neither of us had grown up with a sibling, we had each assumed we were an "only child" and now it was exciting to discover I had a sister, especially one I liked so much.

'You don't get so many cockatoos here,' she was saying. 'When we holidayed at the Gold Coast they were all over the place. Parakeets and parrots too. With bright colours. Do you know what the collective noun for parrots is?'

'No, what is it?'

'A pandemonium of parrots. Isn't that good?'

'Wonderful,' I replied. 'So descriptive and also alliterative.'

'Once, on the beach in Queensland, we saw a whole chatter of budgerigars,' Olivia said. 'I think that's what it's called. Either that or flock. Anyway there were thousands of them swarming all over. The sky was pitch black with budgerigars.'

I had never heard anyone call them that before. Budgerigars. To me, they were always just budgies. And they never flew around. They were only in cages, people kept them as pets.

As a child I'd never had any pets of my own. Not even a budgie. We lived in this tiny flat in south London and it just wasn't practical. I remember that once, in Mr Jeffries's class, we had to do a little presentation where we described our family. Many of the other kids had large extended consanguineous networks – a mother and father, grandparents, aunties and uncles, numerous cousins. They gave detailed accounts of their kinship ties while telling little anecdotes about their favourite relatives. ('Uncle Jack spends every Saturday fixing his Corolla. Then on Sundays he takes us for a drive in the country.') There were even stories involving their pets. ('Rover my dog sleeps all day. When we take him to the park he sniffs other dogs' bums.') That one got a laugh.

But I had nothing to say. No stories of my tribe to tell. It was just my mum and me. (This was before Reg came into our lives.) But then I didn't even have a dog or cat. There was nobody else in our family. Or nobody that I knew. So I wouldn't have been able to say anything. Fortunately, I had told Mr Jeffries beforehand and he let me make up a story about an imaginary family who lived far, far away. There were lots of kids in my pretend family. They always played together and had heaps of fun. The mum was plump and baked all day long. The father could do magical tricks, pull rabbits out of hats, turn water into wine (I got that from the Bible), make bad people disappear and even travel back in time.

And now here I was with my real father. I felt like I was the magician conjuring him out of my imagination, my dreams. But I was just a minor sorcerer with very limited powers. There was so little I was capable of and I certainly could not make bad people disappear or get us to travel back in time. If only I could!

Nevertheless, despite my limited abilities, I had made all this happen. Without me and the actions I had taken none of us would be here together at this moment. My interference had brought us to this point, to this family gathering. I was acutely conscious of the fact that I had disturbed the tranquillity or at least the certainty of their lives. The email I had written to James, my father, had changed everything for these three people. It was like I had carelessly tossed a stone into a pond expecting a small splash and tiny ripples but instead I had unleashed a tsunami of consequences that I had not anticipated.

It reminded me of one of those sci-fi television series where there was this kind of time-warp gate. If you entered it, you went into another dimension or some other planet in a faraway galaxy. The world you entered was one just like our own, a mirror image of it but different in one minor aspect. One small, almost insignificant incident had changed, one little decision had been made that altered everything, made the worlds diverge, set them on disparate courses.

So it seemed with us, with my father and me. If just one little event could have changed, it would all have been different. If my mother had not read that document in Fat Bill's flat, if she had kept silent and not told the ANC about it, if she had already confided to my dad that she was pregnant, if they had gone on holiday a week earlier, if the weather had changed... If any of these were otherwise, we would have lived contrasting lives. It would have been like night and day for all of us.

But it was useless to speculate. The dice had been tossed long ago, the dye cast, the paths immutable. It seemed to me that I was like a character in some real life *film noir,* and that the forces that had brought this into being, that had predetermined my life, were much larger than me. There was nothing I could do to change things. Regret was pointless, self-indulgent, and the kind of "what if" speculation I was entertaining entirely misplaced. It was what it was. Things were as they were. There was no alternative universe. Accept and move on, I told myself.

Nevertheless, I was struggling to comprehend the tactile reality of where I was, on this beach in Australia. It still felt strange and alien. Not just because of the birds. It was everything. The trees, the

217

landscape, the houses all looked different. Similar but not quite the same as home. A fake and noisy England.

For one anxious moment, when the plane landed at Melbourne Airport, I had panicked and wished that I was still back in London. I even sent Jeff, my boyfriend, a text message saying: "Arrived safely but having cold feet. If I could turn around and fly back home, I would." Part of me meant it, part of me was resisting this scary and inevitable meeting with my father. But, of course, another part of me looked forward to it. Embraced the idea. This is what I'd always hoped for, what I'd dreamed about throughout my childhood and adolescence. But which had been so long in coming.

As I waited for my luggage to appear on the carousal I tried to steel myself for this fateful rendezvous. Would I be disappointed? *Of course,* I thought. *You're bound to be. Nothing can live up to your expectations and dreams. Try and set your sights lower. Try not to let your imagination run wild. Try to be realistic.*

But what was "realistic" under these circumstances? What could possibly qualify as normal behaviour? I had nothing to guide me and no way of knowing so I allowed my lips to shape themselves into a tight smile as I collected my suitcase and made my way towards the customs gate.

Walking through the sliding doors of the arrivals hall I was acutely conscious of all the people waiting there. I could feel my smile forced and stiff as I anxiously scanned the faces looking for my father. But he was nowhere to be seen. *What if he's not coming?* I thought. *What if he's forgotten? What if he's changed his mind and has decided he doesn't want to meet me? What if this is just some cruel hoax?* All these kinds of irrational, jittery thoughts jumped wildly into my head.

I fumbled my way past a few people feeling embarrassed and confused. I had travelled all this way, invested so much energy into the trip and had imagined all kinds of airport scenarios but not this. A no-show! I pulled out my phone and sent a text to Jeff: "He's not here!" Fortunately, he replied straight back: "Don't panic. He's probably caught up in traffic."

Then all at once they were all there in front of me. My alternative family. I heard my father quietly calling out my name.

'Sarah. Sarah.'

Then he put his arms around me.

We both just held each other, saying nothing. I had imagined this moment so many times in the past and wondered what it would be like being held by my father. And now that it was happening it did not seem real. I had always thought that I would burst into tears but I was dry-eyed. I felt strangely detached as if I was watching this happen to someone else, a third party. My father, however, was gently weeping. Then he stood aside, wiping his eyes as the two other women in his life, Karen and Olivia, hugged me.

The drive from the airport was a little strained. Both my father and Olivia were very quiet while Karen tried to make small talk. I chatted along emptily as I tend to do in situations like this when I am in unfamiliar territory and feeling uncomfortable. I don't remember exactly what we talked about but it was pretty banal. I think the conversation was mostly about the flight, the English weather, what my boyfriend was doing, if I planned on talking to him soon. That kind of thing.

Their house in Black Rock was a typical Australian bungalow, exactly what I had expected from watching episodes of *Neighbours*. Inside it was very tastefully furnished, the floors adorned with brightly coloured kilims, the walls covered with quirky artwork, polished yellow wood furniture and heaps of African artefacts and bric-a-brac strewn all over the place.

My father showed me into the spare room where a sofa bed had been made up for me.

'I hope you'll be comfortable here. You can share Olivia's bathroom. Sorry the room's a bit small but we weren't expecting a new daughter.' He smiled. 'Actually the whole house is a bit on the small side. We used to have a bigger place but then we decided to downsize now that we're getting older… Are you tired? You must be exhausted after the long flight. Would you like to sleep? Don't think you have to stand on ceremony with us. If you want to sleep, just close the door. We won't disturb you.'

'No, I feel wide awake actually. I'm too excited to sleep right now.'

'Would you like some tea? Oh, I forgot you told me you don't drink tea. Only coffee. I'll make some now.'

'That would be lovely.' I smiled and he gave me a small hug before leading down the passageway into the kitchen.

He put water on to boil and then started rummaging around one of the cupboards.

'What kind of coffee would you like? I've got quite a few. There's a strong Arabica, a mild Viennese blend, some Kenyan stuff. When you wrote and told me you liked coffee I bought some of this Vietnamese weasel coffee for you to try. It's like civet coffee, the weasels or civet cats eat the coffee beans and then poo it out. The farmers then collect half-digested beans, wash it and process it. I know it sounds gross but it's supposed to really enhance the flavour of the coffee. The digestion process somehow changes the chemical structure of the beans. Makes the coffee taste smoother… Do you want to try it?'

'Sure. I'm up for anything,' I said.

He smiled, 'That's my girl.'

That whole first day I felt like I was constantly under scrutiny, like some kind of museum exhibit. The three of them seemed to watch and analyse everything I did – how I drank my coffee, what I said, how I dressed and moved. Everything. It felt like I was an alien who had landed on another planet. They were all warm and friendly but they never stopped inspecting and dissecting me. I know what they were looking for. They wanted to see if they could find my father in me. They wanted to see if genes counted. They were looking for signs of James's daughter.

And now, on the beach, after the cockatoos had flown past us,

Olivia and Karen walked ahead chasing after Danny the dog and leaving my father and me together. It was probably choreographed that way, giving us an opportunity to talk and bond.

So we talked. About everything but mostly the past. There was no awkwardness between us and I felt I could be completely candid with him. It seemed to me as if we had always known each other and we had that easy familiarity that you only get with old friends.

Ever since arriving here I could feel my love for him growing with every passing moment. I had steeled myself for being disappointed in my father but that was not at all how it was panning out. Rather what I felt was this intense and overwhelming affection. It was very strange and I'm not sure I can accurately describe it. I suppose it was a passion, almost a rapture, like those early weeks of idolization you feel when you are first in love. Most peculiar when these emotions are directed towards your father.

I told him about my life and how things had been between my mother and me. He asked me dozens of questions and I replied as frankly as I could but there were some answers I did not know. So I could not tell him everything.

Of course he wanted to know if I had been happy, if I had suffered any hardship or deprivation. I thought about this carefully. Mostly I had experienced a happy childhood but there were times when I had felt isolated and alone. As a youngster I had also been cruelly teased and picked on because of my bastardy, my questionable origins.

I particularly remember one time when my mother and I were in France. There was some kind of party or celebration, I'm not sure what for. It might have been someone's birthday or wedding or some such commemorative occasion but there were a lot of people there and the adults and children were kept separate. I was very young, about six or seven years old and I hardly knew any of the other kids. I also had a rather limited competence with the French language so at first I did not understand what the children were saying to me but soon it became obvious that they wanted to know where my father was and why I didn't have one.

'Is your mother a slut?' an older boy asked. I did not know what to say. It was not a word I knew but I was acutely aware that it was an insult and that they saw me as different from them because I did not have a father. 'Where is he?' they kept asking. 'Why don't you know who your father is? Is he in jail? Is he a thief?'

They crowded around me, harassing and pushing me, asking endless questions that I could not answer. I remember my throat burning, my eyes filling with tears and then weeping copiously. Eventually one of the older children came over, told them to stop, took my hand and led me away. It is a minor event but the pain it caused has never left me.

'It's been fine. I've had a good life,' I told him, 'but sometimes it was hard, you know. Hard not having a father.'

We walked quietly along the beach, then he gently put his arm around my shoulders and kissed me lightly on the top of my head.

'Well, you have one now,' he whispered.

Finally all the suppressed fear and pain and anxiety and happiness I had kept tightly packed inside burst out and I cried like a child would into my dad's chest while he hugged me and soothed me and finally things were as they should always have been.

33

SARAH

'I can't believe this,' my mother said. 'It's so ugly! Nothing like I remember. All these high walls and electric fences! Dreadful!'

We were driving through the streets of Johannesburg. My mother's friend, David, was at the wheel and his wife, Celeste, in the passenger seat next to him. Mum and I were in the back and she was bemoaning the fact that the city had changed dramatically since she had last been here. Of course, that was more than twenty years earlier and I imagine she was seeing the past through rose-coloured glasses, her memory deceiving her, nostalgia altering her perception.

Nevertheless, I had to agree. From the little I could make out, the suburbs seemed dreary. Houses were hidden behind high walls, electric fences and barbed wire enclosures. Some of the streets were closed off to traffic and private security guards policed the area. At all the traffic lights, a mob of young black men would pounce on the car offering to clean the windscreen or attempting to sell us cell phone covers, ripped off CDs or other such junk.

I was expecting it to be more like Australia which I had visited after contacting my father. But it was nothing like that. In

Johannesburg, the streets were dirty and filled with litter. There were lots of beggars and on every corner we saw vendors with broken-down wooden tables selling over-ripe fruit and stunted vegetables, while under-nourished goats stood patiently tethered to the stands. The city had a run-down feel to everything as if it had seen better days. The Third World seemed to be encroaching on the first, colonizing it.

'Unfortunately we are suffering from a violent crime epidemic,' David said. 'As you can see, people have had to barricade themselves into their homes to protect their families. Addressing this crime spree has not been a priority for the new government. They see it as another remnant of *apartheid*. The system created huge disparities between rich and poor and as a consequence, robbery and armed home invasions are almost inevitable. So it's not their problem.'

'It's a little better than it was a couple of years ago,' Celeste said. 'But we still have about thirty carjacks a day. You just have to be careful. Be vigilant and wary. Don't go out alone at night. And don't do anything stupid.'

'I've noticed that nobody seems to park their cars on the street. Is that not a good thing to do?' I asked.

'Never do that,' Celeste said. 'If you visit someone they'll have electric gates and they'll open them for you and let you in once you call in advance on your cell. And if you go shopping, make sure it's at a mall with underground parking and security protection. It's not worthwhile taking chances here as most crimes include some kind of violence. Life is cheap and there are too many illegal guns around.'

'When I visited my dad in Melbourne, crime didn't seem to be a problem at all,' I said. 'My half-sister and I caught trains into the city centre and went to clubs until early in the morning. All young people in Australia seem to do it. They take personal safety for granted.'

'Sarah loves Australia,' my mother said. 'And she and her half-sister, Olivia, get along so well. They really adore each other. I'm very pleased that they're so close.'

I was continually taken aback when my mother spoke. From the moment we landed in South Africa and were met by her old friends at the airport, she started to speak like them, with an Afrikaans accent. It was most disconcerting. Her voice was the same but her pronunciation and inflections were completely different. She no longer sounded like my mum. She seemed subtly altered, changed into someone I did not know. Someone that everyone called Cookie.

I'm starting to get used to it now. This new person. But that first night we were here, it was quite confusing. We were staying with David and Celeste at their new house in Parkview. My mum and I were in the garden cottage which I was told had been converted from the old servants' quarters. It was very spacious and looked out onto the sparkling swimming pool. The grounds were surrounded by high brick walls protected by the ubiquitous electric fence. It was all very well maintained, manicured lawns, flowered garden beds and a large jacaranda tree in full purple bloom.

David and Celeste threw a party in my mother's honour. Dozens of people came, mostly friends from her past. They all wanted to see the stranger they once knew so well. I suppose for many of them, she was a curiosity. Someone who had lived underground for so long, hidden in plain sight. And now she was back and they wanted to meet her. This somewhat exotic creature. Cookie. My mother.

I was surprised by just how many people attended the party. Numerous cars were parked down Roscommon Road and David had hired security guards to protect his guests and their vehicles. Everyone seemed to know my mum or to have heard about her. It never occurred to me that she might be so notorious.

Many of her friends were members of the Melville Theatre Group and I met them all. There was Churchill Khumalo, Dorothy

Makhene, and Zakes Nyeki. Apparently they had acted with my mum in a famous play called *Sunday's Journey* which was soon to have a revival.

'You should come and act in the revival with us,' Churchill said to my mum. 'You're much closer in age now to the character you played then. I bet you can still do the accent.'

'*Vos m'iz geveynt af der yugent, azoy tut men af der elter,*' my mother said.

'Is that Yiddish? What the hell does it mean?' Churchill asked.

'It means the habits we develop when we are young, are what we continue with in old age.'

Everyone laughed. A few applauded. Even though I'm used to her outlandish revelations, I must admit, the Yiddish took me by surprise. How on earth did she know that? But then, of course, I recalled her eerie memory.

The party was mostly outdoors around the pool but it spilled inside to the lounge and dining room. Outside, there was a big charcoal barbecue attended to by a chef who threw massive pieces of steak and large coils of the local sausage, *boerewors* on the hot coals. It was my first *braaivleis*, a cultural eye-opener. A number of servants discreetly placed salads onto the dining room table and carried away dirty plates and glasses to be washed in the kitchen. Everybody, including the black guests, ignored them or took them for granted but, for me, domestic servants seemed both anachronistic and odd.

Later in the evening I met Ruth Jacobson and Rory Callaghan, friends of my mother who had been in her Russian class. I thought Ruth was utterly charming and told her how much I admired her novels.

'Thank you,' she said. 'And how are you finding South Africa? Confronting?'

'It's probably too early for me to say, but based on what I have seen – yes, I suppose confronting would describe it. Certainly different from what I expected.'

'How so?' she asked.

'Well I had certain expectations about the place. From what my mother told me and reading your novels and other books,' I said. 'But I thought it would be more like Australia where my dad lives.'

Ruth was smiling, her face calm but she seemed to be looking inwards, seeing something deep and personal, a memory in her head.

'How is dear James? I miss him so much,' she said tenderly.

'He's great. I miss him too. All the time.'

Just then my mother joined us and swept Ruth away for a *tête-à-tête* and I was left alone with Rory. I felt a little shy and somewhat in awe of him. I knew that he had been to prison for many years because of his political convictions.

'My mum tells me that you're in the new government?' I asked.

'That's right,' he said. 'It sounds more important than it is. I actually work for the Minister of Education, Isaac Spiegel. Advising him. But he does not always listen to me or take my advice,' Rory said smiling.

I remembered the man I had seen on television. The one who looked like Karl Malden, the actor. Only with the big, yellow teeth.

'Didn't someone try to assassinate him?'

'That's the one,' Rory said.

'I believe my mum is hoping to make an appointment to meet with him.'

'I'll try and set it up,' said Rory. 'He's pretty busy at the moment but I'm sure he'll make time to see Cookie. She'll have to come to his office in Pretoria though. What does she want to see him about, if you don't mind me asking?'

Just beyond the pool, the dappled shadows of the jacaranda falling on them, I could see my mother and Ruth talking. They held each other's hands and then my mum leaned forward and the two women embraced affectionately.

'She knew Mr Spiegel in London. In the seventies. I believe my mum wants to talk to him about her testimony. At the Truth and Reconciliation Commission. She wants some advice about what to say and what not to say,' I said. 'Giving evidence against William Saunders, Fat Bill, is very important to her. She feels like he destroyed her life and now she wants to ensure he gets the punishment he deserves. Not only for what he did to her but what he did to others. Even my life was affected by it.'

'The commission's not about vengeance,' Rory said. 'It's about reparation not retaliation. The aim is to achieve *ubuntu*.'

'I understand fully. My mum does not want revenge. She wants justice.'

'Cookie must be careful about her expectations and what the commission can actually do,' Rory said thoughtfully and carefully. 'You should tell your mother not to get her hopes up. Things don't always work out the way they're supposed to.'

His words sent a chill through me. I suddenly experienced a deep sense of foreboding. It was most disturbing. We had come all this way, gone through all this upheaval. Was it all in vain? Whatever happened I did not want my mum to be hurt.

Rory looked straight into my eyes. I thought he wanted to tell me something. I was sure he was going say something more. I just didn't know what it was.

But then some other people joined us and the spell was broken.

34

Now we were on our way to Pretoria to meet with the minister, the Hon. Isaac Spiegel. The man everyone called "Oom" or "Uncle". Was it a nickname? A term of respect? No one seemed to know and, consequently, I never found out.

David had lent Mum one of his cars and she was driving fast and confidently. I was surprised how well she knew her way around Johannesburg despite the fact that the city must have changed a lot since she had last lived there.

Once we had left the suburbs behind, Mum belted down a wide freeway. It was the rainy season and the grass was shamrock green, the hills or *koppies* shimmering in the distance, the rest of the land flat and savannah-like. Apparently this was typical Highveld scenery. Fairly drab if you asked me but my mum loved it. Made her feel alive and vital she said.

Soon we passed the iconic Voortrekker Monument. From the outside I thought it looked rather hideous but a perverse side of me wanted to visit, see what it looked like inside. I had read that it was a strange neo-fascist building and that on a certain day, 16 December, light would shine through a little hole in the domed roof and strike a memorial plaque bearing words that read: "*Ons vir Jou, Suid-Afrika*" ("Us for You, South Africa"). According to my research, the ray of light was supposed to symbolize God's blessing on the Voortrekkers and commemorate both their victory over the Zulu and the covenant that they made with God to keep that day forever holy.

The Voortrekkers had climbed in their oxen-driven wagons and begun their perilous journey to escape oppression and what they saw as a tyrannical regime. In a way they were idealists who believed their God would grant them truth and justice. And, as we headed north, I wondered if it was deeply ironic or completely appropriate that we too were on a pilgrimage which we hoped would end in righteous reparation for the evil deeds of the past.

Once in Pretoria, we drove down Church Street. Some years later it would have its name changed to Stanza Bopape Street after a hero of the Struggle who had been tortured and killed at the notorious John Vorster Square. A little further along, we came up to the front of the Union Buildings, very imposing structures designed (like the South African Embassy in London) by Sir Herbert Baker. The main edifice had a semi-circular shape, with two wings at the sides representing the union of a formerly divided people.

We were searched and scanned by security and then led down a long corridor where Rory was waiting to welcome us. He led us into Isaac Spiegel's grandiose office. The great man came out from behind his enormous oak desk and took my mother's hand in both of his.

'Cookie, so good to see you after all these years. You are looking well. The blonde hair suits you.'

His whole manner was ultra-sincere. He looked directly at both of us and smiled artlessly, his demeanour warmly avuncular. He seemed to live inside himself, in a place that was beyond the everyday scuffle.

'And this must be your lovely daughter, Sarah,' he said taking my hand. 'I have heard so many good things about you.'

'As have I about you,' I said.

He smiled warmly and turned to Rory. 'Thanks, Callaghan, I'll take it from here.'

Rory said goodbye to us and left the room discreetly closing the door behind him. The minister then led us over to a small table, pulling out a chair for my mother. We sat and Spiegel offered us tea.

'I'll be mum,' he said fiddling with the teapot and cups. With his crippled hand he struggled a bit but I thought it would be rude to offer help. Then, after he had completed the pouring ritual, it was straight down to business.

'So, Cookie, after everything you've done for us, what can I do for you?' he asked in that disarming manner of his.

'Well, as you probably know,' my mother began, 'I've come here to take part in the Truth and Reconciliation Commission and to give evidence against William "Fat Bill" Saunders. It's also the first time I've been able to come back to South Africa for many years, so I've brought my daughter here to let her see my homeland and meet some of my old friends as well as her family members that she never even knew existed.'

I thought my mum was handling this graciously and strategically. She was gently reminding Spiegel of the hardships she had endured in order to assist the new government's cause. He watched her carefully, nodding sympathetically.

'We are all deeply grateful for sacrifices you made. I wish there was some way to repay you.'

'I'm not expecting any recompense,' my mum said. 'I knew what I was getting into when I gave you that information about Fat Bill. All I'm hoping for is to see justice done.'

Once again Spiegel nodded sensitively. Despite his apparent vitality, I noticed a thinness in his face, his body angular and emaciated. His eyes pinched, his cheekbones gaunt. *This man is not well*, I thought. *He's ill.*

'Let me just try to explain something to you about the commission,' he said. 'It's not a court even though it does have the power to grant amnesty. And it does not function exactly like a court with the judge and jury weighing up evidence and deciding on guilt or innocence. It does not work like that at all. What happens is that we encourage both perpetrators and victims alike to give testimony. To tell us what really happened. To tell the truth and speak for the record about our brutal history.'

'But some people will still end up being punished,' my mother said. 'Those who committed atrocities will go to jail. There will still be justice. Isn't that what you intend to see happen?'

'Yes, of course, but the Amnesty Committee is an independent body and whatever decisions it makes stand. No one can affect its findings. Its rulings cannot be appealed or overruled,' he said. For the first time, he seemed a little unsettled, awkward. He shifted in his seat but managed to smile through those big, yellow teeth.

'There's one other thing I need to mention,' he continued, 'and you need to really understand this. The end of *apartheid* did not come about as the result of victory in the battlefield. We did not win in the theatre of war. We had to spend a long time, years in fact, negotiating a settlement. And the other side, the old regime, wanted certain guarantees. They weren't prepared to cooperate unless amnesty was promised for some of the members of their security forces. Some of the people at the very top.'

I felt my blood run cold. I could see the colour draining from my mother's cheeks.

'Are you saying what I think you're saying?' Her voice strained, I could see she was struggling to keep her emotions in check. 'That the head honchos, the *binne kring*, are all going to get off scot-free? Escape prosecution?'

Once again, Spiegel shuffled uneasily: 'You understand that this conversation is off the record. If you repeat it I will deny it. But yes, I'm afraid that there will be some people who evade punishment for their crimes.'

'And Fat Bill? What about that prick?'

'I can't say. I don't know what will happen with him,' Spiegel replied. 'That's up to the commission. As you know, Bill has applied for amnesty. But even if I had the power to influence or affect the outcome, I would have to recuse myself. After all, he tried to assassinate me. So my hands are tied,' he said holding up his disfigured left hand. 'I have no knowledge of how the decision will go. Only the Amnesty Committee can decide on that.'

And that's pretty much where the meeting ended. There wasn't really anything more to be said. We left with heavy hearts. My mum was really shaken-up and depressed so she asked me to drive.

We didn't speak much on the road back to Jo'burg. I know my mother's hopes had taken a setback. She had hoped for something much more positive from the minister.

'The door's not completely closed,' I said trying to console her. 'We still don't know what the commission will decide. We need to take it one day at a time.'

'I suppose you're right but I don't think we should tell Ruth about this meeting,' my mum said, squeezing my shoulder gently. 'She's got much more than me invested in this. She lost her husband, Marty, after all. He was a good man, a really good man.'

That night my mother had a few more drinks than usual and went to bed quite late. For quite a while I could hear her restlessly shuffling around in the bedroom next to mine until she eventually fell asleep.

The next morning was glorious, the sun streaming through my window, doves gently cooing, the light sharp and pristine. I awoke feeling surprisingly refreshed and alert. It was still early so I made myself a cup of coffee in the kitchen careful not to make too much noise and wake my mum. But when I went outside onto the veranda, she was already outside in her nightgown, sitting with her feet in the pool, her head tilted back, eyes closed.

'Oh, you're up,' I said.

'*Ja*, I was just enjoying the brilliant sunshine. That's something I always missed in England. The African sun on my skin. Nothing like it anywhere.'

'Are you alright?' I asked. 'I heard you tossing and turning in the night.'

'I'm fine,' she assured me. 'Just a weird dream I was having.'

We were both quiet for a while. Then she said: 'You know I wasn't naïve enough to think that deals hadn't been done. In any regime change, the top brass always manages to get off. The main perpetrators, the ones who give the orders, on both sides, always make sure they're protected. But it was just such a shock. Spiegel coming out and saying it so openly. So blatantly. It took me by surprise. Took my breath away.'

'What was the dream about?' I asked.

'It was kind of confusing. All over the place. My father was in it. Your grandfather… He died about ten years ago. Naturally I wasn't able to come to the funeral. But I miss him a lot. He was a very gentle man. Mad as a hatter but gentle. I wish you had got the chance to meet him. And your grandmother. You would have loved her. You remind me a lot of her. Except for that blonde hair. That comes from your dad.'

I sat down next to her and rested my head on her shoulder.

'In my dream I was in this Mexican village. Well I'm not sure if I was there. It felt like it but I was more of a spectator, watching it all unfold. The village also incorporated elements of a little *dorpie* in it. That's like a small country town. So the streets were untarred. Sandy. My dad was there in the town square. He had on a khaki uniform with a star on his chest. Like a western sheriff. He was marching up and down, doing the goosestep. Shouting out incoherent commands. In the background I could see this dwarf stealing the bell from the church tower. Then suddenly the dwarf was in front of my father. They were arguing about the bell when someone dressed like the Jack of Diamonds appeared and cut off the dwarf's head with a sword… I know it's starting to sound like an early Bob Dylan song but that's what happened.' She smiled and gave me a hug before continuing.

'Then a really obese woman with a half-grown beard waddled down the street. She screamed at the knave and then kicked him in the backside. My father started shouting at her. I tried to hear what he was saying but it was all distorted. Then he and the fat woman began wrestling. They fell on top of the church bell. And then I woke up…'

'Wow! Quite surreal! What do you think it means?'

'I'm not sure. I would probably have to go into analysis to get the full picture. But I'm pretty sure the grossly corpulent woman is some cockeyed version of Fat Bill. I think the bell has something to do with freedom, maybe the Liberty Bell. But I'm not sure about the rest. I always seem to dream about my father when I'm under stress. When I'm nervous and worried about something.'

'It's out of your hands now,' I said.

'Not really. I still have to give testimony. And I need to do a good job. Not just for me. But also for Ruth.'

'You'll be fine. You always rise to the occasion.'

She sighed. 'I hope so… Anyway no more morbid thoughts. Come inside and I'll make you some breakfast.'

35

FAT BILL

'Your test results are all in, Mr Saunders,' Dr Levin said. 'And I'm afraid to tell you that you have Type 2 Diabetes.'

'Oh shit!' Fat Bill swore.

'It's not uncommon in people who are overweight and don't do enough exercise. It's characterized by high blood sugar and insulin resistance. A serious illness like this can result in heart attacks, stroke, blindness and kidney failure. In some instances, we have to amputate an affected limb.'

'Fucken hell. What can you do about it?'

'Well, it is possible in some instances to reverse the process,' Dr Levin explained. 'It's all about diet and exercise. I don't know if we can do that in your case. The disease seems to have progressed fairly rapidly and as you told me, the condition is already causing you to experience some erectile dysfunction.'

The problem had all started, as far as Fat Bill was concerned, one night about a month before. He had gone to his usual hangout, the Adelphi, looking for some action. Sailing into the pub, he seemed to glide across the floor in that elegant manner that only fat men can pull off. (Think Sydney Greenstreet in *the Maltese Falcon*.) His pockets were full of cash and Bill found a rent-boy hanging around the meat rack. Lately, since he'd got older and fatter, he found that, more often than not, he had to pay for it. But he didn't mind dating if the merchandise lived up to its promise. This guy said his name was Frankie. He wore tight trousers revealing that he was hung like a mouse. Just the way Fat Bill liked them.

He bought a few rounds of drinks and negotiated a price. Frankie wanted to know what was involved before he would settle on a figure as he had heard through the grapevine that Fat Bill was into some pretty rough stuff. Bill assured him that it would all be pretty vanilla, just a blow job, some rimming and maybe a dip in the fudge pot.

Soon after they left the club and drove to Bill's Banket Street apartment. In the lounge, he poured them both a drink and went to have a leak. Bill found that lately he had been urinating frequently and wondered if he'd been drinking too much coffee in the office.

When he came back, Frankie had put on a CD, Blondie's *Parallel Lines,* and was dancing around the room. He thrust his pelvis out provocatively and pursed his lips like Mick Jagger while singing along to the lyrics. Bill could see it was going to be a wild night.

He had recently scored some mephedrone and Fat Bill felt like getting really "fucked up". He opened the top drawer of his sideboard and took out a small bag of white powder which he offered to Frankie.

'Is this coke?' Frankie asked.

'Meow, meow,' Bill replied. 'It's very good shit. Makes you horny as all hell.'

Frankie took a large pinch and sniffed it up his nose. Bill followed suit. He could feel the drug burning his nostrils, a warmness washing through his brain, a sense that the world and everything in it was speeding up.

Frankie seemed to be dancing faster, the music a rush of chords and drum beats becoming more and more discordant. The pretty boy had started undoing his purple shirt, one button at a time, swirling and gyrating like a stripper. His chest was hairless, a sly smile on his ruby red lips, eyes sparkling and glowing. Then the shirt was off. Frankie's lean muscles quivered and fluttered. Bill was getting more and more turned on. His thoughts were racing. That old familiar feeling was with him. His tongue thickening, his speech slurred.

The drugs were rushing through both their bloodstreams. With the room slowly spinning in different directions, Frankie kept jiggling and wobbling. He slid closer to Bill, stroked his hair and kissed him on the lips, using some tongue. Fat Bill was getting more and more aroused. Titillated. But something was not quite right. Frankie undid Bill's pants buckle and pulled down his fly, feeling inside, expecting a boner, but the cock was flaccid, soft as a feather.

This did not deter Frankie who fell to his knees and then pulled Bill's trousers and undies down. He slid the phallus into his mouth and began sucking in earnest. Nothing. No reaction. He turned around and came at Bill from behind, gently holding his testes in his hand and licking Bill's anus. Frankie had a reputation as a great rim-queen and this had always worked for him, never a complaint. He pushed his tongue right into Bill's darkstar while moving his hand from the balls up to the penis, caressing it.

By now, Bill was growing frustrated and angry. This had never happened to him before. He willed dark blood into his nether regions but to no avail. Frankie made a small noise. It sounded like a giggle. This drove Bill mad. There was a red flash before his eyes and he could feel an uncontrollable fury enveloping him. All at once, he could smell his stepfather's sour breath on his neck. Feel the pain and wetness in his anus. Nothing mattered anymore except this desperate desire to break free. To lash out. To rage.

He turned and struck Frankie on the back of the head. There was a dull, explosive sound. Bill felt volatile and frenzied. His fists were like rocks beating down on Frankie. The young man cried out and fell to the ground. Bill kicked him on the temple. Hard. Then he jumped on him and rained his thudding fists into Frankie's face. Mercilessly. For a long time. Not stopping until he was exhausted and the body underneath him was silent and still.

Ten minutes later, Bill took out his cell phone and made a call. He used his most secure line.

'Steenkamp?'

'*Ja*, sir. What can I do for you?'

'I need a cleaner. Urgently.' Bill's voice was uninflected. Matter of fact. Calm.

'Sure thing, sir. Where are you?'

'My apartment in Banket Street. You've visited before. Can you get here soon?' Bill asked.

'Definitely, sir. I'll be there in half an hour…Just one question. Is there a body?'

'Of course there's a fucken body,' Fat Bill said impatiently.

'I'll have to bring help. Probably van der Byl. And what about blood spatter?'

'Plenty,' Bill said. 'All over the walls.'

'Okay, sir. Don't worry, I'll be there as soon as I can.'

It was over an hour before Steenkamp and van der Byl arrived at the flat. In the meantime, Bill had showered and changed into clean clothes. A dark, pin-striped suit. He looked immaculate, his demeanour serene and dispassionate.

'You *ouks* took your blerry time,' Bill said by way of a greeting.

'Sorry, sir,' said Steenkamp. 'We had to collect some gear from Chopper's place.'

'The corpse is in the lounge,' Bill said. 'Have you got a place to dump it?'

'No problem, sir,' said van der Byl. 'We'll burn it. I've got a permanent fire going at my farm. It'll be like this *oukie* never existed. Clean as a whistle.'

'Good. I'll leave you to it then,' Bill said, walking out the front door.

And now, a month later the doctor had affirmed the source

of his ED problem. Diabetes. Bill stood naked in his bathroom, looking at himself in the mirror. He could not believe how huge he had got. His belly was bloated and distended reminding him of Marlon Brando at the end of his career.

'I'm going to have to go on a diet,' he told himself, in the knowledge that he had no self-control when it came to eating and drinking. 'What a bore!'

Diane had been nagging him for ages to lose some weight and now a health professional had confirmed how necessary it was. This was bad news but there was worse to come.

That evening when the newspapers were delivered, there was a story on the front page of *The Star*. Hannes Swanepoel, a former policeman and operative in the Civil Cooperation Bureau, had just given testimony at the Truth and Reconciliation Commission. As part of his statement he asserted that Willam Saunders was responsible for ordering the assassination of the Norwegian Prime Minister, Leif Halvorsen. Swanepoel even supplied proof that Saunders had been in Oslo the week that Halvorsen was killed.

Initially Fat Bill found this story devastating and calamitous. It would certainly put his amnesty application at risk. Not only that, but it would bring the Norwegian police into play. They would have to investigate this claim and possibly involve Interpol. It could be disastrous. It was one thing to appear before the Truth Commission but it was something else entirely to be tried in a foreign court.

All the dirt, all the blackmail material regarding his superiors and enemies that Bill had acquired would be useless in a Norwegian courtroom. Worthless. Instead he would be facing an angry and wrathful jury. It was all very troubling.

But then he began to think about it further. He started contemplating it from the point of view of his superiors. The brass who had given him his orders. The higher-ups who had apportioned their seal of approval to terminate Halvorsen. What would they think about this news coming out? Would they want Bill to implicate them? And how could they influence the outcome?

It was simple. It was in no one's interests to pursue this. If it came to light that the *apartheid* regime had been a complete rogue state that sanctioned the assassination of political leaders in other countries, it would be catastrophic for everyone concerned. Not just for the leaders of the old government but also for the ANC high command. It would mean all deals were off the table. It would mean the end of the peaceful resolution that had been agreed upon. This would go nowhere. There would be no investigation into this particular homicide. There were too many people who would want it to remain unsolved.

Bill sighed, realising he was safe. He had nothing to worry about. He poured himself a large Scotch and downed it. *God that was good*, he thought.

36

SARAH

A few days before Ruth and my mum were due to give their testimonies to the TRC, the three of us attended the accounts some other people gave. These hearings were held at the Rhema Bible Church in Randburg which is massive and able to accommodate a large audience.

The proceedings were presided over by Archbishop Desmond Tutu who came across as warm, compassionate and, at all times, empathic. The first person to give witness that day was a middle-aged black woman whose name I missed. She spoke in Xhosa but someone translated what she had to say into English.

I gathered that her story was pretty typical and emblematic. In the 1980s her husband had a minor role in a bus strike. Late one night, while they were sleeping, the police broke down their front door and pulled her husband out of bed. They beat him, threw him into the back of a paddy wagon and drove off with no explanation. That was the last time she ever saw her partner. She told the commission that she just wanted to know what had happened to him. Was he tortured? When did he die? Did anyone know? Could anyone tell her? She forgave the people who had done this but she needed to know where he was buried before she could get closure.

The woman wept through much of her testimony. Despite the fact that the translator had limited skills and the story was sometimes confusing, hesitant and rambling, I nevertheless was moved by the raw emotions on display.

The archbishop called an early lunch break and when we came back Jane Silwayane, a young woman in her thirties, testified. The story she told was horrific and even today I find it difficult to recount. She spoke in English and was highly articulate and eloquent.

Jane had been an ANC activist in the 1980s working to destabilise the *apartheid* government. Someone in her cadre, while being tortured, had betrayed her to the security police and she was arrested and taken to John Vorster Square for interrogation. She was held for seven months, tortured daily and experienced terrible degradation and humiliation.

She was not only assaulted and water-boarded but she was subject to the most awful sexual abuse and rape. She was detained in isolation and never had contact with anyone other than her tormentors. She was stripped naked and the police would demean and embarrass her with vile comments about her body and her sexuality. When she had her period, she was made to stand on bricks while blood ran down her legs. She was denied sanitary towels and soap.

Electric shock therapy was ministered every other day and a cattle prod was applied to her vagina. The men took turns raping her and shoved all kinds of objects into her genitalia and anus. A fist, a tongue, a truncheon. The worst was a dead rat. And all the time these atrocities were accompanied by insults and threats.

Jane told her story and the monstrous deeds that had been done to her in chilling detail. Throughout the telling, the audience sat stunned and awestruck. Almost everyone wept, including Archbishop Tutu. I noticed both Ruth and my mum were shaking uncontrollably, their heads bowed, lips trembling. I kept thinking that I had lived such a sheltered life and that this was my first encounter with unadulterated malevolence. It seemed unimaginable that evil could so easily creep into the lives of good people without their sanction or approval.

The next day was the start of the hearing into William "Fat Bill" Saunders's Amnesty Application. It was a media circus with many press reporters and photographers. On our arrival at the Rhema Bible Church, they bombarded us with questions and the flashlights were dazzling and blinding. I was surprised to see newsreel teams from the SABC, CNN and the BBC. Only high-profile cases were videotaped but clearly there was a great deal of interest in this inquiry.

We were early and had to stand in a little quadrangle outside the church waiting for the doors to be opened. Standing right opposite us was Fat Bill Saunders and his wife, Diane. He did not bother acknowledging either Ruth or my mum but gazed arrogantly and dismissively at the crowd. To me he seemed confident and self-assured, as if he didn't have a care in the world. His wife Diane, however, was clearly embarrassed and kept her eyes lowered. She seemed to shrink within herself.

It was the first time I had encountered the man whose actions had been responsible for so much that had occurred in my life. I was surprised by his size. He wasn't just fat. He was morbidly obese. A walking monstrosity. He took no notice of me but I made sure I was glaring at him, sending him my darkest stare. To me the man was evil personified.

Inside, the crowd was heaving. Ruth's fame had contributed to the palpable buzz of expectation, the almost theatricality of the event. Archbishop Tutu chaired the proceedings and began by reminding the audience that the applicant, William Saunders, had applied for amnesty in respect of offences which related to:

1. The death of Martin ("Marty") Lehman
2. The injuries suffered by Isaac Spiegel

In the first case, the victim had lost his life as the result of an explosion due to an Improvised Explosive Device (IED) concealed in a letter. The victim in the second case had suffered injuries as a result of a similar IED being placed in his motor vehicle.

Fat Bill had only admitted and taken responsibility for these two gross violations of human rights. There was no mention of any other crimes. No mention of Antoine Pienaar, Norman Stern or Leif Halvorsen. No confessions regarding any other assassinations, murders or tortures. That was it. Bill was only admitting to those two.

The hearing would eventually take place over a number of weeks but as we had to go back to England, my mum and I only attended the first few days when she and Ruth gave their evidence. I'll try to summarize their statements.

Ruth spoke first. She had written her story down very carefully and read from her notes. Her prose was elegant and precise and the account she gave dynamic and persuasive. She told how she had first encountered Fat Bill in the now infamous (to me) Russian class. In such a small group, everyone got to know each other very well and Bill had been part of their social circle. But despite his affability, some people distrusted him and kept him at arm's length. Others, however, were taken in and he managed to infiltrate the ANC in England. She went on to disclose how her friend, Cookie le Roux, had exposed him as a spy which forced Fat Bill to return to South Africa and take up a position in the security police.

Ruth moved on to talk at great length about her relationship with Marty Lehman and their deep love for each other. She described Marty in detail emphasising his tremendous talent, his warmth, generosity and goodness. His decency and his altruism. She told everyone in the church that day how passionately she missed him and what a loss he was to her and all their friends.

Then she told us about the bomb and how it had ripped Marty's body to shreds. The horror of that moment was frighteningly portrayed. Her descriptions had a profound effect on the audience.

People gasped in both fear and revulsion. Many were in tears especially when they realised that Ruth was the bomb's intended target.

At one point, Ruth herself broke down and was unable to continue with her testimony. Archbishop Tutu had to call for a break in the proceedings to allow her the opportunity to recover.

When she returned, Ruth emphasized two things. First that Marty's death or her own would have served no real or substantial political purpose. The assassination was rather an act of vengeance designed to silence the country's intelligentsia. And secondly, she pointed out that this was a personal vendetta. Fat Bill had selected her because he had firsthand knowledge of her and had a grudge against her and everyone in the Russian class. The fact that Marty, of all people, had died because of Bill's obsessive hatred and malice made this even more tragic.

Ruth's statements took a few days and then it was my mother's turn to give testimony. Once again the church was packed and the news crews filmed everything. I guess my mum had acquired a reputation because of her many years underground and also for unmasking the master spy, Fat Bill Saunders.

Unlike Ruth, my mum spoke with no notes. I had helped her compose her narrative but once the details were written down, her remarkable memory took over and she just spoke from the heart. Her account was credible, authentic and powerful. She talked about the camaraderie shared by the members of the Russian class and detailed her very close friendship with Antoine Pienaar and the bizarre circumstances surrounding his early death.

My mother then spoke about her relationship with James Morrison, my dad. She said that they had loved each other dearly and had gone to England to study and be together. While there they had once again come in contact with Fat Bill Saunders. She then outlined how she had, by pure chance, discovered Fat Bill's secret life in the security police. In so doing, she uncovered the brutal murder of her friend, Antoine Pienaar.

She told us how she had taken this information to the ANC in exile and that Isaac Spiegel had leaked the story to the press. As a consequence, she was forced to go underground and take on a new identity in order to evade any vengeful reprisal by Fat Bill. My mum spoke of being pregnant with me and of her decision to keep this secret from my father to protect him. Naturally, as this part of the story was so personal to me, I was deeply moved and wept openly. But I noticed that many others in the audience were also crying, tears streaming down their faces.

My mum recounted all the hardships she had to endure bringing up a baby on her own in a foreign and alien land. She finished her testimony by detailing the threats Fat Bill had made towards her and characterised him as a man of violence and vengeance. A truly evil man who would do anything to even the score.

Outside the church, the army of reporters hounded us with all kinds of questions. My mum answered them very politely. There was one objective that both she and Ruth shared and that they wished to make clear to the press and that was, under no circumstances should Fat Bill Saunders be given amnesty. If there was to be any justice in South Africa, he needed to be held to account for his evil deeds. A time of reckoning must come.

Meanwhile, our time in the country was drawing to a close. Mum had to get back to work and university was calling me. I was due to graduate later in the year and had a number of assignments to complete. My boyfriend, Jeff, appeared to be growing impatient to see me and was making all kinds of needy noises. I missed him too.

On our last night in Jo'burg we went to the Market Theatre to see a performance of *Sunday's Journey*. Given what we had experienced at the Truth Commission, the play seemed both topical and relevant. I was swept away by Churchill's amazing performance. He took command of the stage and owned it. The other performers were also excellent but none had the same wild panache.

When the Yiddish lady delivered her lines, I snuck a look at my mother who was mouthing the words under her breath. I could tell that she was entirely caught up in the tableau, cherishing the experience. In the final scene, there was a magical moment, a kind of portent that I'd never felt in any English stage production which left me overawed and giddy. Right at the end of the play, Churchill walked to the front of the stage, raised his fist above his head and cried out in defiance and audacious rebellion: '*Amandla!*' Then there was this extraordinary, breathtaking, theatrical episode when the entire cast and the audience responded in one mighty unified voice: '*Awethu!*' Stunning.

After the show we joined some of the cast for a dinner at an Italian restaurant in Melville. Everyone was in a celebratory mood, buoyant with success, the wine flowed while the lively and convivial conversation swirled around my mother. Later in the evening, she proposed a toast to all her friends. She spoke warmly and movingly, with grace, thanking them for their generosity, courage and love. She looked flushed and I was suddenly very proud of her. Then she asked everyone to raise their glasses and drink to absent friends. We drank silently Marty and Antoine (and my dad James) on everyone's minds. Despite the sadness it felt good to be alive.

The next afternoon when we got to the airport it was raining. A big, spectacular electric storm. In the departure lounge we hugged our friends – David, Celeste, Rory and, of course, Ruth. None of us was sure when we would see each other again. To me, it felt so final and conclusive. I was at a loss what to feel, my emotions deficient and inadequate. In the end, I just gave in to weeping. Then suddenly we were gone, up in the air, looking back down at the flat, green earth.

37

JAMES

Ever since my elder daughter first contacted me, and especially after she came to visit in Australia, Sarah and I have been in regular contact. We email each other almost every day even when there is not much to say. I also phone her at least once every fortnight. It's one way to try and make up for all the time we missed being together when she was younger.

During her recent trip to South Africa, Sarah kept me informed about everything she and her mother had been doing, in particular the evidence Cookie gave at the Truth and Reconciliation Commission. In addition, I had been following Fat Bill's amnesty hearing on the news in Australia. Both the Australian Broadcast Corporation and CNN had given considerable air time to the legal proceedings.

I would have liked to personally attend and perhaps even give evidence to the commission myself but I was tied up at work. Unfortunately, the Australian film industry is no longer as robust and productive as it once was and I had been forced to take a lecturing job at the Melbourne Film School. Not that I don't enjoy teaching but now I am only able to take leave during the school holidays.

Prior to his amnesty appearance, Fat Bill gave an interview in his lawyer's office to a CNN journalist. Watching it, I was horrified by his nonchalant admission of guilt. He casually and arrogantly described sending letter bombs to anti-*apartheid* activists. Fat Bill defended his actions by claiming to be a soldier fighting a war that he believed was just.

'You have to understand the context,' he told the interviewer. 'The Cold War was on and we were fighting on the side of the West. We were protecting western values against the communist onslaught. Not only was it an ideological war but it was an unconventional one. A guerrilla war. The ANC were not fighting set battles. They were bombing power plants and organising riots in the streets. We saw them as terrorists. They weren't playing fair. And so, we had to adopt different methods to deal with them. We also had to stop playing fair.'

I found it chilling to watch Fat Bill defending detention without trial, prison torture and assassination squads with such offhand indifference. 'I was a soldier,' he claimed. 'I was just obeying orders given to me by my superiors.' I remembered that this was exactly the same defence that many Nazi officers had used. It hadn't helped them at Nuremburg.

Then the journalist asked Bill about his superiors. Did the head honchos know about Bill's activities or was he a rogue agent operating on his own bat? At first Bill slid past the question trying to evade it. 'Well, when one is promoted for one's work, when one is rewarded for one's endeavours, when one is lauded and praised, then one assumes that one's superiors are completely *au fait* with what one is doing.'

When he was pressed further, Bill conceded: 'Of course they knew. Of course they approved of what I was doing. In most cases I was doing it at their behest.'

When the time came for him to give his testimony before the commission, Fat Bill more or less stuck to the position he had articulated in his lawyer's office. He insisted on claiming that he had, at all times, been acting on instructions from his immediate superior, Colonel Piet "Klopper" van Wyk. Unfortunately, van Wyk could neither confirm nor deny this because he was deceased.

I tried to research Colonel van Wyk using the new Google search engine which I had only recently been introduced to. There was a comprehensive biography of the man listing some of his most notorious achievements, sensational arrests and counter-intelligence operations. But there was very little information on his death. Google simply stated that he had been killed "under mysterious and suspicious circumstances".

The fact that van Wyk was not around to corroborate Bill's assertions was extremely advantageous and beneficial to Fat Bill. I was struck by the timing of van Wyk's demise. It seemed so fortuitous, almost serendipitous. Everything I knew about Fat Bill told me that very little he did, happened by chance. Anything that seemed random or unplanned should be further investigated.

The paper trail had also been eroded. Bill could not back up his claims of simply following orders with any written evidence. There had been a fire at the Randburg Police Station and all his paper files from before the computer era had been destroyed. In addition, the floppy discs that the police used later on had also perished in the fire.

Bill stated that van Wyk received his orders from the then minister of police and that he had no doubt that van Wyk had the authority to issue orders to him as a subordinate in the command structure to carry out a specified task or operation. And this brought him to talk about the bomb that killed Marty.

He quoted from the *Annual Intelligence Review of 1982*, in particular the section dealing with the Internal Threat. This document stated that members of the intelligentsia were influenced by communist ideology and were using fictional stories to influence people's hearts and minds. Fat Bill said that this reflected the attitude of the time and offered it as justification to

251

prepare a bomb against the novelist, Ruth Jacobson. It was not a surprise for him to receive such an order but it was, of course, a terrible and unpredictable accident that the bomb had killed an unintended victim. Unfortunately, this was simply the kind of collateral damage that could happen in any war.

Bill went on to express regret about the fact that an innocent person had been a casualty but showed no contrition or remorse for sending the bomb to Ruth in the first place. He never once mentioned that he knew her personally or that this might have had anything to do with the decision to eliminate her. He just blamed his superiors.

Watching this unfold on television, I could not help but feel appalled and heartsick. Marty was my dearest friend and a man of conviction and integrity. To have his death so callously dismissed was unforgivable.

Throughout his testimony, Fat Bill came across as both pompous and bombastic. His careless disregard for the lives of both Ruth and Marty, two of the finest people I had ever met, was nauseating. I was so sickened by his performance that I turned the television off in disgust. From what I saw, it seemed obvious to me that Fat Bill's amnesty application would be rejected.

But some months later, the commission published its findings. I was shocked to read that Fat Bill had been granted amnesty. It was outrageous and certainly unwarranted. Clearly Fat Bill had not disclosed all his crimes nor had he been completely truthful before the commission. The three judges hearing his case had been extremely sceptical of his evidence and to be granted amnesty, the accused is supposed to admit to all his offences. Bill had not told the truth nor was he remorseful.

This decision seemed to me to be a savage indictment of the Truth and Reconciliation Commission as well as the ANC. The government had entered into a Faustian pact whereby truth was deemed more important than justice. By pardoning Fat Bill Saunders, the commission lost all credibility and moral authority. It was clear that amnesty in this case meant abandoning the rights of victims and renouncing due process.

The press reports I read were all very critical of the commission's decision. Some of the newspaper articles pointed out that Bill had been implicated in numerous other nefarious activities but no charges had been brought against him. One journalist mentioned that he had been singled out for the assassination of Prime Minister Leif Halvorsen. Apparently the Norwegian police had even come to South Africa to investigate the crime but had found insufficient evidence for a conviction.

Ruth was devastated by the decision and was consulting with her lawyers about the possibility of bringing a legal challenge to reverse the decision. This would entail a judicial review before the Supreme Court. As matters stood, the amnesty granted to Bill meant that he could not be prosecuted or sued for his crimes.

As I read all this, my thoughts turned to Cookie. I knew how much she had invested in getting justice from the commission. She must have been shattered by the decision. This would feel like a seismic event for her. Something she would always struggle to recover from.

It was then that I decided I would have to go and see her. Visit her in England. Ever since Sarah contacted me, Cookie had been on my mind and my whole being longed to see her again after all these years. The following week was the start of university holidays so I was free to leave. But I had to tell Karen. I never mentioned Cookie, instead I said I wanted to see Sarah and that I had promised her I would come to London. This was true but it was not my most compelling motive for going.

The night before I left, I had a disturbing dream. I was a young child and I was walking down a busy street with my mother. I was holding her hand and on my best behaviour. My twin brother was holding her other hand and he was acting up, shouting and swearing at passers-by. I wanted my mother to pay attention to me and see how well behaved I was. But she only had eyes for my brother. She hugged him and kissed him while ignoring me. I was heartbroken. Some dust blew into my eyes and I was blinded. It felt like my eyes were on fire and I cried out. Then I woke up.

The dream was very vivid. I don't have a twin brother so I guess the dream meant there were two sides of me. A good side and a bad side but it was difficult to tell which was which. I was obviously being offered a choice. But which was the right one? It was hard to tell.

I went into the bathroom and looked in the mirror. Softly I whispered to myself: 'Make sure you do the right thing. Be true to yourself.' My face looked gaunt and haggard, my eyes bloodshot red. It felt like I was standing at a crossroad in my life. I wasn't sure which way to turn.

Karen drove me to the airport and we made small talk on the way. The weather had changed radically as it often does in Melbourne. Mist had come in off the bay and everything was hazy. There was surprisingly little traffic on the highway and in the fading light the road ahead seemed narrow and confining.

We said our goodbyes and I kissed and hugged Karen, pulling her in tight. Something in me did not want to let go of her. Before she turned to leave, she sighed and said in a soft voice: 'Look after yourself.'

It was sunset when the plane took off. In the mist, the world seemed bathed in crimson and purple. Looking out the window, I saw the earth turning. The sky seemed to shiver and throb.

38

JAMES

It was mid-morning when I arrived at Heathrow. I caught a cab to Kensington and checked in to a very pleasant hotel near the Gloucester Road Tube station. I was exhausted after the long flight and felt pretty jet-lagged so I spent the afternoon sleeping. After a long shower I was feeling more refreshed and ready to face the world.

I decided to go for a brisk walk along Queen's Gate towards the Royal Albert Hall and then turned into Hyde Park. There was a slight chill in the air and all the leaves on the trees had turned autumnal gold. It felt marvellous to be in London again but my thoughts were jumbled and scrambled. I was running all kinds of scenarios through my head. Finally, I decided that thinking about it was pointless and I needed to take action.

Back in my hotel room, I picked up the phone and dialled. Over the last few years I had called this number often to speak to Sarah but then it was always at an agreed time and my daughter had always been the one to answer. But this time, Cookie picked up the receiver. With my heart thumping in my chest, I said: 'Hi. It's me... James.'

There was a slight pause then she said: 'Just give me a moment. I want to take this in another room.'

When Cookie came on again, she did not seem at all surprised to hear from me. She was taking it all in her stride. She sounded calm, amicable and unflappable. It was almost as if she had been expecting me to call. I, on the other hand, was feeling anxious and uptight. I didn't really know what to say to her.

'I'm in London,' I said. 'I was hoping we could catch up… after all these years.'

'That would be lovely,' she said. It was like we had just seen each other the day before. There was a warmth and graciousness in her voice. 'You know I've thought about this often. What I would say if you ever called me. I rehearsed all kinds of speeches but they have deserted me now. I really don't know what to say except it's so good to hear your voice.'

She was forthright, honest and outspoken. Just like I remembered her.

'Can we meet?' I asked.

'Of course. Where and when?'

'Perhaps tomorrow. For dinner?'

'That's fine,' Cookie said. 'Where are you staying?'

'I'm in Kensington. There's an Indian restaurant near my hotel. The Bombay Palace. Do you know it?'

'I do. The food is excellent.'

'Shall we meet there at 7pm?'

'Perfect,' she said. 'I'm looking forward to it.'

I arrived early and ordered myself a Campari and soda on ice. It was not long before she arrived. Cookie always knew how to make an entrance. The light was behind her creating a halo in her hair, giving her an ethereal, celestial quality. She wore a tight-fitting midnight blue dress that clung to her fine figure. As she walked across the restaurant towards my table, I was acutely conscious of the other patrons watching her. She seemed to glide across the room.

I stood up, watching her with my heart racing. We hugged and gave each other a fleeting kiss on the cheek. Even though I was expecting it, the blonde hair took me by surprise. It was cut short in a style similar to the one Anna Karina has in *Alphaville*. It suited her. She looked stunning.

For the next minute or so, we just sat there not saying a word. I reached out and held her hand across the table, looked in her eyes which were luminous and shimmering. Both of us were on the edge of tears.

'It's so good to see you,' she said.

'And you. It's been so long.'

Soon a waiter arrived and broke our reverie. I ordered wine and we began to make small talk. I asked her about Sarah and Cookie told me in detail about how well she was doing at university and how committed she was to being a writer. In South Africa, she said, Sarah had greatly admired Ruth and hoped one day to follow in her footsteps. There was an easy familiarity between us, nothing strained. We both just seemed to enjoy each other's company.

After we had ordered our food, we moved on to more pertinent matters. I asked her how she felt about the amnesty given to Fat Bill.

'I was devastated,' Cookie said. 'I could not actually believe that the commission could possibly reach such a conclusion. It was outrageous! And, of course, it was worse for Ruth. She lost a husband. Marty was such a good man. She still feels guilt about it. Feels the bomb was meant for her and she asked him to open the letter. She will never, ever get over it.'

'I think the decision was a terrible indictment of the ANC and the new government's will to power. I should imagine that Fat Bill had some leverage over the top brass.'

I knew Cookie was blunt and outspoken but the next thing she said caught me off balance.

'I can understand exactly how Ruth feels because I've lived with guilt for so long. All this time I've been blaming myself for what happened to us. If I hadn't exposed Fat Bill as a spy, you and I would still have been able to be together. We would have had a life.

Not a day goes by that I don't think of that. Not a day goes by that I don't suffer terrible guilt and remorse. It still pains me even now.'

She was starting to get upset. Tears were running down her cheeks. I tried to calm her.

'No, no, you did the right thing. Once you learned about what Fat Bill did to Antoine, you had no choice. The cards just fell badly for us,' I said wistfully.

Cookie leaned forward, close to me, holding my hand in her own. 'I just want you to know that I'm sorry. I'm so sorry that I caused you such pain. It has wracked me apart to know I hurt you. I'm truly, truly sorry.'

Well, what could I say? I, too, understood about guilt. For years I had also been feeling it. I blamed myself for what had happened. If only I had been stronger maybe I could have protected all three of us. Cookie, Sarah and me. But it was a pipe dream. An illusion. Fat Bill would have used all the state apparatus at his command to hunt us down.

Later that evening, through some unspoken mechanism, some intuitive, elemental process we found ourselves in my hotel room. It just seemed logical and fitting. A series of dynamic and robust forces driving us towards each other. It was unavoidable, inevitable. And right.

After we had made love we were lying uninhibitedly naked on the bed. I stroked her arm, kissed her on the shoulder, lay with my head on her firm tummy.

'You know, I never thought I would get over losing you. You were constantly in my thoughts. You were the love of my life. You still are,' I said.

'And you are the love of my life,' Cookie said running her fingers through my hair. 'I thought of you every day. How could I not? Every time I looked at Sarah, I saw you. You in her. Her in you.'

It's difficult to describe what I was feeling at that moment. There was a contentment, certainly. But also a deep sorrow. It was like being at the top of a mountain, seeing the snow below, pine trees reaching up for the pristine blue sky, the sun shining luminously and then deciding to ski down the slopes. To be exhilarated by movement, the wind in one's hair, the bracing chill on cheekbones, everything stripped away, a feeling of freedom and liberation. And, at the same time, an irrational and primal fear seeping into one's gut. I wasn't sure if I could bear losing Cookie again. And yet part of me knew that I would have to.

We made some plans for the short time I was to be there, in England. Cookie would take a week off work and we would go on a trip, like we did so many years ago. Only this time we would head north, towards the historic city of York and stay somewhere on the Yorkshire moors. Like Cathy and Heathcliff.

I asked her what she intended doing about her long-time companion, Reg. Again I was somewhat taken aback by her candid response.

'Oh, I'll tell him of course. I don't like secrets, despite having lived a secret life,' she said. 'Reg is a fine man. He just has a problem with commitment. Maybe this'll spur him on.'

The next day I spent with my daughter, Sarah. We did some tourist things like exploring the British Museum where we had lunch followed by an afternoon of shopping getting her presents. Sarah was very animated, in high spirits and keen to talk about her affection for her sister, Olivia. She mentioned the possibility of coming on holiday to Australia after she graduated. I told her how much we would all love for her to visit.

'Stay as long as you like,' I said. 'It's your home now.'

I had hired a car and the next morning Cookie and I drove north. Our first stopover was at Stratford-upon-Avon as I had managed to buy tickets for a RSC production of *King Lear* at the Swan Theatre.

The production was robust and highly stylized set in medieval times. Lear's narcissism in the first scene was, to my mind, quite odious and repulsive. I had seen the Peter Brook's film version but this was the first time I had seen a live performance and this staging struck me as both ambitious and compelling.

Many Freudian critics have offered persuasive psychoanalytical readings that focus on the absence of legitimate mothers in the play. Although I was aware of these interpretations, they did not resonate with me while I was watching the action unfold. Instead I was acutely conscious of how the play reflected on my own experiences as a father. It was almost impossible for me to even comprehend Lear's treatment of Cordelia. I found myself thinking about both my daughters – sweet Olivia with her generous soul and my new found adorable surprise package, Sarah. All I wanted, as I sat in the theatre with Cookie (the mother of my elder daughter) was to be a caring father to both of them, to give them love and not disappoint them. Ever.

So, by the end of the play when Lear carries the dead Cordelia in his arms across the stage, I was almost in tears. I understood profoundly what it was like to have made mistakes and to have suffered disproportionate punishment. I felt that in the future I had to make sure that I did what was right, what was befitting.

After a late breakfast, we set off, driving at a relaxed pace. We stopped at the Lake District and did some ambling around Derwent Water before heading off to York where we stayed in a fabulous historic hotel set in acres of well-manicured parkland. The next day was spent exploring the ancient city, the Viking Museum, the beautiful Gothic York Minster, the cobbled streets. I thought the city was glorious and all the time that Cookie and I were together I felt a deep sense of contentment.

Then we drove further north to the little town of Ripon where we hired a charming stone cottage. It was not the moors that I was expecting but rather woodland, the tree leaves all russet, amber and burnished in the weak autumn sunshine. We bought some groceries and lit the open wood fire in the lounge. The next three days were idyllic. We went for long walks in the countryside, took turns cooking for each other, and made love.

During all that time, there seemed to be an unspoken acceptance of the fact that I would have to go back to Australia. We both knew that our time together would soon end. But we also knew that it was important for Cookie and I to acknowledge our love for each other. Once again I felt that our choices were limited, that fate had selected a certain path for us and there was little we could do about it. If I was to be the man I wanted to be, if I was to retain my self-respect, I had to go back home to Karen and Olivia. That was the only opportunity available. But at the same time I knew that losing Cookie again would leave me anguished and heavy-hearted.

Soon, all too soon, it was time to head back to London. Neither Cookie nor I said much on the return journey. I think we both felt emotionally drained. This little sojourn of ours had ended too speedily but it was vital and precious. I would never forget it.

I asked both Cookie and Sarah not to come to the airport to see me off. I felt it would be unbearably painful to say goodbye to them.

From my window seat I could see the green English countryside slowly receding as my plane reached altitude. It's difficult to explain the emotions I was experiencing. Of course I was heartbroken about losing Cookie again but, at the same time, I felt strangely optimistic.

In another, earlier era there had been so much in my life that was beyond my control. Big, powerful historical forces had just swept me along. There was very little I could do to change what transpired. But now I had some mastery over the direction my life would take. Cookie had taught me so much. She had shown me how it was possible, in the face of great adversity, to turn misfortune into triumphant accomplishment. She had done this with grace and humility. I realised that what I was facing now was not an ending but rather a new beginning. I needed to walk confidently towards the future.

In truth, I was a lucky man. I had two wonderful women who loved me. One in the past and one in the present. And I had two bright, gentle and individualistic daughters who would have a glorious promise awaiting them if they were honest with themselves. What else could a man ask for?

39

SARAH

A lot has changed since my trip to South Africa. I graduated from university with a First so I'm very happy about that. My mum seemed pleased and told me she was very proud of me.

Jeff, my boyfriend, saw it as an opportunity to buttress our relationship and started badgering me to move in with him. I told him that I wanted to get to know my half-sister better and strengthen my newly formed bonds with my father and stepmother. So my plan was to spend a "gap year" in Australia and if Jeff wanted us to be together, he'd have to come along. Well, he jumped at the chance. So now the two of us will soon be leaving for Melbourne. Olivia, my half-sister, has offered us her bedroom and she'll move to the smaller spare room. She is such a generous and loving girl. I really adore her. I'm so excited to be able to spend time with her.

I asked my mum if she was planning on going back to South Africa to bring legal action against Fat Bill Saunders. She said something which I found rather cryptic and enigmatic. 'No,' she said, 'I have decided, like Robert Graves, to say "Good-bye to all that".'

In any event, her little romantic tryst with my dad seems to have prompted a response from Reg who proposed marriage to her. They tied the knot a couple of weeks ago so I now have a stepfather. It's amazing how quickly my family has expanded. I now have a mother and a stepfather, a half-sister and a stepmum. And, of course, a father. Perhaps I should stop referring to myself as a bastard...

ACKNOWLEDGEMENTS

I would like to express my very great appreciation to my elder daughter, Claire Mansell, for giving me permission to use material from and derive inspiration from her wonderful blog "The Bastard Diaries".

The horoscope quoted in the Prologue was actually published on the Cainer.com website and in numerous newspapers on 6th February 2013. I have taken the liberty of changing the date to 1997 to fit with the novel's timeline.

In Chapter 19, I make use of well-known quotations from the films *Dr Zhivago* and *The Godfather 2*. These can be found at: https://www.quotes.net/movies/3189 and: https://www.imdb.com/title/tt0071562/quotes

It is my understanding that use of such quotes would be considered a *de minimus* use and therefore not bound by copyright.

I would also like to thank my dear friends Dana Kidson and Gavin Ivey who read early drafts of the novel and provided me with valuable insights and suggestions.

And finally, my sincerest thanks to my wife Marian whose editorial experience and advice was most constructive and who supported and guided me through all the backroads, cul-de-sacs and wrong turns I took along the way. I could not have done it without her.

GLOSSARY

accordion
   enlarging penis
Afrikanerdom
   Afrikaner nationalism based on pride in Afrikaner culture and
   conservative values
Afrikaner Weerstandsbeweging
   The Afrikaner Resistance Movement was a neo-Nazi white
   supremacist group
ag
   oh, as in "ag shame" meaning "oh, that's bad luck"
a luta continua
   the struggle continues
Amandla
   Zulu word for "power"
ANC
   African National Congress
Awethu
   to the people
baas
   boss especially a white overseeing blacks
baasskap
   concept of control or dominion of whites over blacks
bakkie
   pick-up truck or ute

267

B & D
  bondage and discipline
Bantustan
  partially self-governing area set aside for blacks in apartheid
  era, a homeland
bashert
  soulmate or ideal marriage partner
bear
  a hairy gay man
blerry
  bloody
boere
  literally "farmers" can be used derogatively for Afrikaners
boerewors
  farmers' sausage
bogan
  Australian slang for uncouth person
bootyhole
  anus
bosbefokked
  shell-shocked
boykie
  small boy
braai/braaivleis
  barbecue
broederbond
  brotherhood, a secret male-only organisation dedicated to the
  advancement of Afrikaner interests
bupkes
  something trivial or nothing
china
  friend, from cockney slang – "mate, china plate"
chow
  food

cinephile
    person who loves the cinema

Civil Cooperation Bureau
    government-sponsored death squad

dagga
    cannabis

darkstar
    anus, also called a chocolate well

die binne kring
    the inner circle

dop
    any alcoholic drink

dorpie
    small town

Durbs by the sea
    Durban

ED
    erectile disfunction

faggot
    male homosexual

fairy
    effeminate male

flamer
    extremely flamboyant homosexual

flip flop
    when two guys are having sex and they take turns at being the
    bottom

fudge pot
    derogatory term for anus

gemors
    rubbish

häftling
    concentration camp prisoner

highveld
>   high altitude plateau

howzit
>   how're you doing

hung like a mouse
>   possessing a negligible sized penis

jislaaik jong
>   exclamation of surprise

joller
>   person who enjoys a frivolous life

jong
>   young person

kaffermeid
>   derogatory term for black woman servant

kerk
>   church

koppie
>   small hill

laissez-faire
>   free from interference

lekker
>   nice, pleasant

los
>   loose, available

manne
>   important, powerful men

meow, meow
>   street name for mephedrone

mephedrone
>   designer amphetamine

Milieu
>   French criminal gangs involved in organized crime

mise-en-scène
>   visual depiction of the story

moffie
> derogatory term for male homosexual

naaiers
> lit. "fuckers"

NUSAS
> National Union of South African Students

oom
> lit. "uncle"

oukie
> guy or man

peri-peri
> a spicy sauce

Pommy
> English

Porros
> Portugese

predicant
> priest, minister, preacher

Randlords
> adventurers who controlled goldmine finance

rimming
> using tongue to stimulate another's anal rim

rim-queen
> an effeminate homosexual who enjoys giving rim jobs

rock spider
> slang, derogatory term for an Afrikaner

rondawel
> African style hut usually circular

rooting
> Australian slang for sexual intercourse

ruse de guerre
> act of military deception

SABC
> South African Broadcast Corporation

SACP
  South African Communist Party
schtupping
  having sexual intercourse with someone
shebeen
  illicit bar selling illegal alcohol
sheila
  Australian slang for woman
shiksa
  gentile woman
Shoah
  the Holocaust
sjambok
  heavy leather whip
skattie
  darling
skeef
  askew
sommer
  just, only
sosaties
  spicy meat kebab
spiel
  an elaborate sales pitch
spook and diesel
  cane spirits and Coca Cola
SRC
  Student Representative Council
Strine
  slang for Australian speech or accent
stoep
  porch, veranda
taal
  language

toyi toyi
  dance used in political protests
tokhis
  Yiddish for arse
tovarich
  Russian for comrade
twink
  boyish-looking young gay man
ubuntu
  philosophical recognition of another's humanity
UDF
  United Democratic Front
uMkhonto we Sizwe
  armed wing of the ANC in exile
vai
  let's go
vanilla
  conventional, boring
voortrekker
  Afrikaner pioneers who migrated north to escape British rule
wanker
  lit. masturbator, generally means an annoying or pretentious person

A NOTE ON THE AUTHOR

John Hookham is an academic and a film-maker. His films have been screened at festivals throughout the world including Cannes, Locarno, Gothenburg, Montreal as well as the National Film Theatre, London and the Cinémathèque Française, Paris. He completed his PhD at Queensland University of Technology. John grew up in Johannesburg but now lives in Melbourne, Australia where he is writing his next novel.